KEEPING THE TARNISHED

BRADON NAVE

KEEPING THE TARNISHED

DEDICATION

For my beautiful wife, Bethany.
You have always been my rock, even when I
didn't know it. Words cannot express how much I
love you, our family, and the life we have built
together. Thank you.

KEEPING THE TARNISHED

CHAPTER ONE

And Then There Was Freedom

The Boy

Midnight. Finally. The moments leading up to it had crawled slower than one of the maggots behind the kitchen trashcan, etching its way blindly through the coffee grounds and eggshells. He grabbed his weathered book bag full of a few clothing items and $188.00 in cash, and then stuck his leg out the window, losing his balance as he fell backward to the ground.

He didn't care. He had been outside of this rundown shack a million times, but never had he been outside and free. Even if this freedom were short lived, and he went in the ground tomorrow, he owned it for this moment.

Quickly, he sprang to his feet, grabbed his bag, and began running in the direction of the cornfield near the end of the farmhouse drive.

The air was eerily still on this night. All was silent

with the exception of a few chanting crickets and the occasional cry of the whippoorwill sounding out over the horizon. The moonlight illuminated the decrepit barn to the north of the house, as every single cornstalk in the field up ahead seemed to be reflecting the moon's rays.

The light bulb atop the wooden pole near the end of the drive was a dingy bright yellow, buzzing in a calming manner. Several fat toads sat at the base, waiting for unfortunate insects to fall to the ground from their dizzy escapades near the globe at the top of the pole.

He ran past the half-built clubhouse his father and Uncle Doug had begun several years prior. He never understood if Doug was actually his uncle, but the men had wanted to build a 'guy's getaway' for the three of them. He paid little attention to the details. He'd seen it all hundreds of times before, and he hoped to never see this place again.

Leaping over old car parts and garbage, he finally reached the corn. Although it wasn't tall enough to hide him completely, it was all the cover he needed to make an effective escape. His heart raced wildly as he ran feverishly over the soft earth through the chest-high stalks. He began to smile through his heavy breathing, running—sprinting—excited as if he were scratching off the winning number on a substantial lottery ticket.

The prospects raced through his mind, and no adversity outside of his former confinements seemed to scare him. Starvation, disease, injury: nothing conjured concern except the idea of returning. He couldn't go back, not now, now that a glimmer of hope had been resurrected.

As he bounded through the field like a fawn that had been mercifully released from the jaws of a predator, he felt as if he were being lifted off the ground; as if he were flying, and nothing in this world or the next could anchor him.

The taste of freedom was that of a bloodied lip, cornstalks, and the occasional mosquito; it was delicious. He knew he would leverage everything to maintain all he had in that moment, which was merely a tattered wardrobe, his father's liquor-cash reserve, the worn clothing in the backpack, and a desperate desire to exist.

Like a thief in the night, lowly and cunning, he darted through the cover, running on what seemed to be an endless rush of endorphins and adrenaline. He was running for his life; this reality gave him wings.

The air was heavy and stagnant and seemed to fill his lungs with a thick, boggy perfume. He knew for certain that, if there were a higher power within the heavens, it would not have him come this far to go back. Even if he were found right now he knew he would die before he went back, and he would die a free man. Yes, a man. No longer a boy and no longer bound to his bedroom—to that shack—by the law. With a head full of dreams and the legs of a gazelle, he shot through the field, promising himself to never look back.

He was certain he had run a decent distance. Lost in the idea of an alternative existence, he had left the house mere moments prior, and already he was nearing the first stop of his journey. This was in face, the only scheduled stop. Just as he began to tire, he heard the faint sounds of motors passing on the two- lane blacktop on the other side of the cornfield. He knew it would only be a matter of minutes; a kind driver would pick him up, and he would be forever free of this field, the shack, and everything else imprisoning him. Finally, he could see headlights, and his future. He felt alive, and overwhelmed with the brand-new taste he had acquired for freedom.

Then he saw it. A very familiar 1987 blue Chevy extended cab pickup was braking just as he had leapt from the field like a bullfrog jumping to safety in the meadow's pond. There was no mistaking that it was the vehicle of his closest neighbor, Bill Clementine, from two miles south. Half of him wanted to jump back into the field and race somewhere else, but there was nowhere else to run. This, he decided, was one of several challenges he would be facing. He understood he would have to overcome it. After all, he was free, and no one could tell him what to do.

The truck grumbled as it came to a complete stop about two hundred feet in front of where he was standing. The truck's lights signaled reverse, illuminating the stalks behind him as he covered his eyes with his free arm from the red glare. Slowly, almost unsurely, the truck reversed down the road and stopped in the center, right in front of where the boy stood. Cautious, he remained put, panting like a winded coonhound, covered in cool sweat, and red from the recent escape efforts. He knew, depending on how this conversation went, that this encounter could either offer assistance, or just be a hold-up.

"Boy, are you okay?"

The escapee understood Bill to be the kind of man and genuine man. Bill wasn't known for being a busybody and was rarely seen at the greasy spoon cafe or coffee shop where those people congregated. Bill seemed only interested in maintaining his privacy and his small farm and livestock.

"Boy," he continued, "is you okay? Ain't you Thomas's boy, yeah, ain't you Johnny?" Bill's teeth resembled shards of butter brickle, and his blue and white striped overalls were stained heavily. The bed of his truck was full of feed sacks and the cab was disgustingly cluttered.

As Johnny caught his breath and continuously glanced back and forth down the two-lane for lights, he finally acknowledged the question. "Yes, sir. I am."

"Well," said Bill, "get in and I'll get'cha back home, you must be five or more—"

"*No!*" Johnny blurted out in a desperate and exhausted voice. "You ain't taking me nowhere, I gotta get away from here, and I don't gotta be there by law anymore!"

Bill looked straight ahead as if he were offended. "All right now, boy. No need to get restless, I'm just being neighborly. I'll bid ya good evenin'," Bill said, as he reached to put his truck in gear.

"Wait, please. I need to get a ride outta here. Can you drop me off a bit up further so I can find a lift? I really need to get away from this field." Johnny felt as though his anxiety was clawing its way free from the confinements of his core.

"A ride to where, boy? It's damn near twelve thirty, anyone out on this road at this hour is either half-lit like myself, or lookin' for you. Go ahead and get in just the same."

"Thank you," Johnny said politely as he reached for the door handle.

Bill, although good-natured, clearly had a love for

the bottle. His pickup cab was evidence of that. Empty whisky bottles littered the floorboard and the ashtray was full of beer caps. Either good luck or good ol' boy reputation had kept Bill behind the wheel for all these years.

"Just where do you plan to go, son? Ain't you got one more year of schoolin' before you're done?"

Johnny merely remained silent a few moments; he had no clue where he was going. Johnny took a deep breath and let it out; he then gazed out the window. He hadn't thought about it much. He honestly thought he would have been caught or worse before now.

"I don't know where I'll go, but I ain't goin' back there. You can just drop me off up here a ways and I'll find a lift," he said softly, pointing up the road.

"Well, don't you got no other family round here? Where did your momma end up?"

Johnny continued his gaze out the passenger window as his mind immediately envisioned his mother on the day she left him. His father had been at the mill that day, and his little brother had turned two the day before. Johnny was only sixteen when his mother left him. He couldn't understand why he couldn't go with her and his baby brother, but he knew his brother couldn't stay.

Johnny was about three when he started to remember things—things that should be etched in no child's memory. Jacob, Johnny's brother, would have been three in one more year. They couldn't stay there. Jacob would be ruined too. He now understood how scared his mother must have been on the night she left. Johnny was horribly frightened, and he didn't even have a child to look after.

"Look, boy. I know you need help. Everyone

knows you need help. You been needin' help a while now. There's a bus station in Shreveport. I got a bit of cash and—"

"I got money," Johnny interrupted. "Why would you think I need money?" Johnny was irritated by the offer. Years of taunting by townsmen and classmates had left him easily offended by the topic.

Bill appeared unsure of how to respond. He looked at Johnny with a scowl and opened mouth, exposing foul breath and massive decay.

"I got my own money," Johnny continued as he folded his arms.

"I'll take you to the station, and you can use your money to take a bus to your momma. Will that work?"

"I can leave now?" Johnny asked in a confused tone. "I can get on a bus and leave now?" He continued to stare at Bill, but he couldn't quite grasp what the man was saying.

"Well, you gotta get your ticket first, and to do that, we gotta go to the station. Now, does that work for you?"

"Yes, it does," Johnny replied.

CHAPTER TWO

The Ticket

And where are you needing to go?" the girl behind the ticket booth asked.

Johnny found the blue-eyed girl attractive, but he was so overwhelmed by all the smells, sounds, and sights of the bus station that her looks alone weren't enough to corral his attention entirely. He felt incapable of controlling his gaze from dancing about the scene, unable to completely connect with the young woman attempting to assist him. The details were surreal to him. The only time he had been to Shreveport was when his grandmother passed away. The change in scenery was oppressively stimulating.

"Louisiana," Johnny replied.

The girl lightly bit her bottom lip, glancing at Johnny from the corner of her eye in a curious manner. She was probably five or six years older than Johnny, but her body language gave him the impression that she was uncomfortable assisting him. "You are in Louisiana," she said, with a slightly condescending smile, "Shreveport, Louisiana."

Johnny broke his gaze from her and looked toward a map of the state, next to a national map on the counter of the booth. "Here," he said, pointing to a small dot on the map. As the girl looked at where he was pointing, she developed a scowl and appeared completely put-off.

As his curiosity calmed, his frustration presented. He didn't appreciate the manner which the young woman spoke to him. She was stern, yet he felt as though she addressed him like a twelve-year-old. Johnny, however, was far from the age of twelve. In fact, he could have very well been the newest legal adult at the bus station. This was his birthday, the big eighteen.

Most eighteen-year-old boys celebrated the monumental milestone with family or friends offering wisdom and gifts. Johnny would celebrate the day with the greatest gift his father could have given him, a ticket to a new scene. Of course, Thomas Tregalis more than likely hadn't even realized his booze stash was gone yet, but he was paying for the ticket just the same.

An elderly black man standing behind Johnny was growing obviously impatient. Leaning on his cane, the gray-bearded man continuously took deep breaths and exhaled loudly in an irritated manner.

"Sir, we don't provide trav—"

"Okay, then here." Johnny cut her off and pointed hastily to a bigger dot labelled Lake Charles.

"One way to Lake Charles. Cash or credit today, sir?" Johnny reached in the book bag and pulled out the wad of cash. The bills were of various amounts, and they were literally presented to the girl in a crumpled ball. He placed the wad on the counter and turned his attention to one of the buses parked near the booth.

A sudden rush of euphoria raced over him. *This was actually going to happen*. He began to think he might actually pull it off.

"Sir," the girl said sternly.

Johnny was a bit startled as her tone snapped him back to the situation at hand.

"Sir, you really need to take better care of your money. This is much more than you need for your ticket," she said as she began to unfold the remaining bills, putting them in order from least to most value. "This is a good way to lose your cash, man."

Johnny heard the girl's words, yet didn't understand why she would concern herself with his welfare. He looked once again at the parked bus as he felt his euphoria slightly give way to anxiety.

"I'm going to put this in an envelope so you can keep better track of it," the girl said politely. "Here is your ticket, and here is your change in this envelope." She handed him the neatly arranged cash and his ticket as he broke gaze from the bus long enough to grab the items and shove them in his book bag's side pocket. "Unless, of course, you have a wallet. Do you not have a wallet?"

"Do I just get on? The door isn't even open," Johnny asked, pointing toward the parked bus.

"No. You don't get on that bus, it's not even operational," snapped the girl in an abrasive tone. "This ticket number correlates to the departure time and bus you will be taking, which is that way. You will present it when asked. Anything else, sir?"

"No," Johnny replied, and he headed in the

direction the girl pointed him in.

CHAPTER THREE

The Ride

"What exactly is it you're needin'?" asked the obese, hateful clerk behind the quick-stop counter. Her short, red hair and acne-scarred face both looked as if they hadn't been thoroughly washed in days. She had sweat stains under either armpit, and she was probably the largest woman Johnny had ever seen. "You just ain't making sense right now," she continued as she rolled her eyes and chewed her gum loudly.

Johnny hated the woman and her unpleasant demeanor, she was hideous, and gratuitously hateful to him every time he walked to the store. He was having difficulty seeing from his right eye as it was nearly swollen shut. His jacket and sweatpants were dirty, but not dingy, just dirty like he had fallen down and rolled around in the dirt. His John Deere ball cap had dirt and muck all over it as well. He wasn't there asking for handouts or even to complain, yet she was still mean to him.

"I need something to cover up this shiner! Why can't you understand that? I got school pictures on Monday," Johnny snapped at the clerk.

"Young man, I can refuse to serve you if you wanna be hateful." She placed her pudgy hands on either side of her extreme waistline. Her dress was atrocious as well. It reminded Johnny of the white and orange curtains his mother once threw in the burn barrel due to their unattractive nature.

"I need some make-up like ladies use to cover up their spots," he replied.

The woman finally seemed to relax and leaned in closer to him so the people behind him couldn't hear what she was saying. "We don't got that, either. What you need to do is call child protective services, young man."

This was probably the kindest tone the woman had ever taken with him, yet he had no idea what this child place was, or why he needed to call. His glance momentarily fell upon his pathetic reflection in the store widow.

"Well, can I use your phone?"

***

"Use my phone? Hell no. I'm roaming and this prepaid bullshit don't come cheap," said the same elderly black man who was behind him in the line earlier. The cantankerous old man ended up sitting next to Johnny on the bus. "Kids are ungrateful shits these days, think the world owes them something," the old man crankily continued.

Johnny turned and looked at the man with his mouth open and eyes widened. He knew he wasn't in the store near his father's house, he was on the bus. He was on the moving bus, sitting by the window near the back. He then realized he must have been talking out loud. He did that sometimes, but the teen had been staring out the bus window the entire time.

After his mother left two years prior, Johnny approached a mental breaking point, as a child's mentality can only bear so much adversity. Once Johnny's one source of security was gone, he began to lose his sense of clarity little by little, though it was never depleted to the point of clinical dysfunction. Johnny began to confuse his dreams and memories with present reality, and would often experience painful flashbacks of childhood trauma, as well as vivid nightmares of more recent atrocities.

When Johnny became lost deep in thought, he often found it difficult to distinguish past from present, and even delusion from reality. He was a prisoner of the chaotic scrambling often associated with people that experience horrific traumatic events. The result was the occasional inability to understand what was really there to hurt him from what was no longer a viable threat. There were even times when he found it difficult to determine if a situation had occurred, if it were occurring, or if it were some wild, anxiety-driven delusion. Maintaining the ability to assure, and reassure, himself was Johnny's saving grace.

Johnny may have angered the man with his question, but he paid little attention to the man's harsh comments as they were mild in comparison to the harassments he had frequently endured. He looked at the old man briefly, and then returned his gaze toward the window.

The bus was filthy, but so were the majority of the passengers, and the old man smelled awfully of body odor and pipe tobacco. The bus window was covered in greasy fingerprints, and what appeared to be smeared dried ketchup along the bottom of the glass. By this time, Johnny's excitement had somewhat faded, and he was slightly fearful. The reality of being without a viable plan was finally setting in to the extent that he was now wondering where he was going to go once he got off of the bus in Lake Charles. Perhaps he would simply buy another ticket and ride the bus indefinitely. The idea was, of course, beyond impractical, but it made more sense than anything else at this point.

He knew something would work out in his favor. With every second, every minute, Johnny was further from his past, and this thought made it all worth it. He could sleep on the streets for years, and it would still be worth it. Leaving it all behind had seemed like a whimsical idea until his mother left. He understood there had to be more out there, and nothing in the world could hurt him anymore than he'd been hurt already. At the same time, he was only teetering on the fence of hope and complete numbness. He felt that with time and distance, part of him could heal. He had not a clue, however, what healing looked like. He only knew that something inside him told him to run, to exist, and to live.

The old man had closed his eyes and leaned his head back as if he was going to attempt to sleep. Johnny took the opportunity to examine the man more closely. He was obviously extremely thin, and his facial stubble was completely gray. His thin, red, plaid, pearl-snap shirt appeared to be freshly pressed, and his jeans were extremely skinny. He appeared to be poor, yet made an effort to be presentable. He had the wasted look that Johnny was quite familiar with.

Many of the fishermen near Johnny's home that brought up fresh catch from the south had the same appearance. Maybe this man used to be a fisherman. Perhaps that was why he was so cranky. All the fishermen seemed cranky. He probably drank a lot when he was younger, maybe he still drank now. Johnny felt sad for the skinny old man. Regardless of how desperate his own situation was, he was still able to feel some form of compassion for a complete stranger.

Many of the passengers were now either sleeping or reading papers, books, or having very quiet conversations among themselves or with themselves. Some were vagrant, some were disgustingly filthy, but they all had one thing in common, they were all leaving something behind. This too brought about a sense of comfort. This escape was his only option. He had no resources, but no other choice, so he had no reason to feel regretful. He thought perhaps he should try to sleep too. Maybe when he woke, things would make sense. The bus had left at seven, and it was only noon now. The night at the station was restless at best, and he still had several hours to go. If the man next to him could sleep, then Johnny thought he would be able to as well. He rested his head on the countless greasy fingerprints and closed his eyes.

"Good afternoon, people!" the male driver announced over the loud speakers. "We're coming up on a stop, you got twenty minutes to grab some grub, use the facilities, and get back on."

The bus exited the highway and the station was just

off the exit. It slowly began to crawl as it pulled into a fuel station, which had a sign that advertised a Taco Bell and A&W within the store.

Johnny stretched as much as he could in the cramped quarters, and let out a big sleepy yawn.

"Yea, I hear ya. I'm dog-tired too," the old man proclaimed.

Johnny had never heard someone say *dog-tired* before, but he got the point. He simply gave the old man a nod and turned his attention to the store outside his window. He thought a hamburger sounded appetizing as he reached for his book bag.

"Hey, son, you don't have an extra dollar or two you could spare an old man, do you?" asked the elderly man.

Johnny looked at the man, and was half tempted to tell him no simply because he had been so grouchy. But he knew all too well the pain of hunger, and the man was very thin.

"Yes, sir. I got a little," Johnny replied. He reached into his envelope and pulled out a five-dollar bill folded long ways. "Here you go. My name is Johnny, by the way." As the man looked at the five-dollar bill, an expression of guilt fell about his face.

"Why, thank ya kindly, Johnny; my name is Bo." The man reached out to grab the five. His fingers were dark, long, and skinny, and his fingernails had a yellowish discoloration, probably from nicotine. The majority of the passengers had already exited the bus. The two stood from their seats, Bo with his cane, and made their way down the aisle toward the front of the bus.

CHAPTER FOUR

Rest

"This is a damn good burger for a fast-food joint," Bo said, ravaging the burger and fries the five dollars had bought him.

"Yea, it is pretty good. So, where are you from, Bo?" Johnny asked curiously as he dipped his fries in a pile of ketchup comprised of about thirty ketchup packets. The booth they sat at was one of about twenty inside the large store. There were two rows of booths running parallel with the large windows in the front of the store.

"I was born and raised in Biloxi. I been in treatment upstate for my drinkin', and now I'm going to stay with my baby sister and my nephew in Lake Charles, and I thank the good Lord every day I wake up sober." The old man had a mouth full of food, and it was obvious his teeth were not real.

"The treatment was just for drinkin'?" Johnny enquired with obvious curiosity in his voice.

"Yes, sir. It certainly was, but I imagine they got a treatment or therapy for just about everything. You just gotta want it," Bo replied.

"So, you wanted the treatment to stop drinkin'?" Johnny asked. "Did they give you medicine for it? How did it work?"

Bo set his burger down and looked at Johnny with a stone-cold gaze, and after a long pause, he answered the curious boy. "I spent over forty years in the bottle. I did things I ain't proud of. They don't give alcoholics no damn pills. They talk to 'em. Get to the bottom of the reason they drink in the first place. Of course I wanted to quit. I went there on my own account."

"Do you think they can actually fix a lot of problems with talkin'?" Johnny asked in a serious tone.

"I do, I do, I do, my young friend. And those people that do the talkin' make the big bucks," Bo said in a friendly voice with a French fry smile.

Just then, the driver came over the loud speakers in the store. "Attention, passengers. Scarf it down, let's get back out there."

Like a prisoner that had just learned of the possibility of a pardon, Johnny rose from the A&W carnage with an extended sense of hope. Perhaps someday he would be free of his past's prison completely, not only in body, but in mind as well.

CHAPTER FIVE

Jackson

The air was muggy, and the sweat stung Johnny's eyes as it hastily invaded from his forehead. There was a light breeze on the air, but it smelled of exhaust and seemed almost suffocating at times. Johnny was walking down Interstate 10, headed away from the bus stop, as the bus had arrived in Lake Charles about forty-five minutes prior.

It was almost six in the evening, and Johnny was completely defeated, walking aimlessly. The sound of the rocks beneath his feet only assured him he was physically desperate, and the situation was only going to get worse.

How could he? There had been the talk of treatment, and the small chat the remainder of the ride. Johnny knew Bo must have done it when Johnny fell asleep. When Johnny had awoken, both Bo and the remaining cash that he had in his bag were completely gone, taken right out of the side pocket of his book bag, envelope and all. Now he had nothing— no plan, and no money.

His initial idea of finding a taxi to take him to the nearest recommended cheap hotel, or even a shelter, was now bashed. He was certain a good night's sleep would improve the situation. Now that plan was stolen, along with his cash. Like an expanding wildfire in the dark of night, it was becoming increasingly clearer the dire state of his situation. The cars flying by him seemed to have little regard to his well-being or location. He was hungry, scared and had no idea where he was going to sleep once the sun went down.

Bo had mentioned a place called The Salvation Army, and Johnny hoped that perhaps they could help him. Bo had said they had helped him in the past, but Johnny had no idea if anything that thieving bastard said was true. Up the interstate on the left was a Shell station with signs boasting a casino inside. Johnny thought perhaps someone inside would know where the salvation place was. He paid little mind to the speeding traffic. In fact, he paid little attention to any of the surrounding scenery. He had never been this far from home. Although it was the same state, this area was quite different from where he grew up. He had too much on his mind to attempt appreciating the local sights or the speeding drivers.

As he walked into the store he noticed the stench of the bus and his own body odor was very evident on him. He needed a shower, a good meal, and a warm bed. There were many nights he had gone without any of them, so he wasn't too concerned about the trivial things he was currently lacking. He was, however, concerned with his uncontrollable emotional state. He had continuously told himself that he was now legally a man. *Men don't cry.*

The reality was that he was a scared eighteen-year-old boy without a plan or a dime to his name. His eyes were puffy, his face was soaked, and he felt about as pathetic as possible. As he stood in front of the counter attempting to speak to the clerk and enquire as to where the salvation place was, he noticed a tall, clean, and charismatic-looking man with dark brown hair approaching him and the clerk. As he approached, he glanced at the clerk and raised his hand with all his fingers extended as if to say, *I got this.*

"Excuse me, bud. Are you okay?"

Trying his best to calm his quaking voice long enough to speak, Johnny was able to make out one clear word, "No."

"Why don't you and I go sit down in a booth over there for a minute, okay?" Jackson asked, as he put his hand on Johnny's shoulder, looking him in the eye. Johnny gave the man an affirming nod, and the two made their way to the row of booths by the entrance of the store.

CHAPTER SIX

To Smile

Jackson

"We can figure it out in the morning. Tonight we're going to get some fried chicken and homemade rolls in your belly. That always seems to do the trick for me," Jackson said with a kind smile. He watched Johnny as he continuously glanced about the man's car, seemingly observing each detail.

The teen appeared a bit concerned by all the heartworm medication boxes and brochures in the backseat of Jackson's car. Jackson had mentioned he worked with animals, but hadn't gone into much detail. Johnny hadn't disclosed too much, either; only that his father had kicked him out, he didn't know where his mother was, he was totally broke, and had no idea why, of all the destinations, he chose to come here, to Lake Charles.

Jackson was aware there was much more to the story, but he also recognized the desperation in his eyes. After about twenty minutes of small talk at the store, Jackson extended an invitation for supper and a bed for the night. He was satisfied Johnny was not in any trouble with the law. When he watched Johnny load up in his car, he briefly questioned what the hell he was thinking inviting a homeless teen to supper.

Jackson's wife, Graye, was always laughing at her husband for bringing home stray dogs. She was hesitant when Jackson called her from his cell phone at the store, but she informed her husband that she trusted him more than any other soul on the planet. She readily agreed to offer a spare room, and some of her home cooking for a young man that was only four months older than her own son, Jared.

It wasn't every day that Jackson brought home a homeless boy. In fact, he had never before brought home a homeless person. He volunteered at the shelters, and knew they had open beds, but there was something about Johnny. Jackson wouldn't take him there—not tonight. He was going to the Everett house. As the car drove past the bus station, Jackson noticed Johnny unzipping his book bag. The man's peripheral vision remained fixed in an uneasy way on the teen as he reached into the bag.

"If you don't care, maybe I can wash these clothes out in your tub when we get to your house. That way they'll be dry when I leave tomorrow," Johnny requested as he opened his bag further.

"We'll take care of those in the wash machine when we get there, bud," Jackson said with an uncomfortable smile. He gripped the wheel and took the curve. As Johnny opened his bag further, sitting on top of the clothing sat a crumpled white envelope. Johnny grabbed it and opened it up, exposing a small assortment of bills. On the front of the envelope was a scribbled note. Jackson watched the boy's amusement and was surprised to hear him mutter the words that had been jotted down.

You, my friend, are a good man. I hadn't eaten in nearly two days. You need to keep this hidden better. Anyone could walk by and snatch it. Good things come to good people. Bo

"Everything okay?"

"He wasn't lying," Johnny exclaimed, showcasing an uncontrollable smile. "I have a little bit of money for you. Sorry, I lost it when I was on the bus," Johnny said as he thumbed through the cash.

"That won't be necessary, sir. All I ask is that you clean your plate and always tell the wife her food is wonderful at least three times," Jackson replied in a joking manner.

"Okay," said Johnny, whose tone gave the impression that he believed the request to be genuine.

"When we get home, I'll introduce you to the family. Jared will like having another guy besides me there for the night. I absolutely hate video games, and he thinks they're the best thing ever," Jackson said as he glanced over at Johnny. "Do you like video games?"

"I played a game once at my friend Bobby's house, but I only went there once because I wasn't supposed to be there in the first place. So, nah, I'm not too good at 'em," Johnny replied as he looked out the window.

"And why weren't you supposed to be there?" Jackson asked curiously, glancing at Johnny as his eyes narrowed in intrigue.

"Well, because he was black," Johnny replied rather nonchalantly as he continued gazing about.

This response surprised Jackson briefly. He knew

this boy had an interesting story, but he imagined it to be painful as well. Either way, Jackson's mind had been made since the store. He was certain this boy needed a great deal of help, and there was no reason for him to have to stay at a shelter the first night away from home. There were certain reservations, of course, but Jackson's natural paternal instinct seemed to cloud his judgment from the practicality of the situation.

"I'll let you take a hot shower and scrub the bus station off of you when we get there, then we'll get you fed, and make sure you get a good night's sleep," Jackson said as he began to yawn.

"Thank you, sir. I'm sorry if I smell bad," Johnny replied as he turned his eyes toward the floor.

Jackson started laughing as he looked at Johnny. "I didn't mean that at all, Johnny. I've been working with horses all day, I probably smell bad."

Johnny broke his gaze from the floor long enough to look briefly at Jackson and smile.

"What exactly is your job?" Johnny asked.

"I'm a concierge veterinarian. That just means I don't work a regular nine-to-five schedule, and my wife teaches English at my son's high school."

"And your boy is my age? You don't look old enough to have a boy my age."

"I just turned thirty-eight. I'm sure the gray will set in soon enough."

"I just wanna say thank you, sir. I really do appreciate this."

"You're going to be grinning from ear to ear when you taste my wife's cooking."

Some souls burn out once they have reached a certain level of adversity. Perhaps Johnny's was close to this point, understandably, but Jackson saw something in him. He saw a recognizable characteristic that he could see in himself and his own son.

As they turned off the highway onto the dirt road, Jackson took notice of Johnny's reaction to seeing the Everett's home come into view. By the American standard, the house was very elegant and quite large; however, it was actually rather modest in regard to the annual income the couple brought in and the inheritance they were sitting on. The drive leading to the two-story, white house was lined with large, white rocks. The house had dark blue shutters, and a huge front porch, complete with a white, hanging, porch swing. To the side of the house was a detached four-car garage, white as well. On the left side of the house was a stable horse with a large pasture behind it. There was also a large, red barn behind the garage with pens.

Four large dogs barked out the warning of the approaching vehicle as they came charging down the drive. "Well, here comes Sampson, Stella, Sunny, and Toby."

Johnny leaned forward, smiling largely as he watched them approach. The dogs appeared to be mix breeds, except one shepherd. There were two yellow lab mixes, and a large black dog too.

"Did you have a dog back home, Johnny?"

"Yea, well, kinda, but she drowned when she was still a pup."

As the car came to a stop, Jackson put it in park and turned toward Johnny, who was now looking out the window, still smiling at the dogs.

"She…she drowned? How did she drown?"

Johnny turned and looked at Jackson with a solemn gaze. "In the pond," he said hastily, returning his glance immediately to the house and the dogs outside the vehicle.

Before Jackson could respond, the front door of the house opened.

The light from the inside of the house lit up some of the plants that were hanging from the ceiling of the porch, which was covered and was as wide as the entire front of the house as it wrapped around the right side of the house and went back several feet.

The evening was completely still. Someone could have lit a long-stem candle in the middle of the yard and the flame would have remained pointing completely skyward. The air was thick and muggy, but the fireflies and singing birds seemed to add a certain enchantment to the property. Behind the red barn was an abundance of trees and thick brush. In fact, other than the yard, and the cleared pasture, all the surrounding acreage was woodland with huge, beautiful trees draped in moss.

As Jackson's son, Jared, came out of the open door of the house, Jackson noted that he and Johnny could almost pass for brothers. They were about the same height, around five foot eight inches, and both had dark hair. Jared was more filled out, he even had a small amount of baby fat on him. This was, no doubt, the product of adequate nutrition.

"Well, there's the man of the hour, Mr. Jared Everett," Jackson said as he smiled at his son, who jumped off the porch and was now jogging toward the car in gray sweatpants and white t-shirt. Jackson assumed Jared was the type of kid that fathers would want their daughters to bring home. He was genuinely kind to about everyone he came across, and was extremely respectable in most cases.

"What's up, Pops?" he asked while smiling in an inviting manner. He leaned into his father's window, bent over slightly with his hands resting on his knees. "You must be Johnny. So, it's Jackson, Jared, and Johnny. That's gonna be confusing as hell for Mom tonight," Jared said, as he was obviously attempting to ease the situation with sarcasm.

"Hey, watch your mouth in front of our guest, dork," Jackson snapped as he ruffled Jared's hair with his hand.

"Yea, yea, Pops. Johnny, I hope you're hungry, man. Mom made enough food to feed a horse, if horses ate fried chicken," Jared said happily as he continued looking through the window.

"I am. I'm *dog-tired* too," Johnny replied.

A little girl came charging toward the car. Jackson adored her precious smile and found her beautiful, even when boasting a mess of brown, ratted hair.

"And here comes Miss Bryce, filthy as ever," Jackson said, shaking his head.

Johnny broke his gaze from the small girl and turned to Jackson.

"Bryce? That's a really pretty name. I like it," he said, as the girl reached the car.

"Well, I like it too, sir. I like it too," Jackson replied as he continued watching his daughter.

"Daddy!" the girl shrieked happily. "Daddy, I wanna see the new boy, I wanna see him." Her little fingers appeared on the window seal of her father's car door as she tried to pull herself up to see.

The new boy. Jackson thought the title almost sounded permanent. He certainly didn't want to give the teenager any misguided impression that the one-night offer would become anything more. "Hold on there, little bit," Jackson said sternly, "that new boy has a name; Johnny," Jackson said to the chipper little girl.

She let go of the door and raced around to the other side of the car to open Johnny's door. She vigorously attempted to open the door, but she didn't have the strength.

Johnny, smiling, opened the door from the inside.

She looked at his face briefly, and then wrapped her arms around his waist, seatbelt and all. "You're very cute," the little girl said with an innocent smile.

"Well, so are you, Bryce," Johnny replied.

"You boys hungry?" asked a lovely voice from the doorway of the house. "You better be!" the voice continued.

Jackson looked up to see his beautiful wife in the doorway of the house. The sun was beginning to set and the string of yard lights on either side of the white porch stairs began to light up. The woman looked angelic while walking down the stairs of the porch. She was slender, had dark brown hair, and a gorgeous, welcoming smile. She was wearing an oversized, white t-shirt and red basketball shorts, and she was barefoot as she walked across the plush, green grass toward the car.

Jackson could sense Johnny appeared understandably overwhelmed. He smiled and seemed to be making a valiant effort to connect with each member of the family, yet he appeared tense and uneasy. The tension seemed to almost lift from Johnny's shoulders as Graye approached him.

"You must be Mr. Johnny," the woman said,

looking down at the sitting guest.

"Yes, ma'am," Johnny said, smiling back at her. "Well, it is certainly a pleasure to meet you." The woman was still smiling as she extended her hand to shake his.

As Jackson watched the interaction, he couldn't help but wonder of Johnny's mother; what she was like, and how she could have simply lost touch with her son. Jackson was typically always aware of Jared's whereabouts and couldn't imagine this kid being halfway across the state without his knowledge. The interaction between his wife and Johnny felt easy and unforced. This began to settle Jackson's nerves too. He was thankful that Graye was receptive to the idea of assisting the young man. He imagined his own boy, lost, broke, and crying at gas station far from home. The thought broke his heart.

"Come on, sweetheart, supper's waiting inside," Graye said sweetly with a comforting tone.

CHAPTER SEVEN

Clean

Graye

As she removed the clothing from the book bag, she noticed not one, but two live roaches crawling about in the bag. The clothes were truly pathetic. There were so many stains, and the shirts were worn and faded. The bag, and its contents, smelled like a stale ashtray. The shirts had several burn holes in them as well. Even if Johnny smoked, there was no way he accidently burned himself that many times.

The laundry room, like the rest of the house, was white, bright, and beautiful, and the bag of disgusting clothing was in total contrast. The room was off the kitchen, and boasted a beautiful granite countertop just above both of the front load appliances. The granite matched that of the kitchen and three bathrooms, a dark brown. It contrasted well next to the bright white walls. The entire house, both stories and the basement, had dark hardwood flooring. Graye was assured everything appeared crisp and clean with a rigorous cleaning schedule.

As she looked at the clothing, she felt an overwhelming urge to cry. What was this kid's story? Although her gut was telling her Johnny was harmless, she had to be practical about the situation. She had to make sure her family was safe; however, she was already thinking along the same lines as her husband. Johnny seemed to have been through so much. He needed a rest, some reassurance, and the love only a happy family could provide. He needed to mend.

There was something that drew her to him. He had only been in her house for about forty-five minutes, and already she was envisioning how they would decorate the guest room to better suit another teenage boy.

"Sad, isn't it?" Jackson asked, standing in the doorway of the laundry room.

"Sad isn't the word. This seriously makes me want to cry and just, just hug the kid," Graye replied with a disgusted look on her face. "Jackson, there are roaches in his clothes." Graye heard the desperation in her own voice as she turned toward her husband, their son Jared appearing with a mouth full of hot rolls.

"Roaches?" Jared mumbled as he chewed his food loudly.

"Jared!" his mother scolded him sharply. "What have I told you about listening in on your father and me? And you are going to ruin your appetite before we all get sat down for supper," she continued as she looked once more in the tattered book bag.

"I doubt that," Jackson said, chuckling as he

looked at his son.

"Mom, how'd he get roaches in his clothes?" Jared asked with concern in his voice.

"We can't keep them in the house. We can't let him wear them, they're disgusting," Graye said as she held up a pair of worn-out jeans, ignoring her son's question. "I'll pick him up some new things when I take Bryce to piano tomorrow," the woman continued assuredly.

"We're buying him clothes? Okay. But if this boy eats as much as Jared, I may have to see about getting another job," Jackson said playfully.

"Mom, he can have my jeans from last year. They're too small thanks to you, and I still have them in my closet. I bet there's at least seven pairs. I'll go look and see." Jared had already offered the newcomer an unopened package of boxer shorts, some socks, some old sweats, and a t-shirt to sleep in, before Graye showed him to the guest bathroom upstairs. "I'm sure I have some shirts I never wear too," Jared said as he turned to head for the staircase in the living room.

Graye watched her son exit, thankful for the undeniably strong and loving relationship she had with him. He truly was a good kid. She and his father had every reason to hold him in such high regards.

"Momma, I'm hungry," said an impatient little Bryce as she came walking through the kitchen toward the laundry room.

"Honey, as soon as Johnny gets downstairs we will sit down and eat 'til it comes out of our ears." Graye was eager to get Johnny fed, as she was unsure when the last time he ate was.

"Momma," the small girl continued, "can we keep

him? Can we keep Johnny?"

"He's not a dog," Jackson chimed in, placing his hand on Bryce's head and looking down at her.

"There will be no more talk about keeping anyone. Understand?" Graye followed up in a scolding tone and disapproving look.

"Yes, I understand." The little girl rolled her eyes as she inhaled deeply and completed a goofy circular ballerina twirl. She then ran back through the kitchen.

Johnny

Johnny was enjoying a much-needed shower. He thought the steam and refreshing water was liberating. He had never been in a bathroom as nice as the Everetts' before. Everything was fresh, clean, and smelled of fabric softener and soap. The water pressure was almost too much, as the hot water washed away the filth of the bus. He felt as if the day was literally washing off him. Completely covered in lathery suds, Johnny washed his hair, yet again. He then heard his stomach growl, reminding him there was supper downstairs.

He hadn't necessarily been plucked from poverty; rather, he coincidentally fell into the lap of a family that was about as goodhearted as they come. In his mind, at this point, he knew his future was uncertain. However, he also knew he was rinsing off in a hot shower, he had a meal waiting for him downstairs, and he had a bed to sleep in for the night. That was more than he could have expected his first night after making his escape.

Stepping out of the shower onto the plush, white

rug, Johnny grabbed the towel Graye had given him off the granite counter. His head remained tilted toward the ceiling until the towel was securely snug around his waist. Of all the things on this earth that horrified him, none scared him as much as the sight of a naked adult man. His own body was no exception. He had not looked at himself in the mirror unclothed intentionally in over three years.

Moving toward the toilet, free of his reflection, he removed the towel and dried off. The towel had a refreshing scent to it, and reminded Johnny of the honeysuckle when it bloomed near the pond by his father's house.

Graye had also given him a brand-new toothbrush. He found it fascinating that the family had a reserve of toothbrushes, deodorant, and other personal items in the towel closet of the upstairs hallway.

Johnny's toothbrush at his father's house was the same one he had gotten from a class trip to the dentist office when he was in elementary school. Johnny took pride in his smile. His personal hygiene was one of the few factors he had moderate control over. He would often scrub his clothing for hours in his father's old bath water. More than once at his father's house he had brushed his teeth with hand soap, as the household was frequently out of toothpaste and other toiletries. He wanted to brush his teeth now. He knew he would be eating soon, but he didn't care, he wanted to brush his teeth with a brand-new brush. Johnny opened the new package of underwear. His underwear had holes, as they were several years old. His mother bought his underwear long before she left. Now he had new pairs, and he would be wearing the fresh, clean clothes Jared had given him. The socks felt so good on his tired feet, and Jared's clothes were so comfortable and fit him just right.

He looked at his pile of dirty clothes by the door and almost felt ashamed to have to wear such things in front of such nice people. He then reminded himself that it was out of his control. His entire existence was out of his control, and feeling ashamed and humiliated would solve nothing. He collected his brand-new toothbrush, the opened underwear package, and the pile of dirty clothes, and opened the bathroom door. Johnny nervously made his way down the hall and down the stairs. Graye placed a large pitcher of tea on the table just as Johnny entered the kitchen. Everything smelled delicious.

Jared and Graye were placing items on the gorgeous oak wood table and carrying on casual conversation. They had to add the leaf to the table to ensure they had enough room to sit all five people comfortably. There was a large serving platter with the biggest pile of fried chicken Johnny had ever seen; a big, square, wooden dish full of fresh green salad; and another bowl full of rolls.

"You about ready to throw down, man?" Jared asked as he pulled out his chair from under the table.

"Throw down?" Johnny asked Jared curiously as he stood near the table with his pile of filthy clothes.

"You'll have to forgive my son. He frequently butchers the English language," Graye said, smiling at Johnny. He could feel water running from his wet hair down the back of his neck. "Let me take these clothes and throw them in the wash with the others." Graye grabbed the clothes from Johnny and turned to walk to the laundry room.

"Thank you," Johnny said appreciatively as she

walked away.

"Why, you sure are welcome, sweetheart. Grab a plate and start loading up!" Graye hollered back from the laundry room.

"Feel better, bud?" asked Jackson, who came walking in from the living room with a fresh-faced Bryce. He had changed his clothes and freshened up too. Maybe he really was dirty from working with horses. Johnny believed the man had only told him that so he wouldn't feel uncomfortable for being so horrendously filthy.

"I feel great. The water here works really good," Johnny replied as he anticipated eating.

"Well, that's good to hear. Here's a plate. I hope you're ready to throw down," Jackson said as he handed a white porcelain plate to him.

"Pops, don't butcher the English language," Jared said sarcastically as he loaded a large amount of mashed potatoes onto his plate. Jackson looked at his son, a bit confused, and shrugged. Johnny had only witnessed the interaction between Jared and his father for half an hour, yet he could recognize several similarities in their mannerisms.

The entire family was now circling the table, loading their plates in a most unconventional manner. The families on TV sat down around the table, and the words, "Will you please pass," were redundantly muttered. Not here, not this family. Johnny didn't mind. The unconventional table manners were nothing to take note of as his father's kitchen was usually cluttered with gas cans, various tools, and the occasional car part.

"Momma, it smells so good!" said little Bryce as she anxiously watched her older brother load her plate.

"Well, of course it does, baby girl. Your momma is only the best cook this side of New Orleans," Graye replied in a confident, sarcastic manner.

Johnny smiled as he placed a chicken leg on his plate. He then grabbed a roll and backed away from the table.

"You're gonna have to grab more than that if we're gonna get through this pile tonight," Jared said as he placed Bryce's plate down in front of the hungry and excited little girl.

Johnny was very hungry, and there was a lot there, even for this entire family and himself.

"I can do that," Johnny said as he reached for what he thought looked like a chicken breast.

"Attaboy!" said Jared with a smile.

Johnny couldn't understand why the family was being so pleasant to him, but at the same time he knew he was in no position to question their friendly generosity. Just as easily as he had ended up in this huge, beautiful kitchen, he could be on the street, or even worse, in a week from now, or even tomorrow. For now, he was going to take the opportunity to quell his hunger, as well as try his hardest to not worry about what tomorrow had in store.

Once he was confident the selections on his plate would appease his rumbling stomach, Johnny turned and walked to the corner of the kitchen, about seven feet away from the table. He then sat down on the floor with his plate of food and his back to the family. He picked up the chicken leg and bit into it; it was delicious. The Cajun spices were so flavorful, and the texture was so crunchy. Johnny was now wishing he would have taken more. Perhaps there would be some left over. He noticed the entire family had halted their plate preparation and was now watching him.

"Um, Johnny," Jared said softly, "we got another place here at the table for you; right here next to me, man."

Johnny, still sitting down, and with a mouth full of chicken, used his feet to swivel around on his butt. "You…you want me to sit at the table?" Johnny asked, somewhat surprised by the invitation.

Graye walked to him, extending her hand to help him to his feet. "Of course, sweetheart. Grab your plate and come sit with the family at the table. We can't have you sitting on the floor on your birthday."

CHAPTER EIGHT

Morning Mumbling

"I really just don't want to talk about it. It doesn't mean anything to talk about it anyways," Johnny said as he sat in the guidance counselor's office.

The walls were exposed brick, and one entire wall was a huge bookshelf that was completely full of books, both large and small. The green floor tile wasn't attractive, but Johnny liked Mr. Benson's office. It smelled like oranges. He always felt comfortable there, at least until Mr. Benson started asking questions. Johnny would never tell him anything that happened at his father's house.

"It doesn't mean anything? What do you mean by that, Johnny?" asked Mr. Benson.

Mr. Benson was a kind man, but Johnny had heard whispers from others that the man had no business counseling anybody. He was thirty years old, tall, slender, often wore suspenders, and was just odd. He had a comb over, and used words that were foreign to Johnny. To top it off, he was constantly pushing his dark-rimmed glasses back up as they slid down his greasy, pointed nose.

"I don't know what you want me to say, Mr. Benson. I can't leave there, and I'm going to be there my whole life. So, that's just that. There's no need to talk about it," Johnny said as he sat in the office chair across from the counselor, looking out the small window on the left side of the office.

"Your whole life? No, that's incorrect, Johnny. When you turn eighteen this year you are no longer required to live there if you don't want to. By law, you are free to leave. There are several available resources and systems in place to assist those that need help getting on their feet. Johnny, your grades are very decent, and—"

"I can just walk out and leave when I turn eighteen? I don't have to stay there no more?" Johnny asked, feeling his pulse behind his eyes, searching Mr. Benson's face for truth.

"That's...that's right, Johnny. Were you told otherwise?" Mr. Benson remained expressionless.

Johnny felt certain the man knew more than he let on. Mr. Benson had filed reports with administration, and had even contacted the local police department. Nothing came from it, as the law enforcement had nothing to go on other than rumors and a shaky counselor's intuition.

Johnny couldn't understand Mr. Benson's specific interest in his case. He recognized the area was riddled with situations similar to his own. He was only one of many sad stories.

"Johnny, did someone tell you that you had to stay at your father's residence your entire life?" the concerned counselor continued.

Johnny stared at his folded hands in his lap.

"How...how long after I turn eighteen can I leave?" he asked quietly, still staring at his hands.

"The day, the very second you turn eighteen you are free to leave. Twelve o'clock midnight, on July 18, you are free to leave and there is nothing anyone can say about it."

***

Johnny sat up in bed. He was sweating and shaking as he looked about the dark room. He was breathing heavily through both his mouth and nose. The room, the smells, the sounds, everything was foreign as he frantically looked in every direction for familiarity. For a moment, he had forgotten where he was. In that moment, he was back in hell. As he evaluated the room, it began to come back to him.

The thick, heavy comforter was the most comfortable blanket he'd ever covered up with, yet Graye had apologized because it had a flower print on it. Johnny often had to wash the mouse urine and droppings from his blankets on his old bed; flower prints were nothing to be apologetic for. The wall next to the door had an oil painting of a woman staring into a mirror. The closet was huge and was full of heartworm medication boxes and other supplies that Jackson needed.

He couldn't hear the dull humming of the swamp cooler that was in the living room of his father's house. He knew he was safe for the night. What was confusing him was his conversation with Mr. Benson.

Deciphering the past from the present was becoming increasingly difficult. The dream was so vivid. Was it a dream? Did it actually happen? Sitting in the bed with his legs bent in front of him, resting his elbows on his knees, he began to reassess. He then reassured himself that the conversation did take place. The meeting with the counselor resulted in Johnny being a few minutes late getting home after summer school.

Johnny lay back and turned onto his side to face the window on the wall directly behind the bed he was sleeping in. This room was on the second floor, right next to Jared's room. Jackson and Graye's room was on the main floor, and Bryce's room right across the hall from theirs. There was a second guestroom on the second floor, and the basement was basically a man cave, although Graye utilized the area more than Jackson and Jared did.

As Johnny looked out the window, feeling the heavy sense of sleep overtaking his eyelids once more, he heard the whimpering of what sounded like a puppy. He quickly pushed himself up and looked toward the lit ground of the yard. A small, black, mixed-breed puppy looked solemnly up at him. Johnny instantly clinched his eyes shut as if he were attempting to keep blowing dirt from them. He opened them slowly. It was gone. He knew it had never been there. "Just stay away," he muttered. Looking once more, assuring himself there was nothing there, he rested his heavy head into the plush pillow, cool and inviting.

Physically, Johnny felt comfortable after he recovered from his elevated heart rate and state of anxiety. The bed was soft; he felt as if he could melt into it. The sheets, the blankets, the clothes, everything about this night was comforting, except his mind's dastardly setbacks. But he was convinced that he was safe. He closed his eyes as a warm blanket of comforting slumber ushered him off to sleep.

***

The floor was cold linoleum that was torn in some areas, exposing the plywood subflooring. The baseboards in the kitchen were disgustingly filthy. Every dish and glass was in the sink as flies swarmed above the pile. On the kitchen counter was a half-emptied package of generic paper plates. The kitchen table was actually a fold up display table. There were four mismatched chairs surrounding it. Where the wall met the floor was speckled with mouse droppings all around the room. The kitchen window, just above the sink, was cracked from top to bottom and was held together with duct tape. The old gas stove was covered in grease, as was the wall behind it, and even the popcorn ceiling was a dark brown from years of grease build up. The cobwebs in every corner of the ceiling were a dark brown from filth.

He sat with his back to the wall on the floor. The bottom of his feet were nearly black, yet he hadn't been outside that day. A cockroach scurried across his right foot and quickly made an escape along the wall. On his lap was a paper plate covered in unheated chicken noodle soup. The house had no clean silverware, so he was using his fingers to pick up the noodles and lift them to his face. His lip hurt every time he opened his mouth too wide. It was healing from being busted, yet again; however, it would crack when he tried to eat. There was a constant noise of scurrying within the walls and under the sink. The entire house was infested.

He would clean the kitchen; he would clean the entire house. He would love to walk across a clean floor. His father would not allow Johnny to touch anything in the kitchen while he was gone. When he was there, Johnny would constantly be accused of misplacing a tool or a random part. Johnny would not dare touch anything of his father's, yet he was constantly reprimanded in a gratuitous manner for misplaced items.

The sound of the swamp cooler often masked the sound of his father's truck engine as it pulled up onto the front lawn. He was constantly listening and observing his surroundings like a hunted animal. Relaxation was only a word to Johnny. Every single day survival was tested in some fashion or another.

He craved something other than chicken noodle soup. He wanted something of substance, something sweet, like cake. Chicken noodle soup was often the only thing he had to eat in the house. When school was in session, he devoured everything the cooks piled on his tray. He pretended not to notice, as did several of his classmates, as the lunch ladies piled just a little bit more on his plate.

As he raised another cluster of noodles to his open mouth, a glimmer of light shimmered through the kitchen window. He dropped the noodles back on the paper plate as his heart raced. He hadn't let his guard down; how did this vehicle approach without any notice? Perhaps he still had time to flee the kitchen. Just then, he heard the truck door slam shut. There was no doubt it was the sound of his father's truck. He didn't have time. He had been foolish and left the can opener out next to the empty dented can of chicken noodle soup. He sat, horrified of what was going to happen. He stared at his half-eaten plate of soup. The paper plate was saturated in broth and had basically lost most of its integrity.

The door in the kitchen opened up to the front yard. Johnny knew that on the other side, walking to the door that very minute was an inescapable source of pain. He sat silently, attempting to remain collected in an almost trance-like state as the door opened. His father's foot hit the floor hard, as did the two steps following the first. Johnny continued to look only at the plate. He could tell by his father's steps that the man was intoxicated.

When his father drank, there was a window of violence. From the time the man began to become intoxicated, to the time he passed out in his room, was the time Johnny dreaded the most. Sometimes, however, the man would drink so much so fast that this window of time shortened dramatically, and the man would simply pass out. Johnny hoped that tonight was one of those nights. Perhaps the man's peripheral vision was so impaired that he would ignore Johnny altogether and head down the hall to his room.

"What the fuck do we have here?" His drunken father's voice was horrifying. He wasn't going to pass out. He was drunk, mad, and Johnny had just handed him a reason for reprimand.

Johnny's hands were shaking as he watched the boots approach him from the corner of his eye. He knew what was coming, yet continued to avoid eye contact with his father.

"I sure did thought I smelt of me a little faggot," the man said under a drunken breath, "and this little faggot is basically trespassing." The man's words penetrated in a cold, deep voice. "What you doin' in here, boy?" the man asked as he used the back of a kitchen chair for balance and raised his muddy boot. Johnny knew he would soon be kicked in the head or face. There was nothing he could say to prevent it. He also knew if he said nothing, it would only anger his father more.

He swallowed hard and answered. "I-I'm sorry. I was hungry. I'm just really hungry."

"Dude, for real. I'm about to get us some breakfast," said Jared as Johnny shot up in bed and used his feet to propel himself to the other side, next to the wall. He looked at Jared in total confusion. He knew he had just been with his father. He remembered Jared vaguely, but the fact that he was not in front of his father was completely confusing to the young man. He continued to stare at Jared as his heartbeat resounded in his throat.

"Johnny, it's okay. I think you were probably having a bad dream. No need to apologize, man. I'm pretty hungry too." Jared was wearing old blue jeans and a torn red t-shirt, with steel-toed boots and an old Budweiser ball cap.

Johnny continued watching him. The room was completely lit, the sun was up, and he imagined it to be at least eight in the morning. Jared took a hesitant step in the direction of the bed with his back arched, and his hand out in front of him.

"Hey, man, you were talking, I came in to ask if you wanted to help me out in the stables today. Do you wanna eat some breakfast?"

Johnny felt the tension ease slightly as he began to recall Jared, Jackson, Graye, and Bryce. Still pressed against the wall, he knew where he was, but he wasn't completely convinced he wasn't in any danger. His respirations were uncontrollable, heart rate was still elevated, and he felt his fingertips ache as his hands attempted to grip the wall behind him.

"Is-is he here?" Johnny asked with a cracking voice.

"Who? Is who here, man?" Jared looked at Johnny, waiting for a response. "Mom and B are in town, and Dad got a call around four, he's been gone all morning. It's just you and me, Johnny."

Johnny finally gained control of his breathing and began to relax. He slowly came to the realization that his father was nowhere near the room or the house.

"I…I'm sorry. I guess I just was having a bad dream," Johnny said as he touched his face, just to be certain it had not been kicked.

"Dude, no worries, you were probably having a night terror because of that ugly-ass bedding," Jared said, grinning as Johnny let out a forced chuckle and the mood in the room began to lighten.

"So, I have about six hours of shit shoveling in the stables today." Jared tilted his head and looked at Johnny, giving him a half smile and raising his eyebrow as he asked, "So, you think you might wanna give me a hand?"

CHAPTER NINE

On The Farm

As Johnny emerged from the bathroom wearing a pair of tattered work jeans and a torn, gray Old Navy t-shirt, and some of Jared's old tennis shoes, he had a plethora of thoughts running through his head. He wondered what Jared thought of him after witnessing his actions. He wondered what he was saying out loud when Jared entered the room, and he was certain that Jackson's son now thought he was a psycho. He thought Jared would now look at him the way some of the kids at his school looked at him.

He made his way down the hallway toward the top of the staircase banister. The floors were always shiny and dust free. The banister and stairs alike were both as dark as the hard wood floors. Johnny took the time to appreciate the beautiful light fixture in the hallway. From the bathroom, he could see out over to the big red barn. The surrounding property was even more amazing in the daylight.

"How those fit ya, man?" Jared asked from the bottom of the staircase as Johnny appeared at the top. "Shoes are a little big, but nothin' too bad," Johnny replied.

"Well, now we both look like hicks," said Jared with a smile. "Come on down, dude, I fixed us some eggs and sausage." Jared motioned Johnny down the staircase with his hand.

Johnny felt a little more at ease, as Jared's actions and tone seemed extremely welcoming. Perhaps he didn't think Johnny was such a freak after all.

As Johnny stepped off the staircase and followed Jared into the kitchen, he noticed that Jared had already prepared Johnny a plate and poured a glass of orange juice on him. "Thanks, man. This looks really good," Johnny said as he eyed the plate of food, walking to the kitchen table. Johnny hadn't had an actual breakfast in years.

"Hey, man, no worries at all," Jared replied, standing beside the table, plucking up pieces of piping hot scrambled egg with his fingers and putting them in his mouth.

"Dude, I totally sleepwalk sometimes. Mom caught me in nothin' but my underwear one night, just standing by the front door. She said it was the freakiest shit she'd ever seen. We all do dumb shit when we're passed out, and most the time we probably don't know it," Jared said, chuckling.

This immediately put Johnny's mind at ease. Even if he were only at the house for the rest of the day, he didn't want Jared remembering him as the crazy guy that said crazy things in his sleep.

"Yea, man. I think I was about to jump out the window when you came in this morning. I totally forgot where I was," Johnny said, smiling as he pulled out the kitchen table to sit down and eat.

"Don't you hate that shit? You wake up and have

no damn clue where the hell you are," Jared exclaimed as he sat down at the table.

"So, she found you by the door? How'd she get you back to bed?" Johnny took a large bite of sausage, which was still extremely hot.

"Hell, I don't know. I guess I walked back by myself. I don't know how I made it up the stairs without busting my ass," Jared said, chewing his breakfast and talking with his mouth full. "I'm glad you decided to sit at the table this morning." Jared looked at Johnny with humor in his eyes.

Johnny didn't know exactly how to respond, as he was never allowed to eat at the table at his father's house, not that he wanted to anyway. He was always forced to eat in the corner of the kitchen.

"Man, I'm just giving you shit. You can sit where you like, I don't mind chillin' on the floor to keep you company." Jared was smiling, but Johnny could tell Jared was serious.

"Every house is different, I guess. At my dad's house I sat on the floor to eat," Johnny said as he stared at his plate of food, avoiding eye contact with Jared.

"Man, that's the truth. Every house is different. I know this girl from school whose family ate the placenta after she was born!" Jared was shaking his head and smiling, as both the boys started laughing lightly.

Johnny looked up at Jared with a comical, yet concerned look, "Why would they eat it?"

"Hell, I don't know. She said her mom baked it in brownies and shared them with her dad!" Jared replied. They both laughed again. The tension was leaving the room as quickly as the daylight was filling it. It was time to get to work.

"Dude, if it's gonna take six hours, we need to get out there," Johnny said, and then finished off his orange juice, placing the glass back on the table. Johnny wanted to help Jared, but knew he would more than likely be leaving today, so they needed to get started.

"Yea, we better get out there," Jared agreed.

CHAPTER TEN

Sweat

The stable was beautiful, but it almost appeared as though the rest of the property's structures had been built long after the stable was erected. The structure stood at least two hundred yards from the house. It contained six stalls and was constructed almost entirely of cement. Foundational cracking was evident all about the building. The doors to the stalls, however, looked new, were made of wood, and were painted a brilliant red, the same color of red the large barn was painted. The stall doors opened up to the huge pasture. Green ivy covered the building from the ground and all the way to the top, and even appeared to be growing on top of the building in some areas. There was damp straw scattered in front of all six doors, two of which were open, and inside every single stall. The Everetts only owned two horses; however, Jackson would frequently board an injured patient within the stalls.

The morning was beautiful, but the humidity was already intense, as it usually is in July in Louisiana. This summer had been relatively mild. There were even some nights that it seemed chilly. Today, however, was starting out as a typical Louisiana summer day. Johnny was almost put off by the fact that Jared's parents had left them in the house alone. He knew he wasn't a danger, but for all they knew, he was a serial killer on the run.

Johnny was carrying two shovels, and Jared was pushing a wheelbarrow. From Jared's description of the task at hand, he was under the impression that the stalls were completely overwhelmed with horse manure. That, however, was not the case. Johnny walked the length of the stable, examining each stall as he passed by.

"Man, this isn't gonna take us no six hours," Johnny said to Jared as he leaned the shovels on the first red door.

"You don't think? Well, that's good anyways; I still gotta school you at some Call of Duty," Jared said, smiling as he rested the wheel barrel by the first door as well.

"Call of Duty?" Johnny asked inquisitively.

"Aw, dude. Johnny, tell me you game. Please, for the love of God, tell me you game."

Jared had a strange smirk on his face as his eyes looked sharply at Johnny.

"You mean video games? Your dad told me you played them," Johnny said as Jared reached for a shovel.

"Dude, we gotta get this shit shoveled. I gotta get you up to speed," Jared said in an enthusiastic tone as he opened the door. "My system is in the basement you haven't been down there yet. It has surround sound and the recliners down there are pimp!" Jared exclaimed from inside the first stall.

"Well, we better get after it then." Johnny happily grabbed the remaining shovel. "Dude, I saw a basketball hoop on the side of the barn, do you ever play?" Johnny asked as he walked into the second stall.

"Oh, hell yea, I love me some hoops when it's not two thousand degrees outside. What about you?" Jared sneezed as he unloaded the first shovel full of manure into the wheel barrel.

"Yea, man. I play. I ain't too good, but I try," Johnny replied.

"Don't let Mom hear you say ain't, it might cost you a quarter," Jared said playfully.

From up by the house a horn honked loudly, and the parade of dogs and their wild warning was heard.

"I guess Pops is home," Jared said as he peeked out of the stall.

"What else do you do around here to stay busy?" Johnny asked as he shoveled manure from outside the stalls.

Jared began laughing an exaggerated, dramatic laugh that was obviously sarcastic. "Dude, there is nothing to do out here. Pop's hardly ever lets me go to town, and when I do I gotta be home by like, nine o'clock on the weekends." Jared looked extremely and happily surprised as he emerged from the stall. "Damn, Johnny, you almost got that thing full! We're gonna be done with this horse shit in like an hour!" he said approvingly.

"Your dad didn't care if you came home at nine at night?" There was a hint of shock in Johnny's voice.

"Ha, that's nothing. I used to be buds with this dickhead, Tyler, and his folks don't even care when he comes home on the weekend. They just leave the door unlocked until he gets home." Jared heaved another shovelful into the barrel. Johnny felt somewhat bewildered by the statement, and then began to shovel again.

"Man, let's go empty this deliciousness and fill the bitch up again," Jared said, smirking, as both the boys started laughing.

"Where do we empty it at?" Johnny asked, looking at the disgusting load of horse manure.

Jared looked at him and then pointed off into the woods across the pasture. "We can take turns pushing it over there, past them trees," Jared said, continuing to point, standing on his tiptoes, and looking off into the distance.

"Wow, that's really a long way away," Johnny replied as he looked off across the pasture.

Jared started laughing again, "Dude, I'm messing with you. I would smell like total ass if we pushed this bad boy all the way over there," Jared said, smiling quite proudly.

"What do you mean you *would* smell like ass?" Johnny replied.

"Ohhhhhh!" Jared yelled as both boys began laughing loudly.

Johnny noticed Jackson up by the house, watching the two guys interact. "Boy!" the man finally yelled out loudly.

Jared sat his shovel down on the ground. "Come on, dude, Pops is hollering." Johnny sat his shovel next to Jared's and began to follow him up to the house.

As Johnny trailed Jared, he felt overwhelmingly uncomfortable. Jared and Jackson appeared so close. Jackson's love for his family was evident in everything he did. Johnny felt like he was intruding as he lingered behind Jared. The urge to draw back finally anchored him as he instinctively placed his hands in his pockets and stopped trudging in the direction of the house. He rocked back and forth on his feet and looked up at the sky looking for birds, clouds, or anything else to focus on.

"Johnny! Come on up, bud," Jackson said loudly from beside the house. He had on green scrubs that were covered in turpentine and excrement. Slowly, Johnny began walking toward the house, with his hands still in his pockets. His gaze remained toward the grass as he approached. He was anticipating that Jackson would tell him he had talked to the salvation place, and that he had found a place for him to stay for the night.

This place was great, but Johnny knew this arrangement was not a permanent thing. He wasn't a necessity here, and the family had gone out of their way to be kind to him. He had eaten more in the last twelve hours than he had eaten the two days before that. They had done right by him, and Johnny was okay with moving on.

Jared and Jackson were already talking lowly before Johnny approached them. He walked up with his head down, and his hands still in his pockets. He couldn't help but wonder what the salvation place was like. He wondered if he would be staying there, or if they found him a place to stay at like a shelter.

"Johnny, you like pizza?" Jared turned from his father and asked. Johnny was caught a little off guard by the question, considering he was expecting a different conversation entirely.

"Well, yea. Who don't like pizza?" Johnny replied,

as he felt his mouth curl into a smile.

"It's settled then," Jackson announced. "We're having pizza and a duty calls tournament tonight," the man said confidently.

Jared stared at his father in a disapproving manner. "Duty calls, Pops? If you don't even know the name of the greatest game ever known to man, then you don't stand a chance. And it's not a tournament, just me teaching two guys the baby steps of playing a masterpiece," Jared said as he playfully socked his dad in the arm.

"Okay. Okay, I see how it is. You hear this, Johnny?" Jackson asked, giving Johnny a friendly smile.

"Yes, sir, I do. Sounds like he might be scared of a challenge." Johnny removed his hands from his pockets and began to feel a little less tense.

"Sounds like it!" Jackson replied as Jared flashed a cocky smile, and shook his head.

"Pops, did you know Johnny is the best damn shit shovelin' fool in Louisiana?" Jared asked laughing as the words came out of his mouth. Both Johnny and Jackson began laughing as well.

"Watch your mouth! What if your mom heard that nonsense?" his dad shook his head again as he put his son in a playful headlock, ruffling his hair.

CHAPTER ELEVEN

Mr. Hops

Graye

Graye hadn't shown Johnny the things she had gotten him that day in town yet. There was never a good time to bring it up as Jared was always around. It was a delicate situation. As she thought about the circumstances in a practical manner, it didn't make sense to give him the things now. That might give the message that they would like him to stay longer. Of course, this didn't make sense. They didn't know him, they didn't know what he came from, and twenty-four hours ago they had never even heard of the name Johnny Tregalis. Now, this young man was playing basketball with her son out by the barn.

As she watched them play and goof around, showing off their rather sad moves, the impractical maternal sense kicked in. Where would he sleep? Would he be warm enough? Would he have enough to eat? All these questions which were heavy on her mind, and she had only known this boy for a day.

The fact she had grown so fond of him so quickly was somewhat troublesome to the woman. Looking at the boys, carefree and happy, she couldn't help but imagine Johnny becoming a permanent fixture at the residence, regardless of how crazy it sounded when she said it out loud.

"Momma, I want juice!" Bryce yelled as she came running into the kitchen. The request startled her mother, who had been in deep thought. Bryce had done exceptionally well at her piano lesson. Her mother had given her quite a bit of praise throughout the day, and it seemed to have fed her ego rather well. "Okay, Miss Thing. You need to say please, and perhaps your request will be fulfilled," Graye replied in a condescending tone.

"Pretty, pretty, pretty please!" the little girl said with a big smile as she looked up at her mother. Bryce was only four, but Graye knew the little girl understood how to work the system.

"Okay then. But only because you added that third pretty to your please." Graye walked to the refrigerator. As she opened it to grab the orange juice, she heard Jared in the living room.

"Yea, man, I'll be right out. I think it's up in my room," she heard her son say as he ran up the stairs. Bryce dashed off toward the living room.

"B, don't bother your brother, he's busy," Graye said passively. She returned to the kitchen counter and poured the orange juice in Bryce's Tinker Bell cup. "B, come get your juice." As Graye called out, she believed the girl to be upstairs, bothering her brother. Jared was always patient with the little girl, but Graye knew her son didn't always have the opportunity to simply goof off and be a guy with other guys his age because of their location. She wanted him to be able to enjoy his game in peace. She was also glad he was outside doing something, rather than being stuck in the man cave, playing games. Graye exited the kitchen in pursuit of her daughter. She walked through the living room and up the stairs to Jared's room.

"Sweetheart, is Bryce not up here with you?" she asked her son, who was on his belly halfway under his bed.

"Nah, Mom," Jared replied from under the bed. "Hey, have you seen my air pump?" He asked as he began pushing himself backward from under the bed.

"Look in your closet," Graye replied as she left the room. As she began her descent down the stairs, she heard her daughter's voice on the front porch. Quietly she walked down the remaining stairs and made her way to the screen door which Jared had left open.

"So, you don't have a sister?" Bryce asked Johnny in an innocent voice. The two of them were sitting next to each other on the first step of the porch. Johnny was sweating and out of breath. He was wearing Jared's old basketball shorts and a black t-shirt. A black t-shirt in this heat seemed absolutely miserable to Graye.

"Nope. No sister. I got a baby brother, though," Johnny said proudly as he looked at the little girl and smiled.

"Where is he?" The little girl was quite curious to learn more about this little brother. Johnny remained quiet for a few seconds.

"Well, that's the thing, Bryce. I guess I'm not too sure where he is," Johnny said with a smile. The little girl was obviously very confused.

"Is he with your momma?" she asked inquisitively. "Yes he is. I imagine they're havin' a good ol' time somewhere on the beach," Johnny said as he looked at the girl again.

"Johnny, are you gonna stay here forever?" Bryce asked as she grabbed his hand and looked at him in a sweet and loving manner.

"I'm afraid not, I gotta get a job and all that other fun stuff you do when you grow up. But maybe I can visit you sometime, Bryce."

The little girl gave him a disapproving look. "You are not a grown up. Jared doesn't have a job. He goes to big kid school. Do you go to school?" the girl asked as if she were scolding him.

"Well, that's a good question." Johnny stared off out into the wooded area.

Graye wanted to interrupt before she asked anything else, but she had developed a lump in her throat from witnessing the interaction. She listened to his words, knowing there was so much mystery surrounding his past. She wanted to know more, but asking up front wasn't an option at this point. Luckily, Jared came barging by.

"I found it, Mom!" the sweaty teen said as he darted out the front door. Graye smiled as she watched Jared jump completely over his sister to the ground. "Let's go, dude," he yelled to Johnny.

"Go beat him!" Bryce said as she jumped up excitedly.

Johnny

The two boys returned to the barn to inflate the

ball.

"Man, Pops should be back with that pizza here soon. I'm about to starve," Jared said as he inserted the needle of the handheld air pump into the basketball and began pumping it to fill it up. Before Johnny could respond, the boys heard something odd. It was high pitched, like the sound made when letting air out of a balloon while pulling either side of the mouthpiece outward. The two boys raced to the side of the barn where the noise was coming from.

By a large, white, rusty, truck-bed toolbox, which was surrounded by ankle-high weeds, was a small bull snake. It had a baby cottontail rabbit by the hind quarters and was attempting to coil around it, but the young rabbit was too energetic for the small snake to overpower immediately. The diamond pattern shimmered in the fading sunlight as the pair danced off for life.

"Let's go, man. I don't wanna see this," Jared said as he turned to leave.

Johnny looked at the rabbit as it was tiring, and the snake was slowly gaining the advantage. It was a pathetic sight to watch the little animal suffer and struggle to live.

"Dude, we should help it. We gotta help it," Johnny said as he stared sympathetically at the small rabbit.

"Man, its nature, let it be. It'll stop squealing in a minute," Jared replied and continued walking away.

"No," Johnny said sternly. "It's just a baby; the damn snake can go find a rat." Johnny pushed Jared from his path and walked to the snake. He bent over and grabbed the snake at about its midsection, holding it out away from his legs. This was all that was needed to convince the snake to release its young victim. The bull snake viciously attempted to bite its capturer, but Johnny released the snake before it could bite him. The serpent was quick to exit the scene, but the young rabbit was not.

"Well, look at you," Jared said as he walked up to examine the shocked little rabbit. "Looks like you rescued Mr. Hops, the luckiest damn rabbit in the world." The small rabbit was lying on its side, panting heavily. The tail end of the small animal was slightly dampened, and there was a small amount of blood. From first glance, it appeared that any wounds were superficial, yet the small rabbit wouldn't move. Johnny sat down in the grass beside the toolbox and watched the rabbit, hoping with all he had that it would recover.

"The little guy is traumatized," Jared said as he stood over Johnny with the basketball resting between his right forearm and his hip. "He'll be okay once he figures his head out," Jared continued as he squatted down next to Johnny.

Those words resounded loudly in Johnny's mind, *He'll be okay once he figures his head out*. How true that was. Everything would be okay somehow if Johnny could just figure his head out. Regardless of where he was or the surrounding circumstances, he would most certainly be able to endure if he didn't suffer mental setbacks.

"Well, I don't just wanna leave him out here while he's like this," Johnny said as he reached over and gently picked the rabbit up with his right hand. The exhausted rabbit offered no resistance as Johnny brought it closer to his chest and used his left hand to get up off the ground.

"Dude, I gotta old shoebox upstairs. Mr. Hops in the house! I'm gonna go grab that box," Jared yelled back to Johnny as he began running toward the house. By that time, Graye was walking to the barn to let the boys know that Jackson had called and was

headed back with the pizza. Johnny watched as Jared ran by her without acknowledgement.

She turned and watched as her son ran up the porch stairs and through the front door. Pursing her lips in curiosity as she continued walking toward the barn. Johnny was cradling the small animal with his right hand, holding the rabbit to his chest, and lightly petting it with his left. He wondered if she would disapprove of his heroic efforts.

"What do you have there?" Graye asked, smiling as she approached.

"I guess his name is Mr. Hops," Johnny answered, smiling. "You can thank your son for the name." He was happy as he looked at the young rabbit, continuing to pet it lightly.

"What happened to Mr. Hops?" Graye asked as she moved closer for a better look.

"A bull snake had him. I couldn't let it eat him. He's too little. I think he just needs a little help, and he'll be good to go." Johnny moved his left hand so Graye could have a better look at the little creature.

"Johnny, that is very kind of you. This little fella has no idea how lucky he is." Graye smiled at the rabbit, but Johnny was sure he noted a hesitant look of apprehension about the woman's face as she eyed the small varmint.

"Oh, I bet he does, ma'am. I bet he's said thank you a million times and I just don't hear it," Johnny said as he began petting the rabbit again.

"Johnny, I'm glad to have you here. I just want you to know that," Graye said.

"Thank you, ma'am. I'm really thankful you guys have been so nice. I want you to know I really do appreciate you feedin' me and letting me stay here last night," Johnny said as Graye began to smile.

"I know you do, Johnny. You're a very sweet boy." Graye reached out and placed her hand lovingly on his shoulder.

"Here's that box!" Jared yelled out as he came running up to his mother and Johnny.

CHAPTER TWELVE

Duty Call

Graye

Graye was loving every minute of it. She and Bryce were upstairs trying out a new recipe she found for no-bake cookies while the guys were downstairs enjoying their impromptu pizza and video game party. The kitchen was cluttered with oats, cocoa, almond pieces, and other various ingredients scattered about the countertop.

The basement stairs were on the opposite side of the kitchen, across from the laundry room. Graye could hear all the ridiculous ramblings from below. She loved listening to the boisterous laughter and the funny banter that took place among a group of guys. There was no doubt about it; they were having a great time.

"Is Mr. Hops gonna be better tomorrow?" asked little Bryce.

Mr. Hops was currently residing in the laundry room in the shoebox. Graye and Jared helped Johnny fashion a makeshift haven for the small animal. The laundry door was shut so the rabbit was not subjected to the constant ruckus from the guys downstairs.

"I'm sure Mr. Hops will be just fine," Graye replied as she handed Bryce a chocolate wooden spoon to lick. Graye was moved by Johnny's desire to help the small animal. She thought it was sweet that he wanted to care for it. She had made up her mind after talking to Jackson that she was going to give him the clothing items she purchased him. This was partly because she had washed the from the filthy book bag, and placed them neatly in a black trash sack in the garage.

Jackson emerged at the top of the stairs and stepped into the kitchen wearing his plaid pajama pants and a gray t-shirt.

"Hey, hun, you having fun playing with the kids?" Graye asked sarcastically as Bryce continued to lick the wooden spoon her mother have given her.

"A blast. How's Hops?" Jackson was smiling as he walked to the sink to get a glass of water.

"He is just dandy. I'm sure he is ready to be free and happy," Graye replied as she walked behind her husband and wrapped her arms around his waist, hugging him from behind. Jackson reached for cabinet door and opened it.

"So, what are you thinking?" Jackson asked his wife as he reached for a glass.

"Well, a lot," Graye replied. Her face was pressed against the back of Jackson's shirt, so her response was rather muffled. She released her husband, exhaled forcefully, and walked briskly to the laundry room, opening the door. She anticipated her husband to follow so that they might converse in private while little Bryce was preoccupied with her spoon.

The man walked in with a peculiar look on his face, clearly wondering what his wife was going to say.

"I am afraid I'm getting too attached, I'm afraid we're sending him mixed signals, then there's this crazy side of me that—well, Jackson, we barely know the kid, but I just feel this overwhelming responsibility for his well-being." Graye had her arms crossed, staring at her husband, as she searched his facial expression for some reassurance or an answer.

"You're so beautiful. Even in pajamas with your hair all messy. You're just so damn perfect," Jackson replied.

"Jackson. Hello," Graye snapped, clearly anticipating an entirely different response.

"I think we should take it day by day. I don't know what to think, actually. I like the kid. I've liked having him here. I know Jared dang sure likes him. I just wish we knew more about him," Jackson said as he gave his wife a half smile.

"I just…I heard him and Bryce talking today—"
"Wait, do you trust him with Bryce?" Jackson asked his wife in a serious tone.

Totally taken aback by the question, Graye looked at her husband completely bewildered as to why he would even ask. "Yes. Yes of course I do. It's…its strange because I hardly know him, but I feel like I trust him with everyone, if that makes any sense at all." Graye said as she stared at her dryer.

"Yes, it does. It makes perfect sense. That's why I'm saying we should just take it day by day," Jackson said as he lifted his wife's chin with his right hand.

"That's what is bothering me, Jackson," Graye

replied as she looked at her husband. "Do you have any idea how scared he must be? He has no clue if we are going drop him off somewhere tomorrow, or if he is going to have a place to sleep a week from now. The…well, just the amount of stress that entails is just unfathomable for a kid that age. If it were Jared—" Graye stopped speaking as she felt her eyes swell with tears.

"I get it, babe. I didn't know what you were thinking completely, and I didn't know how to bring it up. It's all happened so quickly. And no, we don't know him that well yet, but it has only been one day, and why would he open up to us if he thinks this is temporary?" Jackson asked as he looked at his wife, who was beginning to smile. They could still hear the two boys' laughter from the basement. "Let's try it out. He can work with Jared out here. We can clean out the room he's staying in, and we'll see how it works out. If it doesn't work we have options, but there's no harm in trying it out," Jackson said as he pulled his wife in for a hug.

"I never thought in a million years I would be open to taking a homeless, bus-stop boy into my house a day after my husband brought him home." Graye welcomed her husband's embrace. He smelled of bath soap, laundry detergent, and deodorant. She inhaled deeply through her nostrils as she felt an uncontrollable smile fall across her face.

"So, we can keep him?" Jackson asked, chuckling, as he began to sway slightly back and forth with Graye in his arms.

"Um, he's not a dog," a little voice chimed in from just outside the laundry room door as Bryce poked her head around the doorframe with a chocolate smile.

The couple began to laugh. It was settled. At least for the time being, Johnny had a roof over his head.

CHAPTER THIRTEEN

Release

The sun arose shyly over the far horizon, as if for some reason it wasn't quite ready to begin its daily task of lighting the world. Red and orange clouds provided cover as it finally peeked through and blessed the Louisiana farmhouse.

Graye had pried open the guestroom door slightly to see if Johnny had woke yet. He was still sleeping as the sun began to peek through his opened window. She wondered why he had opened it. The cool air from the air conditioner must have freely escaped through the window the entire night. It was then that it struck her. She, her husband, and her children were but a chapter in this boy's tragedy; his story, however, was still being written. She and her husband's decisions and actions could determine the outcome of this young man's future. It was as if the pen that was writing Johnny's story was now in their hands. She was happy he was there. She understood that learning of his past and why he was running was now a priority if he were going to stay permanently.

She knew that not every day would be a day of

basketball and pizza parties, and when he began to face his demons he would need monumental support. She also knew that she and Jackson both were jointly coming to the mutual decision that they were ready to make an impact in this young man's life, regardless of the challenges associated with it. Smiling, she took one last look at the sleeping boy and closed his door. She imagined the look on Johnny's face when he received the news this evening that he would not be needing the assistance of the salvation place he had spoken of, anytime soon.

Johnny

As the door closed, Johnny opened his eyes. He lifted his hand to block the early morning sun's intrusiveness. Even at this early hour, Johnny could tell this day was going to be a good one. He slept the entire night without a single nightmare. There were no cold sweats, no palpitations, and Johnny knew exactly where he was at as he rolled on his side and smiled sleepily.

Suddenly, a small rush of euphoria rushed through him as he sprang from the bed. He had almost forgotten completely about Mr. Hops. He headed for the bedroom door in anticipation of learning the fate of the small animal. He opened the door and walked quickly toward the staircase.

There was only natural light lighting the house at this point. Jackson had been gone for a few hours already, Graye was nowhere to be seen, and both the other kids were sleeping in. It was only seven thirty-eight, but Johnny was excited to see if the rabbit had improved. He raced down the stairs and nearly slipped off the last stair of the case. His socks were slick on the stairs and hardwood floors. He walked quickly through the living room and kitchen to the laundry room.

As he opened the door he saw the box sitting on the washing machine. *Please don't be dead, please don't be dead,* he thought to himself as his heart raced and he walked toward the shoebox. Taking a deep breath, he placed both hands on the box and opened it. There, inside, was a bright-eyed, fat, little rabbit, about the size of a baseball, sitting contently in the corner of the box. Prior to Johnny's interruption, the rabbit had been chewing on the lettuce they had provided it the night before.

Johnny smiled in relief as he reached his hand down slowly to the small animal. As he got close, the rabbit lunged slightly at Johnny, causing him to jerk his hand back. "Hey there, little fella, no need for attitude this early in the morning," he chuckled, smiling at the cranky little rabbit.

"They can be feisty, can't they, sweetie?" Graye asked as she approached with a smile.

Johnny turned around, happy to see someone else awake. "I think he's ready to head back home."

"Good morning, sweetie. Yes, I'm sure he's ready to get out of that box," the woman said as she gave Johnny a brief hug before turning and walking toward the coffee pot on the kitchen counter.

Johnny stood motionless—dumbfounded. He had not been hugged by an adult since his mother left him. He felt warm inside and began to smile.

"You think the dogs will bother him if I take him out now?" Johnny asked.

"Oh, they're put up at night in the barn. They like to roam after the sun goes down, and we got tired of the phone calls from annoyed neighbors six miles up the road."

Johnny turned and closed the box. He carefully picked it up with both hands and began walking from the kitchen.

"I'll start breakfast here in a little bit, Johnny," Graye announced as he exited the kitchen.

"Thank you, Graye. I am pretty hungry," the teen replied. He exited the house through the front door and went down the porch stairs.

Graye

Graye watched Johnny him as he came into view from the kitchen window and began walking in the direction of the stable. She was pleased the rabbit had survived the night and how happy it had made Johnny.

"Um, where's my breakfast, mommaroo?" a sleepy, bed-headed Jared asked as he entered the kitchen. He yawned loudly and hugged his mother.

"Hey now, young man, I was just telling Johnny I was about to start it up," she said as she hugged her son tightly. "But if you want to start demanding I'll show you where the frying pan is."

"Kiddin'," he replied on a half-yawn. "Where is Johnny? I thought he was still in bed?" Jared asked as Graye turned from him and grabbed her coffee cup.

"He is releasing Mr. Hops out by the horse stables."

"Awesome," Jared replied as he looked at Graye with a solemn look on his face. "Mom, are you and

Dad going to take him to the Grace House?"

Graye turned her back to Jared and inhaled deeply, exhaling slowly.

"It's a complicated situation, Jared, but no. Your dad and I are going to offer him a room upstairs while he finishes school." Graye placed her coffee cup in the sink and looked out the window. Before she even completed the sentence, Jared was smiling. "That is, of course, if that is okay with you and B, and if he even wants to stay here with you two crazies," the woman said as she turned to her son just as he hugged her once more.

"That's awesome. You guys are awesome. That is seriously awesome," Jared said excitedly as he hugged his mother.

"I think so too, son."

"Not a word to him or your sister until your father and I speak with him first," she said firmly with a stern gaze. "There will be ground rules that he will be expected to follow, just like you and B," she said continued Jared quickly released her and turned for the front door.

"Yea, yea, I'm gonna go watch the release!" Jared ran for the door happily, hoping he didn't miss the grand release of Mr. Hops.

"I'm serious! Not a single word!" Graye hollered at her boy as she smiled and walked toward the refrigerator.

CHAPTER FOURTEEN

An Invitation

Jackson

"Between what I bought him and the clothes that Jared provided, I'd say he's going to be set up pretty well," Graye said to her husband.

Jackson looked appreciatively at his wife. He was thankful for her secretive efforts as the woman had changed out the bedding in the spare room to something more masculine and moved his clothes into the room without being noticed. She had taken the painting of the woman down, and Jackson had moved the remainder of the heartworm medication into the second spare bedroom. Johnny's new clothes were placed on his bed, and the clothes that Jared had provided were hanging in the closet. Both Graye and Jackson were excited by the idea of inviting him into their home on a long-term basis. The couple had decided the best way to extend the invite was not to embark on a dramatic family meeting; rather, the couple felt a subtle invite with a twist would be less awkward.

"Are you nervous?" Graye asked.

Jackson inhaled deeply, glancing at his wife. "No. I think this is the right thing. I really do. The only time I question it is when I say it out loud because it sounds bat shit crazy." He knew that would make his wife smile. She hugged him as he kissed the top of her head. "I'm going to call him up."

Just as the boys were wrapping up the final basketball game of the evening, Jackson summoned Johnny to the porch.

"Johnny!" Jackson yelled from the front of the house. Both boys stopped what they were doing and turned to Jackson, who was in his scrubs and smiling near the porch swing. "Can I talk to you for a second?"

Even from the porch, Jackson noticed Jared trying to contain his smile, as he knew what this conversation would entail. Johnny, on the other hand, appeared instantly oppressed. Jackson imagined what he was thinking. The thought of Johnny worrying about being taken to a shelter put an ache in Jackson's gut. As he watched Johnny approach with a nervous smile and nearly defeated posture, he knew Johnny must have been thinking he'd outstayed his welcome. "Hey, bud. Can we talk?" Jackson asked with a smile as Johnny walked up the stairs.

"Yea, of course," Johnny replied nervously as he leaned against the porch railing.

"You know we have all been so busy lately, and we could really use another hand around here. I know Jared would sure love some extra help with the daily chores, and I could use another hand sometimes when I get a crazy call. So, well, we wanted to know if, well, we wanted to know if you might wanna finish up your senior year here with Jared and stick around a while."

As Jackson studied the boy's face—he could tell Johnny was completely caught off guard by the invitation. Jackson witnessed an array of emotions flood over Johnny as his mouth remained agape and he simply stared at Jackson with a dumfounded look on his face.

"Um. Well. Yes, sir. I'm not one to tell a person who needs help no, so, yea, I can definitely stick around and help out," Johnny said as his voice cracked slightly.

Jackson extended a friendly handshake, as if they were making a deal. As Johnny shook his hand, Jackson pulled him in and gave him a brief hug.

"It's settled then, bud," Jackson said confidently. "Graye has just about got your room ready upstairs, and she took the liberty of getting you some new threads for when school starts back up." As Jackson spoke, Johnny kept his head down.

As the teen pulled away from Jackson, he attempted to dry his eyes, but the tears kept coming relentlessly.

"I'm, I'm sor—" Johnny attempted to apologize but was unable to speak.

"No worries at all, bud. How about you sneak up to the bathroom and get washed up for supper," Jackson suggested in a friendly tone. He didn't want Johnny to feel embarrassed for crying.

Johnny offered one more appreciative smile before retreating into the house.

By this time, Jared had begun his trek to the porch.

Jackson watched his smiling son approach.

"Daddy!" Bryce yelled as she came flying through

the screen door. "Daddy, what is wrong with Johnny? Why is he crying?" the girl asked hysterically, looking up at her father.

As Jared got to the porch, he became concerned. "He was crying, Pops?" he asked.

"What did you do to him, Jared?" Bryce asked, placing her hands on her hips.

Jackson put his hands up as if to silence everyone. "Kids. Johnny is just really happy right now. Sometimes people cry when they get really good news," Jackson said as reached down and picked his daughter up and watched his son walking up the porch.

CHAPTER FIFTEEN

Country

Johnny

It had been two days since the Everetts asked Johnny to settle in. It had also been two more nightmare free nights of slumber. Johnny felt as though he had gained a small piece of his mental clarity back.

Jackson and Graye had begun the conversations with him regarding the upcoming school year, obtaining school records, medical records, learning more about his father's eviction of Johnny, and addressing the possibility of locating his mother and brother.

For now, Johnny was comfortable with the Everetts' approach to slowly building a mutual trust. Johnny felt the small things like telling him how happy they were to have him, and evening meals around the table, were doing wonders for his psychology. Johnny was told he wasn't the only person benefiting from the arrangement. Jared had basically planned their entire senior year.

Perhaps once the new wore off, the family would remember that every relationship can be taxing at times, and requires patience and understanding. For now, however, there was a great deal of laughter and happiness throughout the house.

Johnny's uncontrollable urge to urinate woke him from yet another nightmare free night. His bladder was so full that his lower abdomen was rock hard. He reluctantly wiped the sleep from both eyes, flung his blue comforter back, and sat up. One leg at a time, he lowered his feet to the cold hardwood floor. Finally, he stood and hastily he made his way to the bedroom door. As he entered the hallway, he could tell there was a light on downstairs as the light was cascading on the wall directly in front of the top of the staircase.

Washing his hands, he couldn't remember the last time he'd peed for that long. He looked at himself in the mirror. He had finally shaved off the scruff. He had what many people would call a baby face. Jared often made envious comments regarding Johnny's ability to grow facial hair. Jared would frequently shave his face in an effort to promote hair growth— to no avail. Johnny thought shaving his facial hair off would be a nice gesture.

He dried his hands on the dark brown washcloth hanging from the circular towel holder next to the mirror and made his way to the hallway. He wondered who was up so early, so he happily made his way down the stairs. For whatever reason, he was wide awake this morning. He and Jared had played Call of Duty until well after midnight, so he should have been tired, but a short, restful night's sleep is always better than eight hours of interrupted rest due to vivid nightmares.

"Well, look at this early riser," Jackson said lowly from the bottom of the stairs as he entered the living room.

"Morning, Jackson," Johnny said, smiling as he descended.

"Have you ever seen a calf being born, Johnny?"

"No, I haven't." Johnny's face lit up as he was truly hoping this was the opening of an invitation.

"Well, if you want to, go throw on some old clothes while I get dressed."

"That's awesome! Should I wake up Jared?"

"Nah. Jared needs his beauty sleep. Just us today." Jackson replied as Johnny ran quickly up the stairs.

As Johnny threw on the dirty work jeans from in his closet, he couldn't help but feel guilty that Jared had not been invited to go. Jared had been so nice to him, and the night before Jared had referred to him as, "the newest member of the family," which made Johnny feel like he was, to some degree, a part of a functional family. After he laced up the old shoes that Jared provided, he made his way out the door.

Johnny made his way down the stairs as Jackson came out of his room in old jeans and an old green scrub top, "Are you sure you don't want me to wake up Jared? I really don't mind," Johnny asked as he stopped midway down the staircase.

"We'll let him sleep in. We'll probably be back before he drags his butt out of bed. We're only going about six miles up the road to a neighbor's."

"To Bill's house?" Johnny asked as he stepped off the staircase and into the living room.

"Who is Bill, Johnny? I don't know any Bill around here." Jackson waited patiently for an answer as Johnny found himself feeling somewhat flustered, his gaze darted about the floor.

"I thought we were talking about someone else," Johnny said as he looked up at Jackson.

"We are going to Emily Lou and Douglas Meer's farm. They would call me if their horse had a cocklebur in its tail, so this is certainly no surprise," Jackson said, walking toward the front door.

Although Jackson appeared to think nothing of the Bill question, Johnny saw this as a reality check. Even though the last few days had been somewhat of a resting period for Johnny's psychology, the truth was that his concern of his father locating him was beginning to become bothersome.

Johnny had continuously reassured himself that there was nothing his father could do, and he certainly could not make him return to the shack if he were to find him. Johnny absolutely hated even reminiscing on his father's atrocious face, but a growing paranoia made it impossible for him to completely relax.

Regardless, Johnny didn't understand what exactly was manifested within his psychology. He knew this was partially because he had no sense of normality. That had never been more clear to him than after he'd been in the lap of normality for the past several days. He understood enough to attempt to control his fear to a point of functionality that he believed was passable.

The two guys exited the house and made their way down the porch stairs.

"Let's head to the barn and grab the truck," Jackson said as he walked briskly in the early morning Louisiana sticky air.

Johnny knew the man was referring to his work truck, the one he took out when his client was of a larger nature. Johnny wondered what the day would consist of. He liked being with Jackson, and his profession certainly seemed intriguing.

"Do you smell a skunk?" Johnny asked Jackson as he trailed closely behind him.

"Ha! The dogs messed with one last night. They smelled lovely when I put them in the pen last night," Jackson said, shaking his head and laughing.

As they approached the barn, one of the penned dogs let out a small bark in alarm at the two approaching humans. Jackson grabbed the black handle of the large, red sliding door, and began pulling it backward, the door making quite a bit of squeaky commotion as it opened. This put the dogs into a frenzy, all four barking and wagging their tails. Between the noise of the door and the barking dogs, Johnny had to cover his ears.

The black, extended cab, 4x4 Chevy was the nicest truck Johnny had ever been in. He thought it quite comical that the leather seats were heated. *Why would anyone want a heated butt?* he thought to himself when Jackson was boasting and describing the vehicle a few days prior.

As Jackson loaded up in his truck, Johnny's peripheral vision captured the silhouette of the sinister intruder lurking in the corner of the barn. Crouched low and confused was a dirty coyote. It was sitting on its hind quarters, partially hidden by an old wooden sawhorse.

As the taillights of the truck lit up the back- end of the barn, the creature began to snap at the sawhorse, eventually biting it. Its tail was damp and covered in diarrhea, and its coat was flattened and not well kept. Johnny stared at the animal, blinking several times, at first unsure as to what it was. The shadows devoured the coyote's outline.

"Johnny? You okay?"

Convinced his eyes and mind had conspired to create the image, he merely shook his head, feeling slightly defeated he climbed in the cab.

CHAPTER SIXTEEN

A Small View

Jackson

What is all that stuff coming out?" Johnny asked Jackson, who was standing behind the distressed cow. The large black cow was penned in a large, blue cattle chute.

Jackson enjoyed watching Johnny's reactions to the situation. Thankful he'd agreed to tag along.

"That's amniotic fluid. It means the calf should be here anytime." Jackson had no sooner offered the explanation, two legs began emerging from the bovine's nether region.

The chute was next to an old white barn with chipping white paint. The barn was huge, even bigger than the one at the Everetts' farm. Jackson had on elbow-high gloves, and had blood and other fluids all over his green scrub top. Within a matter of seconds, the calf's legs had fully emerged, and a wet, ugly little head was now completely out. Johnny stood watching with his mouth agape as the remainder of the calf simply shot out with ease. The slippery calf landed on the ground making a sloppy sound, as Jackson grabbed its front legs and dragged it backward.

As the man leaned down over the nearly lifeless calf, he cleared the calf's nostrils and its face by wiping off the bloody fluid and membrane that was present. He began gently rubbing its ribs in an effort to liven the small calf. As Johnny watched, seemingly amused, Jackson stood up from the calf, which was now clumsily holding its head up on its own, and returned to the tail end of its mother. Johnny seemed to pay little attention to what he was doing with the cow. He was totally focused on the wet, tiny, calf, smiling at it as it looked around from the ground.

As Jackson opened the chute, the bewildered cow slowly exited the other side. As she seemed to gain her sense of awareness back, she slowly made her way to the young calf.

"Johnny, go ahead and stand back by the truck," a filthy Jackson said as he began removing his gloves. The morning sun was barely out, but Jackson was certain it was light enough out that Johnny was able to witness the entire event and see everything quite well. As the mother licked her calf, Johnny walked to the other side of the truck and leaned up against it. Jackson remembered when Jared would show as much enthusiasm for such things. Lately, even convincing his son to go on calls with him was a chore.

Jackson felt the sudden urge to pee. Looking around, the man didn't immediately see Johnny so he proceeded to unzip his jeans. As the man was urinating on the front tire, Johnny walked by.

Johnny looked up and saw Jackson standing there,

the man apologized, but made no effort to stop, he didn't think much of it. Living on a farm for so many years, it was second nature for both Jackson and Jared to find a tree or some other unfortunate inanimate object to pee on when they were outside in the country.

Johnny's nostrils flared, his mouth opened, and his eyes looked immediately away as he turned from Jackson with both hands out, as if he were attempting to push the older man away.

Jackson knew instantly that something wasn't right. As if that very moment provided a view into the boy's past. It was the unmistakable look of fear. The man zipped up his pants and contemplated what his next actions would be. Johnny had returned to the other side of the truck and had his back to the door.

Slowly, Jackson walked around the front of the vehicle. "I'm sorry about that, bud. I didn't realize you were coming around the truck," Jackson said. Johnny said nothing. His expression was still a look of distress. "Johnny?"

"It's okay," he said as he looked at the ground. "I don't…I don't ever piss outside. I'm not gonna piss outside," Johnny said as he turned and looked at Jackson.

"Oh, that's fine, bud. That's just my country manners," the man replied, smiling.

Johnny turned around and looked in the direction of the cow with her calf.

Jackson watched as the cow nudged the newborn in an effort to stimulate it to stand.

"I think she's got it from here, bud. You wanna load up while I gather up my stuff?" Jackson enquired as he slapped the hood of the truck.

"Sounds good," Johnny, responded. As Jackson threw his supplies in the back of his truck, his mind raced with questions. He understood that learning of Johnny's past would be a long and drawn-out process, but recognized that the teen's response to the situation was abnormal. "Not bad for your first day, my young apprentice. I may just make a vet out of you yet." Jackson said.

"Will they be okay if we leave?" Johnny asked inquisitively.

"Indeed, they will, Johnny. We were basically just here in case something went wrong." Jackson put the truck in reverse and turned to look behind him. As they began the drive home, Jackson's expression and tone took a more serious approach.

"So, Johnny, when did your mom leave?" Jackson asked as he looked out over the steering wheel at the dirt road. Johnny appeared almost vexed by the question. His gaze fell on his hands. Jackson watched from the corner of his eye as he began lightly pinching his left hand's fingertips with his right thumb and index finger.

"I was sixteen. I had just turned sixteen." Johnny turned and looked out the passenger window. The cloud of dirt was thick as the tires threw it up on either side of the truck.

"Why did she leave?" The curious man continued. When Johnny didn't answer, Jackson switched tactics. "My mother…my mother was a nurse. She was a nurse for a pain management clinic. She used to come home drowsy when I was younger. I didn't realize she was taking the patients' medication." Jackson paused a moment, noticing he had captured Johnny's attention. "She died from taking too much.

Overdose."

"And your dad?"

"I think he's in Florida. I'm not sure. I always called Graye's father Dad. He passed away a few years ago."

Clearing his throat, he remained silent for a few seconds.

"She had to leave for Jacob," Johnny said lowly in a monotone voice, flushing under emotion.

"And Jacob is your little brother?" Jackson continued as he slowed the speed of his vehicle to around thirty-five miles an hour. "Why did she need to leave for your little brother, Johnny?"

"Because of my dad," Johnny said in a short, defensive, voice. Johnny continued to look out the window. It was obvious to Jackson that the teen wasn't ready to open up about the situation.

"Johnny, I need you to know that I care about you very much. I know we are just getting to know each other, but you can talk to me. I promise I'm not going to judge you or look down on you. Did…Johnny, did your dad hurt you and your brother?"

"I want to. I want to talk to you, I just don't know what to do when he comes back," Johnny said as he finally made eye contact, clearly hoping Jackson could make sense of what he said.

"Who comes back, Johnny? Your dad comes back? Who, who comes back?"

"Yes. Sometimes both of them. I just can't talk about it right now," Johnny said in a low, withdrawn tone.

"Johnny, if…well if your father hurt you, well, you needn't worry about him coming back to hurt you again. No one is going to hurt you again. Please,

Johnny, just answer me. Did he hurt you? Is that why your mother left?" Jackson felt his blood pulsating in either side of his throat, as the thought of a grown man hurting the kid in his passenger seat angered him deeply.

"Yes," Johnny muttered as he returned his gaze to the window. "My mom was afraid my brother would get outta line like me. But he was too little." Johnny said softly. "I done said too much. I can't. Please."

"Did he hit you? Is that what happened to your lip?" Jackson had a death grip on the stirring wheel, and his jaw was clenched.

"I was in the kitchen when he wasn't home. I shouldn't have been in there while he wasn't home." Jackson heard pure tension on his voice, as several beads of sweat collected on his forehead, regardless of the cool air conditioner. Johnny bit his lower lip and continued pinching his fingertips. "I don't wanna talk anymore about it right now. Not today," Johnny said as he turned toward an infuriated Jackson. "I'll talk to you. I will, but I just can't right now. I can't today."

"That's, that's fine, bud. But I need you to understand that there is nothing out here that you need to be afraid of, and you are totally safe with my family. Do you understand that?" Jackson placed his right hand on his left shoulder, waiting for a response.

Johnny's shoulder was rigidly stiff as the boy remained seemingly uncomfortable.

"I understand."

"Good."

"I'm pretty tired. You mind if I go back to bed for a bit?" Johnny asked as they turned off onto the driveway. It wasn't even nine o'clock yet.

"Of course not, bud." Jackson smiled and ruffled the boy's messy hair, the same way he often ruffled his son's hair. The man's blood felt like it was boiling, but he tried his best to compose himself so Johnny couldn't tell.

"I'll put your breakfast in the refrigerator so you can heat it up when you wake up again."

"I know what I came from, but that don't mean that's what I am. If that makes any sense," Johnny said solemnly.

"It makes perfect sense, young man."

CHAPTER SEVENTEEN

Hero

Johnny

The chicken coop had a certain charm to it. Johnny often felt the coop was cleaner than the shack of a house. The building was a good size for a chicken coop. The paint on it was old. There were several layers of paint including an avocado green, a red, and a white layered one on top of the other. On certain boards, all three colors were present as the layers began to curl from years of exposure.

The chicken wire was secure all the way around the outside enclosure so the chickens could exit the building without being threatened by stray cats, coyotes, and skunks.

Johnny sat on the north side of the chicken coop with his back leaning on the outside wall of the building. In his hand, he held a hatching chick. Its tiny beak had been working vigorously in an effort to break free. Johnny had been lightly breaking tiny pieces of the shell, attempting to assist the exhausted hostage. Johnny smiled as he gently peeled the white membrane off the tiny bird's beak so it could breathe. As he looked at the tiny hatchling, a shadow appeared over him. His heart began to race as he looked up.

"Just what the fuck do you think you're doin'!"

Johnny couldn't see the man because the sun was directly behind him, but he knew it was his father and immediately looked toward the ground beside him.

The man reached down and grabbed the boy violently by the hair. He pulled him viciously to his feet with two hands full of hair.

Johnny accidentally dropped the hatching chick as he was pulled rapidly to his feet.

"What the fuck is this you ignorant piece of shit?" the man asked, slamming his face into the side of the coop. He continued to maintain a strong grip on his hair.

Johnny watched helplessly as the man raised his left foot high, and smashed it down on the hatching chick, crushing it to death.

***

"No!"

Johnny shot out of his bed and began looking all about the room. The space was well lit. He hadn't remembered that he went back to bed after his morning with Jackson. His heart raced as he remembered the chick and his father. His eyes, wide and wild, searched the room for some sort of clarity. It didn't make sense, he knew his father was there, and there was no talking himself out of it.

He bolted from the bedroom door and ran down the hall. He flew down the stairs like a fox fleeing from an angry pack of hounds. His feet hit the stairs so hard as he descended that it sounded like someone was beating down the front door of the house. As he reached the bottom of the stairs, he stopped instantly. He held the rail, searching the room for an explanation.

Breathing hard, he felt reality slowly slipping back into his psyche as the living room and its surroundings were gradually offering a comfortable sense of familiarity.

Although he wasn't completely convinced his father wasn't there, he began to reach the point where he could rationally dissect a situation and pull the reality from it. That was when he saw her.

Graye was on the couch in the living room with Bryce. They were cuddled up on the rich dark leather piece of furniture, reading a book until Johnny had come racing down the stairs like a madman, startling the both of them.

"Johnny? Sweetie, is everything okay?" Graye asked as she sat the book down on the couch.

Johnny stared at the two of them in confusion—relieved to learn that his father wasn't actually there, Johnny felt the humiliation mounting.

Rapidly, he blurted the first excuse that came to mind. "I, we didn't let the dogs out this morning. I need to let the dogs from their pens." Johnny studied Graye's face, hoping his answer would satisfy her need for an explanation.

Little Bryce sprang to her feet, shrieking, "I wanna go too!"

Johnny knew the dogs had been sprayed by a skunk the previous night, and also knew it was best if they remained penned until the stench was tolerable.

However, nothing else seemed to come to mind. He could tell by the way Graye was watching him that she was still a little startled.

"Well, let's not let them out just yet, but if you two would like to go check on them, I think that would be a good idea," Graye said as she looked down at her daughter. She gently kissed the little girl on the forehead and began to stand up from the couch.

Johnny was standing at the bottom of the staircase. He was looking at the floor and had placed his hands in his shorts pockets.

Graye walked toward him and gave him a hug. "Are you okay?" she asked lovingly.

Johnny imagined that Jackson had shared what little information he had gathered that morning about his painful past with his wife while Johnny had been asleep.

"Yea, it was just a bad dream, I think." Johnny looked at the concerned woman as she pulled away and placed her hand behind his head, lowering his head to hers. She kissed him on the forehead; the same way she kissed her own children. Johnny smiled and instantly he felt better.

As he pulled his hands from his pockets, he looked over at Bryce.

"Let's go check on them dogs, little buddy," Johnny said to the messy haired little girl. She jumped off the couch with an enthusiastic smile and ran across the living room to Johnny and her mother.

"Well, let's go, buddy!" the little girl shrieked and laughed. The two began for the front door.

Hand in hand, Johnny and Bryce walked down the porch stairs and headed in the direction of the big red barn. Johnny turned to see Graye watching from the open screen door. The large door was still open on the side of the big red barn. Jackson's truck was gone, Johnny believed he must have been called out again. Johnny looked down at the little girl and smiled.

"You know these dogs smell real gross?" Johnny asked with a huge smile as they approached the barn.

Bryce suddenly stopped walking and began pulling back on Johnny's hand. Johnny, watching the small girl, noticed her facial expression change rapidly.

"That's not one of our puppies!" Bryce yelled loudly. As Johnny looked up, he saw a most horrific sight as a ravenous-looking coyote had exited the barn and was attempting to run toward them. The animal was having extreme difficulty as it would stagger a few feet and then nearly fall down. Its mouth was gaping as if it were choking on something. It would randomly snap at the air as if it were biting at invisible flies, and was making high pitched yipping sounds as it attempted to get closer to Johnny and Bryce. Its eyes appeared to be unable to focus on the two, and its mouth had bloody saliva dripping from it.

Johnny heard Graye scream from the front porch, *"Run! It's rabid!"* He saw the woman come running down the porch stairs frantically and hoped she would reach Bryce before the crazed coyote did. Bryce was now crying as the animal was almost upon them.

"Run, Bryce! Run to your mom!" Johnny yelled as he ran in the direction of the coyote. He watched her run to her mother screaming as Johnny ran toward the animal, waving his hands and yelling loudly.

The coyote lowered its head and had a death-lock stare on him with its bloodshot, sunken eyes. It was filthy, covered in feces and dirt, and the front of its mouth was badly injured, as if it had been smashing its muzzle into rocks or cement.

Johnny was relieved to see Bryce reach the safety of her mother as he saw Jared, startled by the commotion, running out the front door of the house in his pajama bottoms.

As the animal found its footing, it attempted to lunge at Johnny, but it merely fell to its side, snapping at the grass and weeds. The coyote was obviously weakened by the disease, but it was still capable of inflicting deadly damage as it managed to find its footing again. It snarled and snapped at the air, concentrating on Johnny once more.

Johnny turned and ran in the direction of the barn in an effort to divert the animal from the family. As he raced inside the open door with the clumsy coyote in pursuit, he could hear Jared yelling his name over the barking dogs. It was then he saw it: an old shovel next to the dog pens to scoop up the waste.

As Johnny ran for the pens, the coyote seemed to become discombobulated due to the loud barking. Johnny grabbed the shovel and turned to the animal.

The coyote nearly fell on its side again as it bit its own leg multiple times very rapidly.

Johnny raised the shovel above his head, and brought it down with all his might on the animal's skull. With a sickening thud, the animal's suffering was over.

As Johnny attempted to mentally digest what had happened, Jared appeared in the doorway. "Johnny!" he yelled loudly as he ran toward Johnny and the dead coyote.

"Yea," Johnny replied in a shock-like trance, although his response went unheard.

"Holy shit! Dude, are you okay? Did that thing fucking bite you?" Jared grabbed Johnny's shoulders with both hands and looked at him eye to eye.

Johnny shook his head no, and motioned that they head for the door to escape the deafening noise of the barking.

Both boys looked at the dead coyote as they walked entirely around it, as if it at any moment the animal would resurrect itself. As the boys exited the barn, Graye came running up without Bryce.

"Johnny! Jared! What, what the hell happened? Where is it?" the woman asked as Johnny watched her attempting to catch her breath. She saw the dead animal through the doorway by the pens.

Sunny, one of the yellow lab mixes, was dead. Her throat looked like it had been ripped out, and blood covered the cement flooring of her pen. The two animals must have fought through the pen's fencing.

Johnny watched as Jared noticed his mother's expression and turned his gaze toward the inside of the barn too. Jared saw the dog and was instantly devastated.

"No!" Jared yelled out as he bent over with his elbows to his knees and his hands covering his eyes, and let out a wailing of cries as Johnny watched helplessly.

It was clear to Johnny that Graye was torn between her frightened daughter crying on the front porch, and her boy bawling at the sight of his dead dog. Johnny was beyond thankful to see Jackson's truck pulling into the drive.

CHAPTER EIGHTEEN

Stars

Johnny understood why no one had spoken anything of substance the entire time they were sitting at the dinner table. Jared's eyes were still bloodshot, and he had spent the majority of the day curled up on the couch. There was no denying that Sunny was Jared's favorite dog. Seeing her like that must have been traumatizing for the young man. The family attempted to comfort the distraught teen, but it wasn't until Johnny offered to play a game in the basement that he finally got off the couch.

Johnny felt as though he were basically interrogated by Jackson, as the man repeatedly asked if he had been bitten, scratched, or even touched in any fashion by the rabid animal. The remaining dogs were now officially quarantined. Although they were vaccinated, Jackson said he would take no chances because he had seen the horror this illness could inflict.

The coyote was in the cooler, and Jackson would

be taking it to the appropriate destination in the morning.

After Johnny gave the best description he could offer of the awkward behavior exhibited by the coyote, Jackson was completely positive the results of the testing would prove the coyote was sickened with the deadly disease—rabies. The man claimed there had not been many cases of rabies reported in the area, and seemed surprised no one had noticed the animal lurking around the barn or country back roads prior to the attack.

He couldn't consider himself a hero. Johnny felt that his failure to identify the animal as an actual threat was partially responsible for Sunny's death, and Jared's turmoil. When he'd initially seen the emaciated and horrific-looking animal, he was certain it was merely a cruel device set into motion by his ailing psyche.

Johnny felt horrible for Jared, but he couldn't find the words to communicate that effectively. As he watched his friend get upset off and on throughout the day, he never once felt that Jared was weak for being upset, and this confused Johnny. He knew if he had ever cried in front of his father, he would have been called several names or something worse. Johnny only felt sympathy for his friend. He also felt sad that Bryce had had to witness the chaos the coyote had inflicted. He knew this day would be a day that stuck with her for the rest of her life.

***

Dinner had been served late, and it was already dark outside by the time the family finished up. "May

I be excused?" Jared asked as he looked at his mother. He hadn't touched much of his spaghetti and bread. Johnny looked at Jared's nearly full plate.

"Yes, sweetheart, you may," Graye replied as she looked toward her pathetic looking son. He hadn't changed out of his pajama bottoms.

"May I be as well?" Johnny asked.

"Yea, bud, you're good too," Jackson replied as he gave him yet another appreciative look.

As Johnny set his plate in the sink on top of Jared's, he turned to follow him from the kitchen.

Little Bryce was sleeping at the table. It appeared the day had been a long one for her too, as she was simply too tired to partake in family supper.

Johnny retreated to his room upstairs.

Sitting on his bed, he stared out the window, studying the roads leading to the house. The day had been a major setback for him mentally, and his mounting paranoia prevented him from curling up in bed and attempting to sleep.

He knew that logically his father had no idea where he was, but something within him continued to insist that there was actually a reason to remain hypervigilant.

Johnny was thankful that the early morning conversation with Jackson, and the incident in the living room with Graye and Bryce, had been completely overshadowed by the coyote and the death of poor Sunny. As he continued to watch the roads for headlights, he once again heard the whimpering of the puppy. This was almost instantly followed by the sinister sound of his father's truck engine. He raised his hands to his ears. "Please just stay away."

Johnny heard a knock on the door. He turned to the

door as Jared stuck his head in.

"Hey man, can I come in?" Jared asked from the doorway.

"Yea, dude, come on in." Johnny turned from the window and began putting on the shorts while sitting down. The sounds were gone. The room and the world outside were serenaded by wildlife, but not puppies or old truck engines.

Jared entered the room, walked toward Johnny, and sat on the bed.

"You lookin' at the stars?" Jared asked as he looked to the window as well.

Of course, Johnny was not going to admit that he was suffering from paranoid delusions of his father driving to the farm and finding him.

"Yea."

"Well, come on, there's a better view from out here." Jared pushed up on the window to open it further, which lead out to the roof above the front porch. He put his arms and head through the window and slowly inched his way out of the room onto the roof. Once there, he sat with his legs crossed and gazed up at the stars.

Johnny was soon to follow, carefully climbing onto the roof. The air outside was still hot and thick, and the night was totally alive with the sounds of crickets and other insect life. The sky was clear, and every star seemed visible in the atmosphere.

"Dude, I'm glad you're here," Jared said as he continued looking skyward.

"Me too, man," Johnny replied. That simple comment made Johnny feel welcomed, as the two young men were basically inseparable after not even a week. Johnny assumed the week had been eventful and overwhelming for everyone involved, not only him. He was thankful he had a friend he could goof off with and get his mind off of everything else.

As Johnny became accustomed to the normality of a functional family, he grew more frustrated with his mental instability. He felt if he could mend his mind he would be completely happy, and nothing would hold him back from achieving complete fulfillment.

"I'm sorry about Sunny, Jared," Johnny said as he looked over at the stargazing mourner.

"Yea, me too," he replied quietly.

As the two sat on the roof, enjoying the Louisiana summer night, Johnny noticed Jared watching him from the corner of his eye.

"What are you so scared of, man?" Jared asked suddenly, catching Johnny off guard.

"What?"

"I just think you're scared of something. You act like you're scared of something out there." Jared laid back on the roof with his hands under his head.

"Nah man, I'm just lookin' around I guess," Johnny said as he too began to lay his head backward on the roof to look at the stars.

"There are millions of stars out there. It's like we're nothing," Jared proclaimed in a dark tone of voice. "Do you ever just feel like it's all pointless, like there's no reason for us to even be here?" Jared pondered out loud.

Johnny looked at Jared, unsure of how to respond. "I think you're gonna do great, man. I think you're gonna do something awesome. You're not pointless," Johnny responded with the only words that came to mind.

Jared yawned loudly and closed his eyes. "Man, oh

man, am I beat," Jared said as he yawned again. "I really hope you can sleep tonight, dude. I would probably have nightmares about that damn coyote acting all crazy," Jared continued quietly.

Johnny turned his head to the side and looked at Jared. He felt comfortable around his friend, and felt like maybe Jared could help him get some answers, especially since he'd brought up the topic of dreaming. "Do…do you ever feel like your dreams just, like, continue even if you think you're awake? Or like you're in two places at the same time?" Johnny asked, instantly regretting his question.

"I guess I don't follow, Johnny. But you shouldn't put too much into it. There's been a lot happening here lately. You're staying in a new place, you're around an entirely different group of people, and you almost got ate by a psycho-ass coyote. Don't stress about it."

Jared's kind words brought some comfort to Johnny, but he was still afraid his father was desperately searching for him. Even more, Johnny was afraid of what his mind would conjure during the night if he found sleep.

Graye

Graye reached over and gently grabbed Jackson's hand. She looked seriously at her husband. "If he hadn't been there…if Bryce had been playing by the barn by herself. It…it all happened so fast, and if Johnny hadn't been there," Graye said, as her eyes began to swell with tears, again. She felt her throat tighten.

"I know, I know, honey. We owe him so much."

Graye felt her husband's callused hand slide atop of hers.

"He's supposed to be here, you know that, right?" the woman continued as a few tears escaped her eyes. She gently ran her finger over her husband's blistered hand. He had buried Sunny very deep in the ground because he didn't want wild animals digging up the carcass and causing his family further trauma.

"I know he is," Jackson replied, lifting his wife's hand to kiss it.

CHAPTER NINETEEN

Awake

Johnny

He heard the knock on the door, yet it wasn't registering that he needed to open his eyes, that he needed to wake up. Finally, he cracked his eyes open as he heard the door handle turn.

"Hello? Sleepyhead? Are you hungry?" It was Graye, peeking her head in the door and smiling.

Johnny had fallen asleep looking out the window. His head had been resting on his folded arms on the windowsill. The last time he looked at the alarm clock it said it was after four in the morning. He had persistently kept a vigilant watch the majority of the night. He was exhausted, but he hadn't had any dreams.

As he looked at Graye, he smiled with puffy eyes and yawned. "What time is it?" he asked as he sat up and stretched his arms, yawning again.

"Well, you slept in a bit today. It's almost ten.

Jared and Bryce went with their dad to look at some boxer puppies." Graye began shaking her head. "Jared tried to wake you, but he said you were zonked out. I told all three of them the last thing we need around here is another mouth to feed," Graye said as she entered the room. Her face gave the impression that she instantly recognized those to be a poor choice of words.

Johnny immediately diverted eye contact and look down toward his bedding, unsure of how to respond.

"Johnny, I didn't mean that in any way toward you. I only meant we have so many dogs." The woman sat down on the bed next to him. "You are very special to me and this family. I will be happy to feed you as long as you can stomach my cooking."

Johnny could feel the woman's friendly smile, begging for forgiveness. He looked at her and returned the smile, as he knew the woman would never intentionally say something that hurtful to him.

"I know I can *throw down* on some food, so I appreciate you keeping me fed," the boy said as he started to chuckle.

"Oh, no. It spreads like a virus!" Graye said, placing her palm on her forehead as she began to laugh lightly.

As she headed out the bedroom door, Johnny couldn't help but wonder, again, what had prompted this family to be so kind? He had nothing to offer them other than miniscule assistance on the farm. He once again reminded himself that he shouldn't question, but be grateful.

Johnny looked once more in the direction of the window. He consciously understood that the paranoid behavior was completely unproductive and hoped the would be able to momentarily turn it off and enjoy the day as it came.

The coyote, the conversation with Jackson, and Sunny's death were all things that were out of his control. Johnny understood there was nothing he could physically do to alter the events that occurred the previous day. It puzzled him how well he could rationalize digesting an entire day's worth of trauma because it was out of his control, and then stare out the window for hours in a panic fueled frenzy. As he turned from the window, he stood from the bed and headed for the door.

When he walked down the hall to the stairs, the smell of hickory-smoked bacon became increasingly present. He wasn't even very hungry, but he hadn't eaten bacon in years. He thought of how the family used mealtime as a social gathering, a reassurance of unity. The times around the table were basically a chance to disclose the day's events and reminisce on funny stories. He loved sitting at the table with the family.

He walked down the stairs, hearing Graye humming some tune and the sound of dishes being placed in the sink. He felt his cheeks lift in an uncontrollable smile. He loved it here. He loved how the family rallied together and overcame adversity as a team. They supported each other and helped one another when needed. Johnny loved being able to witness how a normal family functioned and existed.

As he entered the kitchen, he saw his plate on the table. Perhaps he was hungry after all as he eyed the two large, homemade biscuits smothered in white gravy.

"Do you want some orange juice, or maybe some

milk?" Graye asked as she watched Johnny walk into the kitchen. Beyond the smell of breakfast, the smell of lavender dish soap was lingering as Graye rinsed the suds from her hands under the sink water.

"Um, I'll take some milk if that's all right," Johnny replied as he approached the table.

"That's just fine," Graye said sweetly as she grabbed a drying glass from the counter and walked to the refrigerator.

"Sweetie, I have to run into town today to grab a few things. Would you like to go with me just to get out of the house?"

"Yea, that sounds good," Johnny said as he pulled his chair out from the table. He was hoping that the trip wouldn't produce another line of questioning. He sat down and began cutting into one of the biscuits.

"Are the dogs still penned up?" Johnny asked with a mouth full of food.

"Yep. They seemed pretty shook up, so we let them out for a few minutes this morning, but then it was back to the pen. I'm surprised the house doesn't smell like a family of skunks." The woman sat Johnny's glass of milk down by his plate. As Johnny chewed his food, he looked up at Graye.

"Do you think they know Sunny is dead?" Johnny asked, still chewing.

"Well, I think they have their own way of mourning loss, but I'm sure they don't completely understand what happened."

As Johnny ate, he looked at Graye and wondered again of his own mother. He found it strange that Graye would go so far out of her way to let him know how much he meant to her, and how much she appreciated his existence, and his own mother made no effort after leaving to return and rescue him. He understood the woman had her own setbacks to overcome, but he'd always prayed she'd eventually return while his father was at work to collect him. He understood there were several things that were out of the woman's control, but being with Graye for the short time assured him that his mother could have done more. She didn't have to leave him. She could have protected him, ruined or not. As Graye opened the fridge, it reminded Johnny of the coyote.

"Is the coyote still in the cooler outside?

"No, Jackson took it into town when they went to look at the pups. I'm sure they'll be coming home with one of them," Graye said, shaking her head again.

It came over him faster than a swarm of vengeful wasps. His heart rate soared to the point that he felt it pounding in his fingertips and eyeballs. He swallowed a large piece of crisp bacon without chewing it completely. He could feel it slowly moving down his esophagus, scraping all the way down. He looked to Graye as she walked to him with a look of concern plastered across her face.

"Are you okay, sweetie?"

"Are…are you gonna answer that?" Johnny heard himself blurt out.

Graye looked confused, as if she had no idea what he was talking about.

"Answer what, Johnny?" she replied as Johnny stood from the table.

"There's someone at the door, what if it's him? I heard someone at the door." Johnny walked backward in the direction of the laundry room, convinced someone had knocked at the door. He was horrified at the prospects of it being his father.

Graye placed the milk back in the fridge as Johnny retreated to the laundry room.

The sound of his father's truck engine was not only humming in his ears, it invaded them in an oppressively resounding loudness. The way the truck would nearly stall, and sputter—it was too clear to be anything but real. Johnny was certain he was here. His father was here.

"Sweetie, there's no one there. Nobody was knocking, and there are no vehicles outside," Graye said as she entered the room. "Johnny, what's wrong, sweetie? Honey, are you afraid of your father finding you here?" The woman's soft words overpowered the delusional sounds of the engine, replacing them within his head as Johnny lowered his shaky hands from either ear.

He looked at Graye. He knew she wouldn't lie, but convincing himself that there was no immediate danger lurking at the front door was proving difficult. "I'm sorry. I'm really sorry. I just, I just thought I heard someone knocking. There was…I thought I heard knocking and the truck. There's no truck? There's not a truck out there nowhere?" Johnny asked with a shaky voice.

"Sweetheart, no one is going to find you here, and if they do the only way you are leaving with them is if you want to." Graye's words seemed to calmly bring Johnny out of the manic state of confusion. "And, Johnny, just so you know, we have a lot of ammunition in this house if someone wants to try."

Johnny felt his stomach contents settle once again in his belly as his heart rate steadied to a normal pace. "You want to try to finish up your breakfast?"

Graye asked in a calming tone. "Yes, ma'am."

"And Johnny, you have nothing to apologize for, okay?" the woman said reassuringly.

With that statement, Johnny felt he was more concerned with what Graye thought about his behavior, but her comments were kind and reassuring and seemed to ease his tension.

CHAPTER TWENTY

Bitty

The remainder of the day had gone by without incident. Johnny was correct in assuming Graye would question him regarding his past, yet Johnny didn't find her approach nearly as intrusive as Jackson's. He told her of his mother's battle with addiction, and of how much he missed his little brother. Johnny didn't disclose anything about his father; but then, Graye hadn't really pushed him to talk, she simply asked open-ended questions and let him disclose what he felt comfortable discussing.

He now sat in the living room, feeling mentally exhausted and in desperate need of sleep as the evening was well underway. Graye's assumption that her family would ultimately bring home yet another puppy was correct.

The boxer pup, Bitty, was quite a handful. Jared seemed to appreciate the pup's playful antics, but Johnny found her fondness for toes and her needle-sharp teeth to be almost too much. He was thankful the pup wasn't black. She boasted the typical boxer color pattern. She looked healthy and bright-eyed.

The entire family sat on the large leather couch as Johnny watched the fat puppy bounce about the room, looking for toes to bite mercilessly.

"I think I'm gonna turn in early tonight, if that's okay with everyone," Johnny proclaimed. His eyes felt as though they'd been under a blow dryer. He understood he was exhausted from the previous night's road watch.

"You feel okay, man?" Jared asked as he continued to allow his feet to be used as chew toys.

"Yea, I'm just sleepy," Johnny replied.

"Maybe we should all turn in early. It's been a long couple of days, and I know someone is going to be getting up early with Bitty," Jackson said as he looked at his son.

"Night everyone," Johnny said as he stood from the couch.

"Goodnight, sweetie," Graye replied with a smile. "Goodnight, bud. You want to ride with me if I get a call in the morning?" Jackson asked as Johnny walked past them.

"Yea, that'd be awesome." Johnny was genuinely excited about the invite, but instantly hoped any such trip wouldn't result another interrogation.

"Hold up, man. I'll head up with you." Jared said as he stood up from the floor, holding Bitty. He handed the wriggling puppy to his father with a smile. "You have fun with that," he said and quickly walked to the stairs, laughing.

"I see how it is," Jackson said, smiling. The two boys headed up the stairs.

As they reached the hallway at the top, Johnny felt Jared staring him down. "You sure you're okay, man?" he asked Johnny yet again.

"I'm sleepy. That's it, dude." Johnny smiled and lightly socked Jared in the arm.

"All right, all right," Jared replied as he made two fists and air boxed by Johnny's head.

"Goodnight, dude," Jared said as Johnny headed down the hall to his room.

"Goodnight, man," Johnny replied, yawning.

As he crawled into his bed, he avoided looking at the window. He pulled the covers up to his chin and almost instantaneously, he felt his eyes grow heavy. He put either of his index fingers in his ear canals in an effort to drown out any outside noise, real or not.

***

The puppy was just a mutt. Johnny had no idea what kind she was. He only knew that she needed something to eat. The pup's ribs were showing, and her black coat was filthy dirty and she was infested with fleas. The puppy had followed him from the convenience store as Johnny walked home. The cranky clerk with ugly red hair had no idea where the dog came from. During the walk, the puppy would grow tired and fall behind. Johnny was torn. He knew his father would not allow him to keep the dog, but he also knew the puppy needed help.

Thankfully the pup liked the chickens, and they didn't seem to mind her. Johnny had taken some bread from the kitchen, removed the molded portions, and mixed it with several eggs from the coop in a bowl. Johnny sat in the straw with the small dog inside the chicken coop. The pup wolfed down the mixture as the sun was setting and the inside of the coop was getting dark. Johnny watched the small pup yawning contently after she finished her meal. The boy tucked the puppy in straw and the old towel he took from inside. He knew he needed to get inside the house and to his room before his father got home. The puppy yawned and laid her head down as Johnny pet her one more time, and then stood up to go inside. The exhausted puppy made no effort to follow him out the door. Her swollen belly was huge, as this was probably the first time the pup had eaten in at least a few days.

He left the chicken coop, taking the time to look around and enjoy the calm, quiet evening. As Johnny looked at the outside of his father's house, he was once again ashamed to have to live in such atrocious conditions. The boards on the back of the house were warped, and some had fallen off, exposing the insulation underneath. The roof overhang had several holes in it where animals had chewed through and taken residence in the attic. As he looked at the yard, he couldn't help but feel embarrassed. When people drove by, they had to think poorly of the property in general. There were several large metal pieces of cars, scattered garbage, and even an old mattress. Johnny was not allowed to touch any of it, let alone attempt to clean it up. For whatever reason, his father was convinced he needed everything there.

As he headed to the door, he heard his father's truck from down the road. Johnny hated the sounds and sights of the old truck. Every time he heard it, he knew that his father was home, and there was no chance for any type of relaxation.

Quickly, Johnny rushed through the backdoor and through the kitchen. As he made his way down the hall, he heard the grumbling from the engine as it pulled into the drive. Johnny made it to his room and closed the door behind him in plenty of time. He heard the creak the old truck door made when it opened, and then he heard it slam. He then heard his father whistling some tune. Johnny hoped the puppy wouldn't respond to his father's whistling. He was hopeful that his father might be in a decent mood, as he rarely whistled. He listened as the back door came open, and then the thud of his father's boots as he took a few steps inside. There was the sound of a paper sack crinkling in his hand. Johnny assumed his father had gone to the liquor store prior to coming home. As he sat on the bed, he prayed his father would drink heavily and quickly, and that he would pass out quickly as well.

Johnny's heart felt as though it had stopped in place as the sound of his father's boots were coming down the hall at a quick pace—right to Johnny's room. As the door flung open, Johnny did everything possible to avoid eye contact with his father.

"If you're hungry, I got some shit from the quick stop," his father said in a relatively pleasant manner. Johnny was actually a bit shocked by the offer.

Reluctantly, he arose from his bed and made his way to the hall, following his father. His hands were shaky as he walked toward the disgustingly filthy kitchen. On the table, amongst the random objects, was a white paper sack, next to it was a pizza pocket on one of the disposable plates.

"Well, don't just fuckin' look at it. That shit costs money. Eat that motherfucker," his father said from

the sink. The man walked to the fridge and opened the freezer door with a red plastic cup in hand.

Johnny was very hungry. He hastily made his way to the table, picked up the hot, baked, hot pocket and bit into it. It tasted so good to him, he had always wanted to buy one when he went to the store because they smelled so good. He devoured the baked morsel in a matter of seconds. He looked at his father, who had his back to him as he was grabbing ice from the fridge.

"Yea, I thought I'd be nice and grab you some dinner. That's the kind of father I am," the man said as he reached for the bottle of whiskey on the top of the fridge. "That fat, ugly-ass bitch at the store said you was in there this afternoon." The man turned to Johnny, filling his glass with Wild Turkey.

Johnny's heart raced and the lump started developing in his throat. He knew his father knew about the pup. Johnny didn't care if he were to be punished, but he deeply feared for the puppy's well-being.

"Here, I do my best by you. Stopping to grab your lazy faggot-ass something to eat, and then I learn you went behind my back and brought home another lazy-ass, good for nothin', piece of shit!" the crazed man yelled. He then chugged the whiskey from his cup, taking large gulps until Johnny could hear the ice fall back down to the bottom of the empty cup. The man was covered in dirt and grime. His face was bright red and sweaty. His overalls appeared as if they hadn't been washed in ages. The man's body odor was so strong that it smelled like someone was mincing rotten onions in the kitchen. He looked at Johnny with the cold, cruel stare which Johnny was so

accustomed to. There was no escaping it, the night was going to be a long one.

"Where is it?" Thomas asked in a deep tone that sent chills up Johnny's spine.

"In...it's in the coop," Johnny said in a shaky, horrified voice.

"With my fuckin' chickens?" the man screamed belligerently as he threw the cup to the floor. His eyes were peeled as wide as they could open. He turned back to grab the bottle on top of the fridge and removed the cap again, throwing it in the kitchen sink as he began drinking straight from the bottle. Although there was at least one-third of the liquor still in the bottle, his father drank it down like it was raspberry soda. He then looked at Johnny and threw the bottle violently at him. The bottle sailed by the trembling boy's head before Johnny even had time to react, and it shattered against the wall behind him as pieces of the broken glass showered Johnny's back and shoulders and hair.

Thomas, clearly in a heated fit of rage, stormed to his bedroom down the hall. From the kitchen, Johnny could hear the enraged man. "I do my best by you, and this is how you treat me. No fuckin' respect, none at all. You're gonna learn, fag!" His voice became louder as the man came storming back into the kitchen holding a filthy pillowcase, which was covered in dried saliva stains, and God only knew what else. Johnny stared at the floor, which was covered in filth and glass, as his father charged in his direction. He felt his father's powerful grip around his throat. Thomas slammed his son into the wall.

"What do I have to do? Why can't you listen! Look what you make me have to fuckin' do!" the man

screamed in the horrified boy's face. The veins in his forehead looked like they could rupture at any moment. Johnny said not a word as he continued to look in the direction of the floor. He felt dizzy as his father's grip became tighter.

Suddenly, the man released his son's throat and grabbed a hand full of the boy's hair, yanking him violently toward the back door. He kicked the door open, nearly taking it off its hinges.

Johnny was bent over, trying to keep up with his father, nearly losing his footing as the man dragged the trembling teen out the door. Finally, Johnny's feet went out from under him and he was unable to regain his footing immediately. His father was dragging him. Johnny could feel a popping sensation on the top of his scalp as he was being pulled like a sack of potatoes across the yard. Johnny desperately tried to find his footing again, but then they were at the chicken coop. His father threw him to the ground, and Johnny's face hit the dirt hard. As the dazed boy rose to his hands and knees, his father unlatched the coop door and flung it open.

The chickens inside clucked and flew about. Several of them exited the building from the opening to the outside enclosure. Thomas reached down to the frightened pup, which hadn't moved from the spot where Johnny had left her, and violently grabbed the dog by her loose hide. The confused puppy began to yelp in pain and terror. As Johnny looked up at the scene, he could no longer contain his nerves and began vomiting the only decent nutrition he had had that day. He watched as his father shoved the frightened puppy into the disgusting pillowcase and heaved it over his shoulder. "Get up, you pantywaist!" the man yelled at Johnny. Johnny rose to his feet as quickly as he could. Thomas grabbed him by the back of the neck and began leading him forcefully in the direction of the truck.

Johnny was absolutely horrified at what his father might do to the innocent puppy. As they approached the truck, Thomas shoved him hard to the passenger door.

"Get in, you son of a bitch!" the man said as Johnny scrambled for the handle. Thomas then tied the top of the pillowcase in a knot so the pup couldn't escape, and then threw the pillowcase in the back of the truck rather forcefully. The pup let out a yelp, and then it was quiet.

Johnny still felt quite nauseated as he climbed in the passenger seat, but he had nothing left in his stomach to expel. His heart was racing so fast he felt it could explode.

His father jumped in the driver's side and started the old truck. Throwing it in drive, he went speeding through the yard like a mad man. As he flew by the chicken coop, he spun out attempting to turn the truck around. The pillowcase hit the side of the truck bed with a sickening thud. The belligerent motorman finally got the truck straightened out as he tore off through the yard toward the dirt road. Johnny knew exactly where they were going. He was going to the pond about a half a mile up the road from the house.

Johnny desperately wanted to beg for the puppy to be spared, but he was too frightened. He had urinated himself, and he knew as soon as his father saw his wet clothes, it would only get worse. As the truck approached the pond, Thomas slammed on the brakes, sending Johnny's face slamming into the dash and bloodying his nose. The pillowcase, and its unconscious contents, slammed into the front of the truck bed as the truck came to a screeching halt, cascading the scene in a cloud of dust. The man looked at his shaking son. "That's a nice sound, ain't it, fag?" he said in a deep, horrific tone as Johnny bled uncontrollably.

"Get the fuck out!" the man yelled. Johnny was shaking profusely as he exited the vehicle. Thomas left his truck running and parked in the middle of the road as he grabbed the pillowcase from the truck bed. There was no sign of life from the puppy, and Johnny hoped she had died from the force of hitting the metal truck bed.

"Get walkin', asshole!" Thomas yelled as Johnny headed in the direction of the pond. Thomas raised his foot and kicked him in the rear, nearly knocking him down. The pond was shallow, and only about one hundred feet from the road.

"I swear to God if I get ate up by those damn mosquitoes because of you, you're gonna pay!" the man yelled at Johnny. As they approached the still body of water, his father grabbed him by the hair on the top of his head and yanked him backward.

Johnny let out sharp cry as his neck popped from being yanked so violently, his nose still bleeding. The man then held the pillowcase out, insinuating that he wanted Johnny to take it.

"You did this to yourself. You killed this pup. Just you remember that, ya pussy," his father said in a cruel, low voice.

Johnny, trembling, grabbed the pillowcase from his father, just as there was a slight movement from inside.

"Please," Johnny muttered as the blood cascaded from his nose, down his face and off his chin to his clothes and shoes.

"Boy!" his father yelled at Johnny as he bowed up to him. Johnny turned from his father as the puppy began to whine quietly, he inhaled deeply, closed his eyes, and tossed the pillowcase through the air. As it landed about ten feet off the bank, it made a loud splash and sank quickly.

"You sure do throw like a girly fag," the man said with a maniacal smile, as he watched the entire event in pure and utter delight.

Johnny stood staring at the pond as the ripples continued to make their way to the outer edge of the bank. The bullfrogs and insects had all momentarily halted their nightly serenade, as if they were honoring the fallen pup.

"You know what's happening when we get home, don't cha boy?" his father asked, as once again he grabbed the back of his son's neck, but this time he leaned in closely. "I hate fags in my truck. You got five fuckin' minutes to be in your room, you better get to running."

Johnny awoke from his sleep. Without even attempting to analyze or process, he jumped out of his bed and ran for his bedroom door. Part of him knew he was indoors, but his mind was still there— with his father, and he knew he had to get away from the pond, and back to his father's house. As Johnny burst into the hallway, he ran head-on into the wall directly across from his door with a force so hard it knocked him backward, flat on his back. As he rose to his feet in the pitch-black hallway, he ran in the direction of the stairs. As he grabbed the railing, he lost his footing on the second step, and tumbled all the way down the stairs, hitting his head hard at the end of the staircase on the wood flooring.

"Stay here! If anything happens, call the police!" He heard Jackson yell out from the master bedroom, but he didn't immediately recognize the man's voice. Johnny raced to the front door as he saw Jackson enter the living room behind him, but it was too late. Johnny had managed to get the front door open, and was now sprinting down the driveway in a delusional race against time.

"Graye! It's Johnny! Something's wrong!" Johnny heard Jackson yell out as the raced out the front door after him.

"JOHNNY!"

Johnny could hear Jackson's voice, but at this point, nothing made sense, he only knew he needed to get past the pond and to his room.

"JOHNNY!" he heard the man yell again. This time the voice was closer; Johnny knew he was being pursued. As he reached the road, he plunged even further into the chaotic confusion. He understood he needed to get to his father's house, yet he had no idea which way to go. His lungs burned from the stagnant air and his body ached from the fall. He looked back and forth down the road, simply standing still, unsure of what direction he should take.

Total fear had overtaken any rational sense. He placed both hands on either side of his head and squeezed. "Where? Where is it!" he cried out in between breaths as Jackson ran up behind him.

"Johnny! What's wrong?" Johnny heard as he hit his knees and covered his head with his hands in a fetal position.

"I can't find it! I'm sorry! I don't know where it's at! I can't find it! Please! I'm sorry!" he yelled out repeatedly. He focused on the man's feet while attempting to cover the back of his head in anticipation of being beaten. He then heard the familiarity of Graye's voice approach as the woman called out.

"Jackson! Johnny! What is wrong? Johnny turned to see the bottom half of her nightgown approaching him.

"Jackson! What is it?"

"Johnny. Johnny, look at me," Johnny heard Jackson demand of him as he felt the man place his hand on his back.

"Johnny, what is going on? What happened?" Jackson asked concernedly.

"He's here!" Johnny yelled out as his gaze danced about the country backroad looking for his father.

"Who? Who is here, Johnny?" Jackson demanded again.

"Johnny, sweetie, who is here? Your father?" Graye asked as she kneeled down and began rubbing Johnny's back.

"Is he here?" Johnny asked as he heard his own voice begin to crack. He looked at both Graye and Jackson, waiting for an answer.

"No, bud. No one is here. No one is here but us," Jackson said.

Johnny felt himself shaking violently and his clothing was soaked in urine.

"You're okay, sweetheart." Graye's words were strained but reassuring.

"I'm sorry! I'm so sorry." The boy began to sob. "I saw him at the pond, we were just at the pond," Johnny proclaimed with absolute certainty.

"Bud, the only pond is miles from here. You're safe. No one is going to hurt you here," Jackson said as Johnny looked to him and Graye.

"I don't understand. He was just here. He was just *fucking* here!" Johnny wailed as he began to cry harder. "My head! My mind ain't right!" the boy cried out. He the felt Graye touch a tender goose egg on the back of his head. It shot pain through the back of his skull and up into the side of his face.

"Oh, sweetie. You did a number on your head," he heard her say softly.

"It's nothing we can't work on, bud. Everyone needs help from time to time, Johnny. We can get you help," Jackson said as Johnny looked up at him through his tears.

"I, I understand if you want me to go," Johnny muttered as he attempted to stop crying.

"No. You're not going anywhere," Graye said confidently as she placed her other hand on his shoulder.

"No, you're not. This is your home now," Jackson said in a reassuring voice. "Johnny, I'm not sure why you're so afraid of your father. If you would just talk to us, maybe we could try to understand. But you need to know that you're safe here. No one is coming for you out here," Jackson said as he began to stand up. As he regained his footing, he offered a helping hand, assisting Johnny from the ground. "Come on, bud. Let's go get you cleaned up," Jackson said as he motioned in the direction of the house.

CHAPTER TWENTY-ONE

Unrest

Graye

He's passed out. I'm sure the warm milk helped," Graye said to her husband as she entered the kitchen.

Jackson was sitting at the kitchen table; his hands covered his mouth as his elbows were resting on the tabletop. "What the hell happened to him? Who the hell could…I just don't get it," Jackson said as he stared across the kitchen at the backsplash above the sink.

"I'm going to call Brian tomorrow. I'm sure he can offer some insight," Graye replied as she grabbed the empty glass from the table and walked toward the sink.

Brian Mulberry was a dear frriend of Graye's and Jackson's. He was also the school psychologist for the school system Graye taught for. Brian had been involved with thc family extensively throughout the years. When her father passed away, Brian was there for her and her family, acting both as a professional counselor and a genuine friend.

"He needs help, Graye. But I meant what I said about this being his home." Jackson broke his stare from the wall and looked at his wife.

"I agree completely. I'm happy that he's here. But we need to get him the assistance he needs," Graye replied, thankful her husband was so receptive to helping Johnny through his mental debilitation.

Jared entered looking a little surprised to see both his parents in the kitchen at this hour.

Graye was not as surprised to see him, as he would often raid the fridge at night.

"Is everything okay? Why are you guys up?" he asked as he sleepily made his way into the kitchen, slapping his bare feet on the hardwood floor as he entered.

"What are you doing up, young man? It's nearly two in the morning," Graye snapped halfheartedly.

"I was just a little hungry, so I thought I'd grab a midnight snack I guess. Am I interrupting something here?" he asked his parents as he began to look concerned.

"No, bud. You're fine. I think there's still some leftover bacon in the fridge. Knock yourself out. I think I'm going to try this sleep thing again," Jackson said as he stood up from the table.

Graye watched as her son walked to the fridge and Jackson put the boy in a gentle head lock, kissing the back of his head.

"Pops, dammit." Jared chuckled as he broke free. "Good night, you two. I love you guys," Jackson said as he exited the kitchen.

"Night, Pops," Jared said as he opened the fridge, looking for the leftover bacon.

Graye quickly walked to her son and kissed his cheek, hugging him tightly. "Good night, son. I love you so much, sweetheart."

"Love you too Mom," he replied, smiling as he bit into a slice of cold bacon.

Graye smiled, and then quickly followed her husband out of the kitchen.

As she pulled the bedding back, she looked at her husband, who was obviously deep in thought. "What are you thinking?" she asked with a half-smile.

"What could have happened that was so horrible it would cause a fear like that in an eighteen-year-old kid?" Jackson asked as Graye searched her mind for answers, disgusted by the thoughts it conjured.

"I'm sure it was horrible. I don't understand how someone can suffer so much, and still be able to smile and try to be happy," Graye replied as she fluffed one of the pillows. "I think that is what breaks my heart the most. He wants to be happy, but he's haunted by this fear that his father is going to find him."

"It's more than just that. Something else is going on. He genuinely thought the man was here, he thought he was with him tonight," Jackson proclaimed passionately.

"I'll call Brian in the morning. Maybe he can come for supper some night next week or something," Graye replied as she walked toward the door to shut the light off.

"Are you afraid of what he is going to say?" Jackson asked as his wife flicked the light off.

"No, we need to know. That's the first step to Johnny getting better. Like I said, I trust him, and I want him here, but he does need help. If he is going to have a productive school year and, well, a productive future, he is going to need help now." Graye climbed into bed as they heard Jared place a dish in the kitchen sink. She kissed her husband goodnight as she listened to her son walk into the living room and up the stairs.

Johnny

As Jared got to the top of the stairs, the bathroom door opened. Johnny came into the hall, heading to his bedroom.

"Man, you can't sleep either?" Jared asked as he approached Johnny in the hallway. That simple question let Johnny know that Jared was not yet clued in on the evening's events.

At this point, Johnny fully understood that his father was nowhere near the farm, nor had he been at any point in the evening. He was once again back to his best mental clarity, although he would not allow himself to drift off to sleep again after the late-night rendezvous.

"I guess not. Roof?" Johnny asked as Jared yawned and leaned up against the wall. Jared scratched the back of his head.

"Nah. I guess I better not. I just ate and had some milk and I'm actually kind of sleepy now," Jared said, patting his stomach.

"All right then. See you in the morning." "Night, man."

As Johnny entered his room, he found himself feeling embarrassed by the night's events. At the same time, a depressing sense of discouragement came over him. He sat down on his bed and put his back to the wall on the right side of the window. He had finally escaped the clutches of his father, and from the shack of a house. He was finally free, yet it seemed like the further he got from that day, and the more time that passed, the worse his mind got. Then he thought about the incident in the kitchen. He was so sure that there was someone at the door that even Graye had difficulty convincing him otherwise. He knew that the Everetts were right, he needed help.

The only gratifying aspect about the situation was the idea of possibly obtaining mental stability. Johnny knew that the life he was living now was by far the best one he had ever lived. This past week had actually been beyond his greatest expectations. He smiled slightly at the thought of living at the Everett place and not having nightmares or delusions. The idea seemed almost unachievable, but he took comfort in what Jackson and Graye had said. Everything they said they were going to do so far, they followed through with.

Johnny drew his knees up to his chest as he sat on the bed. He knew this would be a long night, and he hoped it would pass quickly.

CHAPTER TWENTY-TWO

Good Morning

As Johnny yawned and listened to the playful banter taking place downstairs, he contemplated going down and telling good morning to everyone. He had heard Graye and Bryce, but had yet to hear Jared or Jackson. Every time he decided to get off the bed, something held him back. He was exhausted, and knew his face more than likely showed it. He intentionally stayed awake all night for fear of the nightmares.

His eyes felt scratchy, and his mouth was sticky and dry. His head hurt from where he hit it on the hardwood the night before, and after a detailed examination he found he had several small bruises on his limbs from the fall. He thought little of it, as physical bruises seemed to only sting a short while, and then fade away. He heard footsteps coming up the stairs. He yawned as he watched the doorknob, anticipating it opening and one of the family entering to say good morning.

He heard the footsteps reach the top of the stairs

and quietly make their way down the hall to his room. Rather than wait to be surprised by whoever was about to enter, he got off the bed and headed to the door. He was anticipating Jackson inquiring as to whether or not Johnny would like to go out on a call with him. He was somewhat surprised when he opened the door and found Graye preparing to knock.

"Oh," Graye, startled.

Johnny imagined she had been up for a while, as she was wearing a nice pair of jeans and a graphics T-shirt. Her hair was fixed nicely, and she even had a small amount of make-up on. Until this interaction, Johnny hadn't seen the woman in make-up.

Johnny smiled with puffy, tired eyes as he opened the door wider.

"Morning, sweetheart," the woman said as she smiled warmly.

"Mornin'." Johnny smiled as he headed back for his bed.

"Sweetie, I was wanting to talk to you about a few things," she said as she entered the room.

"Are you mad at me for last night? I really am sorry, I don't know—"

"Absolutely not. There is no need for apologies. None whatsoever. The last thing I want you to think is that I'm upset with you in any way."

The time with her had Johnny longing for his own mother. Even though she would be considered a horrible parent by most any societal standard, Johnny truly his mom and felt she loved him.

"Do you think you can talk to someone? I have a good friend, and he is amazing when it comes to talking. He's the psychologist at my school. I called him this morning, and we are going to meet for brunch to catch up. I was going to ask him to meet you sometime this week if that was okay with you."

Johnny was uncomfortable with the conversation, yet he knew things had escalated to a point where they could no longer be ignored or even downplayed. He understood completely that he needed help that even the Everetts couldn't offer.

"I want to talk to you. I want to talk to you and Jackson. I just can't," Johnny said softly as he looked at the floor, the heat from his anxiety wetting the palms of his clasped hands. "I wanna make this better. I'll meet the guy," he said as he looked up at Graye. He knew he would eventually have to talk about his past.

"He is a great guy; you are going to like him. Pancakes?" she followed up.

"That actually sounds really good." Johnny, feeling anxious and excited about talking with this friend of Graye's, looked up, and smiled.

Leaving his bedroom, Johnny had a small sense of hope. The tiny euphoria almost compensated for the lack of sleep.

As Johnny walked down the hall following Graye, Jared opened his door.

"Boo yea!" Jared yelled at Johnny, eliciting a chuckle.

"Pancakes are on the table, boys," Graye yelled out as she continued walking down.

"Man, let's eat and go game after we eat," Jared suggested as he walked into the kitchen.

"Sounds like a plan, dude."

After breakfast the boys sat in the dim lit basement and while Jared clicked buttons on the controller.

"Dude, we should go check on the dogs," Johnny

said.

"I don't want to. I'm just not ready to go out there yet, I guess," Jared responded dejectedly.

"Sunny?"

"Yea," Jared said, staring at the screen.

Johnny noticed Jared hadn't been much for conversation. Rather than question continuously how to play this particular game, Johnny decided to watch intently. As Jared was in the process of losing to the generated team, he pushed pause and set the remote down, exhaling in an almost irritated manner.

Johnny instantly figured that Jared needed his space and that he was growing irritated at being around him constantly. Just as Johnny had made up his mind to leave the basement and give Jared some room, Jared turned to him.

"We got her when I was fourteen," Jared said, looking over at Johnny. At first, Johnny was confused; he had no idea what Jared was talking about. "Pops brought her home; she was even smaller than Bitty. He found her right before the sun went down on a dirt road coming back from a call. She was covered in big, fat-ass ticks and fleas. We scrubbed the hell out of her with dog shampoo. Pops said her belly was swollen from worms, so he treated her."

As Jared spoke, Johnny noticed his friend's eyes swell with tears. Johnny realized Jared just wanted to talk about the loss of his dog. "We put her in the laundry room after we got her bathed and dewormed. Pops said I could keep her if I took care of her. The first night we had her she cried and cried, so I snuck downstairs and brought her upstairs to bed with me. Dude, the next morning I had puppy shit and worms all over my bed, in my hair, and all over my pjs."

Jared began laughing as he described the situation.

Johnny began to chuckle too, although the thought of waking to intestinal worms in his hair had him cringing and shivering.

"I had to help Pops on weekend calls to pay him back for her vaccinations. She was seriously the best dog—" Jared's voice began to crack, and he was unable to finish the sentence right away. "She was the best dog ever. I hate that fuckin' coyote, and I hope that fucker is burning in hell," Jared proclaimed as he gripped his hands together tightly. A look of absolute anger came across his face, and a few tears finally escaped his eyes.

Johnny had so many thoughts compiled, yet none of them seemed capable of forming into words. He felt horrible for his friend. He could tell that his friend was going to be distraught over the loss of his dog for quite some time. What Johnny couldn't understand was how easily Jared confided in him. He had absolutely no reservation in expressing emotion in front of Johnny and talking about his feelings.

This was a strange concept for Johnny, and he didn't know how to respond immediately. He desperately wanted to communicate with Jared and relate his feelings of loss from when he lost the puppy because of his father, but the last thing he wanted to even think about was anything that happened there. Johnny knew the black puppy for but a few hours, Sunny was Jared's companion.

"I'm sorry, man. I hope it's in hell too," Johnny blurted out.

Jared broke his gaze from the paused video game and turned to Johnny.

"Fucker, you better not give me shit for cryin' like

a bitch."

"I wouldn't do that, man. That was your dog."

Although Johnny didn't quite understand how or why Jared was so open to disclosing how he felt to him, he did take a valuable lesson from the conversation. He had listened to Jared as he talked about his dog, and watched him cry. Johnny realized that not once did he think badly of Jared for crying. He didn't think he was a *pantywaist*, he didn't think he was a *pussy*, he merely felt bad for his friend and wished he could do something to make him feel better.

"So, you bout ready to get your ass kicked at this game?" Jared asked in a much more chipper voice.

"It won't be hard. I don't know how the hell to play," Johnny said as he smiled and picked up the controller. He heard Jackson coming down the stairs. The man walked in looking annoyed and stood right in front of the boys.

"So, you guys know what the first thing I did when I got out of the shower was? Well, I guess the second thing, because the first thing I did was grab a towel," he said as Johnny stared, completely intrigued.

"Nah, Pops. What was the second thing you did after you took a much-needed shower?" Jared said as he smiled from his chair.

"The second thing I did was step in a huge, mushy pile of cold puppy shit!" Jackson said as he started laughing. Both of the boys started laughing too. "It was smashed between all my toes, it was basically awesome," the man continued as all three of the guys continued laughing. "What exactly do you mean, a much-needed shower, Jared? I don't think that hair of yours can get any greasier.".

"Ooooww!" Jared said in protest.

In all actuality, the boy's thick, brown hair was sticking out and up in no specific direction, but Johnny didn't think it looked greasy, it was just messy.

"You boys want to go with me to town when the queen gets back? I need to get supplies," Jackson asked as he headed for the stairs.

"I do," Johnny said first, hoping that Jared would say he wanted to go, as well.

"Yea, Pops. Count us in. Oh, and ah, Pops," Jared continued as a mischievous smile came across his face.

"What, dork?"

"Watch where you step. I can't ride with a guy that stinks like dog shit!" Jared yelled up to his ascending father, who started laughing from the top of the stairs.

CHAPTER TWENTY-THREE

Advice

Jackson

Jackson turned on the radio as the three guys headed to town. He and Jared rode in the front seat of the truck, and Johnny was in the back. As the truck turned off the dirt road and headed to town, Jackson noticed the two guys appeared somewhat less than enthused to be leaving the sanctuary of the air-conditioned man-cave. From the time it took to walk from the front porch to the truck and get the air conditioner adequately cooling the vehicle, the guys were all perspiring.

"So, what the hell are we getting?" Jared asked in a grouchy tone as he leaned his seat back.

"Hey, I asked if you wanted to go. I never said you had to. If you like, you are welcome to get out and walk back home," Jackson replied. Although he would never make his son walk home in the heat, his tone was somewhat grouchy too. "I need to pick up some materials at the hardware store. Your mother wants me to fix the missing boards on the barn so that we don't have any more surprise visitors."

"When will they know what was wrong with the coyote?" Johnny asked from the backseat.

"Well, it depends. Could be tomorrow," Jackson replied as he looked at Johnny in the rearview mirror. He noticed that Johnny looked worn out. He knew Johnny had had a late night the night before, but today he looked as though he could use several more hours of sleep. "Based on what you told me, and my experience, I can assure you the animal had rabies," Jackson said in a serious tone. "I have seen quite a few cases over the years. I'm just glad you and Bryce were not bitten. I'm glad you were there when it happened, but I'm thankful it didn't bite you. You would have had to get shots for about six weeks," Jackson continued as the truck continued to town.

"Can we talk about something else?" Jared snapped. Johnny was now looking out the window and was obviously in a foul mood.

"How about you don't talk at all, shit britches," Jackson said as he looked over at his moody son.

Jared ignored the comment and continued to look out the window.

Jackson noticed Johnny smiling in the rearview mirror. Johnny obviously thought the comment was funny.

As the truck entered town off Highway 210, Jackson looked over at his son, who had his eyes closed, head tilted back, and mouth wide open. He was glad Jared was able to catch a catnap. When Jared was a baby, his parents would take him for quick joyrides in the car to put him to sleep. Nearly eighteen years later, Johnny seemed to be just as susceptible. It seemed to never fail. Unless Johnny was driving, he usually fell asleep during trips to town, or anywhere for that matter.

Jackson looked in the rearview mirror to see Johnny gazing straight ahead out the windshield. His eyes appeared fixed, like he was deep in thought. Jackson continued to glance at Johnny's reflection. He was going to insist that Johnny take a long nap when they got home.

Jackson noticed his exit up ahead and turned on his turn signal.

"Johnny, bud, you okay?" a concerned Jackson asked as he continued watching him in the rearview mirror. As Jackson began to move into the turning lane, he heard Johnny muttering something. Johnny's eyes were open, but he appeared to be in a trance and saying something under his breath. Jackson continued to glance at Johnny, and then glance back at the road as he pulled onto the exit ramp.

"Bobby, man. Drop me off here. Not too close to the house," Johnny said in a shallow, nearly inaudible voice, as he leaned forward. He was pointing out the front passenger window with his left hand right by Jared's sleeping head.

Jackson watched Johnny curiously as he slowed the vehicle, preparing to turn.

As Johnny withdrew his hand and leaned back, he began looking about the interior of the truck. While doing so, Jackson noticed the boy glance in the rearview mirror from the backseat, making eye contact with him. The boy's mouth opened slightly as he slowly broke eye contact and looked out the side window of the truck. He sat there for a second while Jackson continued watching him, and then looked back up at the man in the mirror, giving him a halfhearted smile.

"So, how much do we gotta get?" Johnny asked Jackson, who was still trying to figure out what was going on. He had no idea if Johnny realized he was not with anyone named Bobby.

"Well, um, how much of what, bud?" Jackson asked, as he pulled into the store parking lot.

"How much wood and stuff to fix the barn."

"Oh, well, not much. There's nothing too significant," Jackson said in a relieved tone. "I'm sure the coyote actually got in through the front door of the barn. If there were too many large holes, the cooler wouldn't keep the barn as cool as it does," Jackson continued as the truck came to a stop.

By this time, Jared was snoring softly. "Let's let him nap with the truck running while we grab the supplies," Jackson suggested as he put the truck in park. Jackson met Johnny at the front of the truck and began walking to the front of the store. The heat was horrible. Immediately, Jackson felt his forehead being kissed with tiny beads of perspiration. "So, Bobby, he was your friend, right?" Jackson asked Johnny as they walked closer to the entrance.

"Yea. Good guy," Johnny replied in a reserved voice.

As Jackson looked at Johnny, Johnny developed a look of suspicion. Jackson remembered Johnny briefly mentioning Bobby several days before, when they first met, but it was clear to the man that Johnny had no clue he'd been conversing with an imaginary Bobby only moments prior.

"So, did Bobby give you rides home often?" Jackson probed as the front doors of the hardware store automatically opened. The store expelled a scent of cut pine and other wood, and a cool, refreshing gust of air.

"Yea. He did." Johnny stopped walking just three feet or so inside the store's entrance. Johnny's nostrils were slightly flared, and his brows pointed toward the ground in an irritated manner. He seemed hesitant to follow Jackson any further into the hardware store.

Jackson, looking at Johnny from about fifteen feet in front of him on the lighting aisle, noticed Johnny's uneasy stature. "You coming?" He instantly recognized that his questioning was bothersome. With dark circles under his eyes and his haggard-looking complexion, Johnny diverted eye contact. Judging by appearance alone, Jackson was certain that Johnny was in need of sleep.

"Yea," Johnny said lowly as he placed his hands in his gym shorts pockets and looked toward the smooth, cement flooring. He stood still for a second more, and then walked toward Jackson.

Jackson noticed immediately the change in stance, and the way Johnny carried himself. He decided then that the way he was going about getting Johnny to open up was ineffective, and possibly even pushing him away. As Johnny walked up and stood next to the man, Jackson decided to make light of the situation.

"You all right? Or do you got shit britches too?" Jackson asked jokingly. Johnny laughed a little as he continued his downward gaze. "Hey, you all right?" Jackson asked as he leaned his head down in an effort to make eye contact with Johnny.

"Was I talking about him or something?" Johnny asked. Johnny's expression was a combination of exhaustion, despair, confusion, and even irritation.

"No. Nah, I was just curious about your buddy is all." Jackson stumbled through the words. He was under the impression that Johnny knew he was lying. "You know, Graye and I have both decided that we couldn't be more happy having you here to help us," Jackson said, trying to lighten the situation. "I won't ask any more questions about anything. But just know that if you ever need to talk, I'm here. Deal?" Jackson asked as he literally watched the depressive posture lift.

"Deal," Johnny said with an extremely sleepy smile.

"You know, you and Jared are gonna have to stop sneaking out at night and chasing girls once school starts. You got to be awake for class," Jackson said jokingly as he turned to continue his quest for supplies.

"What?" Johnny asked as he removed his hands from his pockets, following Jackson.

"Yea, I don't think so," Johnny finally replied. "So, what all do we need? I bet Jared don't sleep too long," Johnny continued as he followed Jackson.

"Well, we've got a couple projects. Patching the barn, and then we're gonna make a simple cross for Sunny's grave." Jackson pointed in the direction of the lumber. The guys headed toward the extensive selection.

"Do you think Jared is gonna be all right? I know he really loved his dog. He told me all about her," Johnny said with genuine concern in his voice.

Jackson looked at Johnny. The fact that he was concerned for Jared's well-being, even though his own was so desperate, only reaffirmed to Jackson what kind of a person the young man was at core.

"Yea, Johnny. I think he'll be fine. I think we'll all be fine."

CHAPTER TWENTY-FOUR

Tyler

Johnny

The family stood around Sunny's simple cross, staring at the soft earth. Johnny's deep appreciation for the strength of the family was stronger than ever. Sunny meant the most to Jared, yet the entire family united to comfort him. This was something Johnny had rarely witnessed, and had only mildly enjoyed during his time on earth. He felt as though he had experienced more support and love from the small time with the Everetts than he had in his entire life. This was only further motivation for him to embrace the help the family was attempting to give him. If he could only get his mind right he felt he would be the happiest boy in the world.

In the distance, the coyotes began their eerie cries. This irony seemed somewhat too much for Jared. He was clearly bitter toward the coyote that had taken Sunny's life. He had informed his father and Johnny

that if he were to see one of them anywhere near

the farm, he was getting his shotgun out of his closet and blowing it away. As the coyotes continued calling, Jared excused himself and headed for the porch.

Johnny watched as his friend walked past him with his head down. Johnny assumed Jared needed time to himself. It had been a long day, and erecting a cross probably evoked a greater feeling of loss. As Jared walked to the front of the porch, he looked back at the family, still standing by the grave.

"Hey, Johnny. You wanna go to the basement?" Jared asked, looking back at Johnny.

"Sure thing, man." The teen began jogging in the same direction and the two boys disappeared around to the front of the house.

Johnny was glad that Jared had asked him, yet he was somewhat surprised. Although Johnny wasn't good with words, he hoped his presence offered at least some comfort to his friend during this difficult time.

Johnny had been able to take a nap after the guys had returned from town. He slept for two solid hours without a single nightmare and was feeling refreshed.

As the boys made their way downstairs, Jared turned on the light and plopped down in the overstuffed recliner.

"Dude, you're by far the coolest friend I've had in a long time," Jared proclaimed as he looked at Johnny, much to the latter's surprise as he had anticipated Jared wanting alone time rather than summoning him to play video games.

"Thanks, man. You are too." Johnny appreciated the way Jared and the rest of the family communicated and expressed feelings, but sometimes it made him feel awkward.

"Yea, so this dickhead, Tyler, is gonna be here Friday night. I'm half tempted to just punch that bitch right in the face. Just knock him smooth out," Jared said as he made a fist with his right hand and punched the palm of his left.

Johnny sat down the in the other recliner. This was the second time that Jared had mentioned Tyler. There was obviously some bad blood there.

"Why is he coming here?" Johnny asked curiously. "Mom and Pops have a crawfish boil every summer. They usually do it at the beginning of the summer, but this year has been too crazy. This Friday, all our damn neighbors, and some of Pops' clients, will be here 'til like, eleven at night. Hell, maybe later. Tyler's parents live about ten miles from here, and they've already said they're gonna be here." Jared had a scowl as he looked in the direction of the hardwood floor.

"What did Tyler do that you hate him so bad?"

"Look, dude, I'm not stupid. But the way I see things is different than how other people see things. Sometimes letters are backward, or even in the wrong place. It's called dyslexia, and I can't read very well." Johnny studied Jared's facial expression. He could recognize that this information was something Jared found difficult to offer.

"Mom has worked really hard with me to keep me up to speed with the rest of my class, but I still go to a special class in the afternoons to make sure I don't fall behind. Well, Tyler was supposed to be my bud. Hewas always over here, or he would drive us to town, or I would go to his house. I thought he was a cool guy."

Johnny was certain by Jared's expressions and body language, and the way his cheeks flushed red, that this wasn't easy for him to discuss. He heard someone in the kitchen. Either someone had come in to grab something, or everyone had come in.

"Tyler was always asking me why I had to go in the afternoons. Finally, I just told him. That douchebag waited until we were in homeroom, and then he wrote on the blackboard for everyone to read.

Did you know Jared is a dyslexic tard?

But he turned the letters backward and some were upside down. I couldn't believe he did that. He thought it was funny, but I didn't go to school for two days, and when I did, I told him to fuck off every time he tried to apologize or even talk to me. It's been a year, and I still hate that bitch." Jared was glaring at the floor as he described his hatred for the boy who'd humiliated him.

"Dude, you're not stupid. Probably one of the smartest guys I know. And if that asshole does show up, I'll punch him in the damn face," Johnny said as he realized how tormented Jared had been by the Tyler ordeal. Johnny had been made fun of in school most his life. He never had nice clothes, he never had money, and kids were cruel. He knew what it was like to be belittled publicly. The fact that this Tyler kid was supposed to be Jared's friend made it even more despicable. "Well, dude, that's why you're my bro," Jared said, still looking at the floor.

"You too."

Graye

Neither of the boys knew, but Graye was at the top of the stairs, listening to Jared's story. The woman only caught the last part of Jared's confession, but she was absolutely livid. The thought of that little bastard, Tyler, humiliating her son like that set her blood on fire.

As Graye listened from the top of the stairs, part of her wanted to barge into the basement and grab her son and reassure him how absurdly intelligent he was. She knew all too well that this would not produce the desired outcome of reassurance, and would only embarrass him in front of Johnny. Another part of her wanted to call Tyler's mom up and give her an earful, but she understood this would only embarrass her son too. She understood the only thing she could do that was practical was vent to her husband, and be thankful Jared had such a great friend in his life. She was becoming increasingly thankful to have Johnny.

CHAPTER TWENTY-FIVE

Bobby

Johnny

"Dude, what the hell? I don't mind buyin'. It's a damn corndog," Bobby said as he and Johnny were standing in the Quick Stop, looking in the greasy glass warmer, which was full of deep-fried food. The fat, redheaded lady wasn't there, but the racist old man was behind the counter. Johnny was under the impression that everyone that worked at the run-down store was related. He disliked most of them, but the store was in walking distance.

"I don't need you to buy me anything," Johnny said defensively.

Bobby was a tall, slender, black boy that lived a few miles from Johnny, just inside of town. He was a nice enough kid, and Johnny knew Bobby's situation was extremely similar to his. Bobby's alcoholic father was too weak and sick to be much a physical threat, but Bobby claimed to have suffered greatly when he was younger and his father was healthier.

"Man, I need to get two potato wedges and two corndogs," Bobby said in a friendly tone to the toothless, gray-bearded old man behind the counter as Johnny stood back, watching the interaction.

"Johnny, your dad know the company you keep?" the old man asked Johnny over his glasses." Johnny looked at the old man, afraid to answer in front of his friend. Just before he responded, Bobby began laughing at the comment as the old man took the food from the warmer and set it on top of the grease-covered case.

"If it's not too much trouble for ya, can I get that in two sacks?" Bobby asked the old man.

Johnny knew the trashy man was never one to turn down business, but he despised any person of any color other than white.

He angrily shoved the wedges into two separate white sacks, and then tossed the corndogs in on top. He didn't bother wearing gloves while handling the food.

Johnny didn't care, and Bobby didn't seem to. The conditions he usually ate under were much less sanitary than this place.

The old man slowly walked the sacks to the register. As he peeked over his glasses at the keys on the register, he pecked them with his finger like a chicken pecking at the ground.

"Four eighty-eight," the old man snapped. Bobby had a crumpled up five-dollar bill. He threw it on the counter.

"Keep ya mothafuckin' change, old man!" Bobby snapped back angrily.

Johnny, completely shocked at the way Bobby spoke to the old man, was quick to exit the store through the door.

The old man was obviously shocked as well, as he said nothing in return. He only stared as Johnny exited the building with his mouth agape.

"Dude, what the hell?" Johnny asked as Bobby was laughing.

Bobby started walking to his father's maroon 1992 Grand Prix, which Bobby usually drove.

"Get in. I'll take you home," Bobby said as he reached for the handle, still chuckling.

"Man, I better walk. It's a little late," Johnny replied. He wouldn't risk his father seeing him in the same vehicle as Bobby.

As Bobby opened the car door, he sat one of the white sacks in his seat, and tossed the other one at Johnny.

Johnny caught it with a look of irritation on his face.

"Just shut the fuck up and eat. I'll see you at school tomorrow," Bobby said as he climbed into the driver's seat.

Johnny turned and began walking home. It was hot day, but not excruciating.

As soon as he heard Bobby's car drive away behind him, he tore the bag open and grabbed at least four wedges and shoved them in his mouth. He barely chewed them before he swallowed. As he finished off the wedges, he grabbed the corndog and tossed the white sack. He devoured the corndog within a minute. Although he acted irritated, he was incredibly thankful that Bobby bought him food. Cold chicken noodle soup was anything but appetizing.

The blacktop leading to the dirt road and his father's house had thick trees and other vegetation on either side. The sun was already attempting to hide behind the tree line. Johnny took the time to enjoy the evening. He liked walking from the store. He was a little worried his father would be at home before he made it there. For whatever reason, Thomas Tregalis hated it when his son was not at home when he got there.

The sounds of buzzing locusts and bullfrogs croaking from the spillways were already prevalent. Johnny loved the noises of nature. He turned on the dirt road leading to his father's house. His stomach made several strange grumbling noises. Johnny chalked it up to inhaling his food and barely chewing. He truly hoped his father wasn't home. If he knew for a fact the man was still at the mill, he would have walked slower and enjoyed the time out of the house.

As he walked past the old, abandoned house a mile before his father's place, Johnny couldn't help but think the abandoned house looked more presentable than the house he lived in. He stopped a moment and looked at the old house. It was overgrown with ivy. All the windows were intact, and the house itself seemed interesting. It was small, white, and had probably been empty for quite a while.

As he stood staring, the familiar sound of his father's truck sent Johnny's heart racing. He had the sudden impulse to run to the house and hide behind it. He knew that it wouldn't matter in the end. Either his father would drive past him, or he would harass him to some degree. The truck turned on to the dirt road like a bat out of hell. Johnny watched as Thomas came flying down the road like a belligerent moron. Johnny knew his father was in rage. As the truck got closer, Johnny descended into the ditch. The man slammed on the brakes, sending his truck sliding down the dirt road. As the dust flew, Johnny heard the creak of the door as the man exited the truck.

"What did I tell you about bein' seen with the likes of that trash! You think you're a man now and can do as you please?" Thomas was cloaked by the rolling dust as he stormed around the front of the truck, running full speed at Johnny in the ditch.

Johnny stood still in a horrified trance, unable to move as his father approached. He knew the old man had told his father what Bobby had done.

The man grabbed Johnny by the shirt and threw him down in the ditch. Thomas was violently enraged. As he stood over the frightened teen, breathing hard with his chest bowed out, Johnny actually feared for his life. "Get up!"

Johnny slowly stood to his feet.

"Look at me!" the man yelled at his son.

As Johnny made eye contact, his father's fist came flying at his face

***

."Dude, wake up. Dude."

Johnny sat up straight, looking at Jared. Johnny swallowed hard as he looked all around the basement. "Johnny, dude. We crashed in the basement, it's like three in the morning."

Johnny continued to look all around the room.

"Man, you were having a bad dream."

Johnny remembered they had fallen asleep in the recliners in the basement. Johnny looked at Jared, but said nothing. Johnny then stood from the recliner, breathing heavily, still looking around.

"Johnny, man. It's all right, dude. It was just a bad dream."

Johnny looked at Jared and nodded. Luckily, for whatever reason, he was able to regain the reality of the situation rather easily. Perhaps Jared's interruption aided somehow. As Johnny went through the process of reassuring himself that he was in fact safe, his father was nowhere around, and he had not been anywhere near his father at any point in time.

He noticed at some point in the night Graye must have snuck downstairs and covered them with blankets as they slept.

"My bad, man," Johnny said as he sat back down in the recliner.

"It's all good, dude. Night," Jared replied as he pulled his blankets to his chin.

"Night." Johnny was scared to try to sleep, but he was just too tired to fight it. He felt better having someone familiar close by. He closed his eyes and drifted to sleep once more.

CHAPTER TWENTY-SIX

Breakfast

Graye

"How do you do it without getting the shells in the bowl? I've never been able to do it right," Johnny asked as he stared into the bowl of fresh egg whites and yokes with several white pieces of shell. Johnny had flour on his face, some in his hair, and more all over the front of him. Although he'd donned one of Graye's aprons, his black gym shorts and blue t-shirt had managed to become covered as well.

Graye was more than amused by the situation. As she watched Johnny trying his hardest to help her make breakfast, she was all smiles. "It's a learned skill that comes with years of practice, my young chef," the woman said, smiling happily as she began to open a package of hickory-smoked bacon.

Jared was still sleeping in the basement, and Bryce decided she wanted to sleep in as well. Jackson was called to a neighbor's house around six thirty to euthanize an extremely injured horse. He told Graye he didn't want either of the boys to see that, so they were left sleeping.

It wasn't until around three in the morning that the woman had gone to the basement to cover the boys. With her own lazy children fast asleep at eight, Graye was more than happy when a chipper, well-rested Johnny entered the kitchen and asked if he could help. The two had been laughing and talking loudly as she showed him the basics of breakfast.

She loved Johnny's innocent charm, and she couldn't help but notice how he seemed to naturally fit right into the family, regardless of the setbacks which had taken place.

The conversation the boys had the night before weighed heavily on her mind. Jared never talked about his dyslexia openly. The fact that Johnny was there for him to discuss it with was monumental. She was also eternally grateful for the boy's selfless acts of courage as he protected her family from the coyote. She learned that morning it had tested positive for rabies.

"Not too shabby, sweetheart. Did you do a lot of cooking back home?" Graye asked as she reached in the lower cabinet by the stove for a frying pan. Johnny was still smiling as he plucked tiny pieces of eggshell with a fork from his bowl of cracked eggs.

"No, I never went in the kitchen unless my dad said it was okay." Immediately Johnny halted what he was doing as Graye witnessed his smile fade, as if Johnny had said something he shouldn't have.

Graye didn't push the topic, as she could recognize the sudden discomfort.

"Well, I do believe your biscuits are ready to go in the oven, sweetie," the woman said as she began placing the bacon into the frying pan. "So, did Jared tell you we are hosting a boil this Friday?" Graye asked as she handed Johnny a whisk.

"Yep. He said you guys do it every summer." Johnny began smiling again as he grabbed the whisk from the woman. "I just beat 'em until they're all yellow, right?" Johnny asked as he looked down at his bowl.

"Yes, that's right," Graye began to chuckle. "So, did Jared tell you his old friend, Tyler, was going to be here?" She witnessed a stone-cold look fall across Johnny's face as he looked up at her. She was fishing for a reaction, and she instantly obtained it.

"Yep. He did." Johnny shook his head as he returned his gaze to the eggs.

"Well, I will be sure to get you introduced to the neighbors," Graye said as she opened the heated oven. "What the hell have you done to this man?" Jared asked as he entered the kitchen from the basement. Jared appeared to still be half asleep. His eyes were half closed, his hair was wildly messy, and his arms were crossed as he smiled at the sight of his friend dressed in his mother's apron.

"Hey now. You wanna eat this morning?" Johnny asked, smiling as he headed to the oven with a large pan of biscuits.

"No complaints here, man. I think having another cook around is an awesome idea," Jared said as he entered the messy kitchen.

"Jared, sweetie, I think a hot shower is calling your name," Graye said as she kissed her sleepy son on the cheek.

Jared stretched his arms to full extent and yawned loudly.

"All right, all right," Jared said. "Johnny, what you wanna do today after you're done with the Betty Crocker thing?" Jared asked as he headed toward the living room.

"Betty who?" Johnny asked with a confused smile. "Man, I don't care. I'm up for whatever," Johnny continued as Graye watched the interaction, sipping her coffee.

"Sweetheart, breakfast will be ready in a few minutes," Graye said from the stove, prompting her son to get upstairs.

Before Jared left the kitchen, a bouncing Bitty came full force at him from Bryce's room. "Hey!" Jared said softly as he grabbed the ornery pup from the kitchen floor. "You could use a shower too."

Graye watched as her greasy son left the kitchen. She began showing Johnny how to scramble eggs and cook the bacon completely. Johnny diligently watched her. She could tell that through the course of the morning his mood had shifted slightly. Johnny had seemed to be all smiles and upbeat when they first began cooking.

"My dad…my dad didn't want me in the kitchen if he wasn't home," Johnny said in a nervous voice as he watched the bacon grease popping.

Graye inhaled deeply through her nostrils, attempting to keep the clamorous questions in her mind caged.

"He had a lot of important things in there that he didn't want me losing accidentally," Johnny attempted to explain. "He, he wouldn't come home some nights, so I would sneak in there and get soup or bread or something."

Graye was unsure of how to respond as she

listened to Johnny's comments. "He had a lot of documents he kept in the kitchen?" she asked as she looked at the uncomfortable boy. Johnny was breathing a little heavily, and she could tell he was distressed by the conversation as he avoided eye contact. She contemplated ending the discussion as Johnny seemed to be growing extremely uneasy.

"No. He had cans, and, um, car parts, and pieces in there."

Graye couldn't stop looking at Johnny. She didn't want to pass up the opportunity to communicate, but she didn't know what to say. "Did he cook for you? Did he cook a lot for you, your father?" Graye asked inquisitively. She was nervous herself. She watched Johnny bite his bottom lip. It was clear he didn't want to talk to about it anymore, but he didn't stop himself, either.

"The stove wasn't right, he just couldn't really cook," Johnny said as he looked at Graye. "Is that okay?" he asked, pointing to the nearly charred bacon. "Oh. That is very well done." The woman gasped as she moved in front of Johnny and removed the pan from the burner, placing it on an unlit one and shutting the gas off.

"So, what would happen if you went to the kitchen?" the woman asked as she removed the popping bacon from the pan with a fork, and placed it on a plate with a paper towel on it to collect the hot grease. "What would your father do if you were in the kitchen when he wasn't home?" Graye removed the last piece and then focused her attention strictly on Johnny.

This question seemed to be too much for Johnny. His face reddened and he began pinching his fingertips with his right hand. He looked away from Graye and from the stove altogether.

Graye reached out and touched Johnny on the shoulder. "Hey, sweetie. You're fine. If you want to talk to me about anything at all, we have all the time in the world to talk about whatever you want." Graye said.

"I will."

CHAPTER TWENTY-SEVEN

The Run

Jared

The Louisiana heat was at an all-time high. There was absolutely no breeze, and not a single cloud in the sky. The dirt road looked as if it continued into oblivion, and for all that Jared knew, it actually did. He had never been on this particular road. The trees that lined either side of the road were beautiful and huge. The thicket at the trunks of the trees made viewing even ten feet off either side of the road nearly impossible. In fact, the road itself may have been nearly invisible from an aerial view, as many of the tree branches cascaded out high over the road, creating almost an enclosed atmosphere. The trees were like those surrounding the Everett farm, they were beautifully decorated with hanging moss, and large conk mushrooms were growing from almost each of the numerous trees.

The muggy, thick air was almost suffocating. As the rubble made crunching noises beneath Jared's feet, the two boys continued their steady pace down the road. They had decided to run for a mile or two. This turned into an indefinite run that had lead both boys several miles from the house. The numerous insects were relentless, regardless of the fact that both of the guys were saturated in bug spray.

Jared decided against wearing a shirt, and thought his belly and chest looked disgustingly greasy, oiled in bug spray.

Johnny had on the same attire he had on while cooking breakfast. His shirt appeared soaked in sweat. Occasionally the two would run through a swarm of mosquitoes or other small swarms of insects. They would stick to their skin, as they were covered in sticky repellent.

The run was exactly what Jared needed to clear his mind and get out of the house. He kept an even pace with Johnny, and so far had not stopped for even a breather. They had been running for at least an hour. Jared felt he was physically able to run for miles and miles, and was impressed with Johnny's ability to go stride for stride. Typically, the heat would have been a factor, but they didn't seem to allow that to affect them today. The shade from the overhanging trees aided in keeping the sun from directly shining on them.

As they ran side by side, keeping nearly perfect pace, Jared muttered out, "Do you hear that?" The two continued for a few more seconds.

"What?" a breathless Johnny replied.

Jared stopped running suddenly, throwing his hands behind his head and inhaling deeply into his burning lungs. Sweat profusely entered his eyes, stinging them as he attempted to wipe them clean.

Johnny stopped running and he too placed his hands behind his head. They both stood in place for a moment before either of them spoke. "Hear what?" Johnny asked again. He was clearly out of breath as well.

"Water," Jared said as he nodded past the trees on the right side of the road. The boys continued to catch their breath. "You wanna check it out?" Jared asked as he put his arms down by his side. He'd always been drawn to nature and random bodies of water.

"Are you crazy? We come across a gator's nest, and it ain't gonna be pretty."

Jared ignored his friend's warning and headed in the direction of the babbling water. He heard the disruption in the thicket behind him and turned to see Johnny following him. Jared wasn't concerned with the idea of walking across an alligator nest. He had seen the animals several times throughout his life and found them less than menacing.

"Dude, you need to be watching for poison ivy," Jared heard Johnny warn. The brush and thicket were so thick that Jared could hardly see five feet in front of him.

"There's a clearing up here, dude," Jared replied. He was far enough in front of Johnny that it was difficult to see his friend as he turned, looking for the other boy. He saw him continuing to forge through the endless greenery, until finally he was right behind Jared again.

"It's gorgeous," Jared said, staring at the large creek. The bank led into the water, which was clear, and appeared around knee deep in the center. There were thousands of river stones on the bank and in the water. It appeared as though the creek ran parallel to the road the boys had been running on.

Johnny seemed more difficult to impress as Jared searched his face for a sign of appreciation for the beautiful surroundings. Jared understood that Louisiana had random bodies of water all throughout the entire state. But this certainly wasn't the typical swampy scene that is so highly associated with the southern state. He failed to see how his friend was unable to see the beauty of the clear creek.

"Yea, man, it's great. I'm sure the millions of cottonmouths that live here think it's awesome too," Jared heard Johnny say. It didn't stop Johnny from unlacing his shoes and removing his socks.

"Dude, your panties must have crawled all up in your twat during that last mile," Jared proclaimed loudly, smiling and looking up at Johnny from a squatted position. Johnny seemingly thought the comment was humorous as well, as he smiled and shook his head. "I'll turn my head the other direction so you can pick 'em out if you want." Jared was laughing quite proudly as he removed his sock.

Johnny began to chuckle too as he squatted down to take off his socks and shoes.

"I ain't going all the way in," Johnny said as a barefooted Jared began carefully walking down the stone covered bank to the water, feeling the soothing water encapsulate his toes.

"Hell no, dude. Running all the way back with wet boxers and shorts would be miserable," Jared replied, as he took his first real step into the cool water. A small frog leapt from the bank and into the moving creek as Jared entered. The cover from the trees' overhanging made it difficult for the sun to shine on the water. Millions of minnows retreated from the boy as he slowly made his way toward the center of the water. The creek was only about thirty feet across, so Jared reached his destination rather quickly.

Johnny followed Jared's lead as he stepped into the water. "This place is pretty nice," Johnny finally said approvingly, much to Jared's delight.

"Yea, man, I want this in my back yard," Jared replied as he watched Johnny reach the middle of the creek, then down the waterway. It appeared to go on forever.

"You don't got ponds or streams on your land?" Johnny asked.

"Not on the property itself, but there's a huge-ass pond about three and a half miles south of the house. It's damn near impossible to get to, and God only knows what the hell is livin' in that thing." Jared bent down and cupped his hands in the water. He stood up and splashed his face, rinsing the sweat from his irritated eyes.

"We should go check it out some time," Johnny suggested with curiosity in his voice.

"I guess. I hope you're fond of ticks. Me and Pops were covered in them last time we went out there," Jared said as he began walking toward the bank. Johnny splashed around the water with his feet and then headed toward the bank as well.

As the guys reached the bank, they sat down on the river stones and enjoyed the beautiful view. Neither of them spoke for several minutes, they simply sat silently with their feet in the water and relaxed.

"Holy shit, dude. I didn't even see that little bastard," Jared proclaimed as he pointed at a juvenile alligator.

Johnny leaned up and glanced at the reptile as well.

The small animal had gone unnoticed in the center of the creek.

"We must have been standing right next to him," Johnny said, smiling.

Jared felt the day seemed to have been flying by until now. The calming waters and the beautiful surroundings were therapeutic. He stood to his feet and walked up the bank. As he approached the tree line, with his back to Johnny, he pulled down the front of his shorts and began urinating on a small tree. Johnny seemed to pay no attention to Jared's actions as he stared out at the water with his feet still soaking.

When Jared was done, he walked back to where Johnny was still sitting. "You 'bout ready to head back?" Jared asked, standing over Johnny.

Johnny seemed to completely ignore the question. "Johnny, dude. You about ready, it's a long run back." Jared was kneeled down by his friend, but Johnny continued to ignore him. His mouth was slightly open as he stared off into the water. As he squatted down by Johnny, Jared cautiously touched Johnny's shoulder.

Johnny immediately sprang to his feet, looking wildly around the creek bed. "What time is it? I gotta get home, now!" Johnny yelled out as he looked hastily about. "What time is it? I need to know what time it is!" Jared sprang to his feet as well, and was totally taken aback by Johnny's sporadic actions.

"The fuck? I…it's almost three," Jared said as he stepped away from Johnny, gazing briefly at his wristwatch.

Johnny had a strange look of confusion on his face as he stared at Jared.

"Okay," Johnny said softly as he looked at the

ground with a dazed look on his face.

"Dr. Mulberry isn't coming to the house until seven. We got plenty of time, dude," Jared said as Johnny looked up at him. "You all right, man?"

"Yea, yea, I'm good. I just…I just lost track of time."

Jared continued to watch his friend in an uneasy manner. The heat was becoming nearly unbearable. Even after the lengthy break in the water, the guys continued to sweat. "Dude, you might wanna take your shirt off for the run home. It's bad out here," Jared suggested as he walked to his socks and shoes.

"Nah, man. It's cool."

The boys sat down on the ground next to each other and began putting on their socks and shoes. Johnny appeared slightly embarrassed by his actions.

"So, what's that Brian guy like?" Johnny asked while he put his socks on.

"Dr. Mulberry? He's a cool guy. He's black, but he was born in England, so he has a funny accent."

Johnny appeared instantly surprised. "He's black? Your folks got black friends?" Johnny asked as he looked at Jared with a curious expression on his face. Jared chuckled a little, but it was more out of shock than anything.

"Well, yea, man. They have all sorts of friends. He's gay too, oh my," Jared said sarcastically. "Mom and Pops go to dinner with him and Tracy sometimes. Tracy is his boyfriend, or husband, or whatever. I don't know why they decided to have them over rather than get out of the house."

"Dude, we need to run more often. It feels good to get out of the house and just run like hell," Jared said as he rose to his feet.

"Yea man, anytime."

Jared extended his hand to assist Johnny to his feet. Johnny grabbed his hand and stood up. "Next time, let's not go in the middle of the hottest day ever,"

Johnny said with a smile as both boys headed for the thick brush and trees.

"Here," Jared said, as he slid the silver watch from his wrist, handing it passively to Johnny.

"What's this?" the teen asked, reluctantly grabbing

it.

"Just so you don't lose track of time. No biggie, I got two more," Jared replied.

"I can't take your watch, man. This thing is…this thing is too nice. I can't take this."

"Dude. It is no big deal. I got two more almost exactly like it. Let's get the hell out of here. I'm sweatin' my balls off out here," Jared said, attempting to change the subject as he watched Johnny hesitantly slide the watch over his hand.

CHAPTER TWENTY-EIGHT

Brian

Jackson

"So, how deep was the water?" Jackson asked his son impatiently as they sat at the kitchen table. They were picking at the bountiful array of food Graye had been setting on the table.

"Where we were at it was about two feet deep at the most." Jackson and Jared both had on nice khaki shorts and polo shirts.

"It's probably not the smartest decision to go traipsing around ponds and creeks this time of year," Jackson lightly scolded his son.

"You sound like Johnny. That guy was worried about gator nests, snakes, poison ivy, and just about everything else," Jared said, smiling at his dad.

"Well, at least one of you is smart." As soon as Jackson said this, he wished he wouldn't have. He knew his son was extremely self-conscious about people thinking he was less than intelligent. Jared immediately looked away from his father; he was obviously a little shocked by the comment.

Guilt emerged in Jackson's gut as he reached over and squeezed his son's bicep. "I didn't mean that you're not smart, son. We both know that's not the case. I just don't want you boys getting hurt so far from the house."

"I know, Pops. My bad." Jared's facial expression and soft tone let Jackson know that he got the point.

"You check your sac for ticks?" Jackson asked sarcastically with a smile. Both the guys started laughing.

"Jackson!" Graye snapped from the sink. She was wearing an elegant white sun dress, and her long, dark hair had been neatly straightened. "That is not appropriate table talk," the woman scolded.

"I'm good, Pops. Not a tick anywhere." Jared was still chuckling at his father's crass comment.

"And stay out of the food until everyone gets here," Graye snapped again. As if on cue, the doorbell rang.

"I'll get it!" little Bryce yelled from her bedroom.

Jackson heard the little girl bolt across the living room floor with Bitty in hot pursuit. He arose from the table and walked to the living room.

As Bryce opened the door the little girl developed a smile of excitement. "Brian!" the girl shrieked as she grabbed the man's legs and hugged him.

"Bryce, darling. How are you my sweet girl?" Brian asked with a thick British accent as he picked her up in his arms. Brian was very tall, at least six foot six inches. He was completely bald, by choice, and was very slender.

"There you are. Thank you so much for coming," Jackson said from the doorway. "Where is Tracy?"

Jackson asked curiously.

"He's actually just about to leave the office and head this way. They are right in the middle of a grant reapplication." Brian entered the house with Bryce still in his arms.

"Ouch." Jackson replied as he welcomed Brian in.

"Brian," Graye said, smiling and raising her arms to extend a hug.

"Hello, gorgeous," Brian replied as he leaned into the woman's embrace.

Jackson believed if he were not clued in, he would probably have not realize that Brian practiced an alternative lifestyle. Brian's partner, Tracy, however, was extremely flamboyant.

Graye wrapped her arms around both Brian and Bryce as well.

"It smells delicious," Brian exclaimed as Jared walked in the living room from the kitchen, extending a hand to Brian. "Jared, you certainly have grown this summer," Brian said as he shook his hand.

"Hi, Dr. Mulberry," Jared said, smiling.

"I think that was Brian's way of telling you you're getting chubby," Jackson said, smirking at his son. Jared didn't seem to take offense to the statement, probably because there was no reason to. The boy was athletic and stayed in shape. The small amount of belly fat was to be expected as his mother was a master at comfort food.

"Not at all. Jared is a healthy boy, nothing wrong with that," Brian replied as he sat Bryce down. "Tracy said to start without him. He should be here within the hour," Brian announced as the group headed toward the kitchen.

Johnny

Johnny heard the commotion from the bathroom. His hair was still a little wet, but the shorts Jared gave him fit well. As he stared at his reflection, he broke his gaze from the large mirror and looked down at his shaking hands. He was extremely nervous about meeting Brian, as he was afraid the man would think he was crazy and needed to be sent away, and he wasn't sure how the process of *getting help* actually worked. He took one last deep breath in, and then headed to the bathroom door. As he entered the hallway, the smell of the delicious food lifted his spirits. After the extensive run with Jared, he was extremely hungry, despite his nerves.

As he walked down the stairs, he experienced an almost overwhelming sense of anxiety. He felt he was acclimating rather well to the family, and he was growing attached to them more every day. The thought of something like an opinion coming between him and them was frightening to the teen. At the same time, the thought of gaining mental clarity was very exciting.

As he reached the bottom of the stairs with his hand on the rail, he drew in a deep breath and looked out at the living room, waiting for his nerves to calm prior to entering the kitchen. The large family picture on the wall above the couch was beautiful.

Bryce was probably only two when the picture was taken. The rest of the family basically looked the same. Johnny wished he had a picture of his mother and Jacob. Some days he felt like he was forgetting what they looked like, especially his mother.

Standing on the staircase, Johnny could hear the

family talking in the kitchen. He could hear the strong British accent from Brian. In Johnny's mind, most all doctors seemed to have some kind of accent, so it only made sense that this man would have one too. Johnny was impressed with how the family seemed to accept everyone. The Everetts not only welcomed Brian into their house, but they were obviously extremely fond of him.

Johnny stepped off the staircase and slowly walked through the living room to the kitchen. As he appeared in the entryway, Jared saw him and greeted him by socking him in the arm. Johnny was taken aback by the force of Jared's gesture, but the hit seemed to clear his mind rapidly—for which he was thankful. Both the boys started laughing at Johnny's surprised reaction.

"You must be Johnny," Brian said as he walked past the kitchen table.. The tall black man stuck his hand out to shake Johnny's as he promptly obliged.

"Yes, sir. You must be Brian," Johnny nervously replied as Brian delivered a firm handshake.

"Here, and in my office, yes. When you start school next month, you'll have to address me as Dr. Mulberry. I'm quite conceited, and the title feeds my ego."

Johnny was uncertain if what the man was saying was sarcastic or serious as he stared at his face.

"It was a joke," Brian said as he began to laugh. Johnny attempted to produce a smile and force a laugh, but felt his nerves overshadowing, impacting his voice and trembling hands.

"Brian, we really don't mind waiting on Tracy," Graye said as she retrieved several bottles of dressing from the refrigerator.

"Absolutely not. You have a growing family and they need to be fed, as do I," Brian said as he turned to the rest of the family, clapping his hands together loudly.

"No objections here!" Jared said, smiling as Johnny watched his friend eyeballing the mountain of food Graye had prepared. As the group gathered at the table, Johnny's nerves began to give way to his hunger.

CHAPTER TWENTY-NINE

Tracy

Graye

"He's certainly not disengaged. He seems connected, happy, and intelligent. I would assume Johnny had a decent, if not splendid, relationship with his mother. I would also assume he had a few other key people in his life that have contributed greatly to his psychological well-being. I certainly feel your structured family may be working wonders for him and his mental state."

Brian appeared quite professional as he spoke to Graye and Jackson as they were all three in the living room. Brian sat on the large coffee table in front of the couple who were sitting on the large couch. Bryce and Bitty were playing on the front porch, and Jared and Johnny had retreated to the basement to allow their food to settle.

"I'm so glad to hear you say that," Graye said, smiling as a sense of relief came over her. "Please keep in mind, I would like to see him by myself. He does not appear to be socially inept, but his demeanor is somewhat reserved. Jackson, the description you gave of his reaction to the sight of you urinating, and his reluctance to talk about what happened to him makes me think he could be suffering from post-traumatic stress disorder," Brian continued. "I absolutely hate to speculate, but I would almost bet my license Johnny was abused physically, sexually, and emotionally."

"How can we help him if, if he won't talk to us?" Graye asked as she searched her friend's face for a quick response.

"Graye, darling, you are helping him. You have to keep in mind that if he is suffering from PTSD, he will need ongoing professional help. The nightmares, the potential flashbacks, they won't just disappear with kind words and three-square meals." Brian's tone was serious as he looked at her, but she knew this was exactly what she needed to hear.

"Yesterday he was talking to someone. He was talking to Bobby while we were driving to town. But, of course, Bobby wasn't there," Jackson confessed with his hands folded.

"What? You didn't tell me that," Graye said as she looked at her husband with look of disapproval.

"What do you mean, 'Bobby wasn't there?' He was carrying a conversation with someone who wasn't there?" Brian asked.

"Yes, he was exhausted, he seemed like he was in a daze and he asked his friend Bobby to drop him off while we were in my truck going to the hardware store." Graye made it clear to her husband through a series of disappointed glances that she was displeased with his reluctance to tell her.

"Look, occasionally people that have experienced extremely traumatic life events develop PTSD. Symptoms can include horrific nightmares, flashbacks, extreme paranoia, and in some severe cases there may be a certain level of psychosis. I have seen patients suffer from horrible flashbacks that seem to take them directly back to the situation that inflicted their mental dysfunction. Often, they will do whatever they can to avoid talking about the trauma."

"You need to ask yourself how much you are willing to invest in this situation. You also need to ask yourself if your household is the best healing environment for this boy. Regardless of where Johnny ends up, it's going to take a lot of time, effort, and resources for him to actually begin to heal, and he may never actually heal completely from his trauma." Brian's words were hard for the Graye to hear, but she was expecting that or worse.

"He's not going anywhere," Jackson said with a certain level of defensiveness in his voice.

"We have time, and God has blessed us with more than enough resources," Graye said, supporting her husband's statement.

"No, he sure as hell isn't going a damn place," Jared announced loudly from kitchen entryway.

The three adults all looked at Jared, who was obviously upset by Brian's statements.

Graye hoped her son wouldn't lose his temper and say something foolish.

Jared looked directly at Brian. "Dr. Mulberry, you may just be trying to help, but that's my friend and I'd appreciate it if you'd stop talking about him like he's a damn freak," Jared snapped angrily as he pointed at Brian.

"Jared!" Graye yelled at her son as she stood from the couch.

Jared merely shook his head and stormed up the stairs to his room, his feet falling loudly on the staircase.

"Let the boy go. He is very loyal to his friend. Does Johnny exhibit the same level of loyalty to him?" Brian asked, seemingly unfazed by Jared's comments and outraged actions.

Graye knew that Brian was used to being snapped at, as the man dealt with angry teenagers all day. She had witnessed his partner, Tracy, become passionately offended several times at past gatherings, screaming at Brian like a lunatic for all to bear witness to.

"Yes, he's been excellent for Jared. Just last night I overheard Jared talking to him about his dyslexia. He doesn't even talk to us about that," Graye said as she sat back down.

"That is actually a significant breakthrough for Jared. He was never comfortable talking to me about his struggles with his learning disability," Brian said, smiling.

"He's been good for all of us. He's actually a well-mannered, even-tempered, loving, and polite kid," Jackson said as Graye felt him take her hand.

"If you both are absolutely certain this is what you want to do, then I would like to start working with Johnny immediately. You need to begin the process of obtaining medical records. If I can help, I will, if I can't, I have several colleagues that specialize in working with victims of trauma," Brian said, smiling at the couple.

"One hundred percent certainty," Graye said as she

heard a vehicle approaching outside.

Jared was heard coming down the staircase, with his basketball in hand. As he stepped off the last stair and headed toward the kitchen, he stopped briefly and turned to Brian and his parents. "Sorry," the teen said reluctantly, and then continued on his route to the basement. Graye understood that Brian had worked extensively with Jared. She knew they were actually quite close, and Brian had seen the boy act out before. "Tracy!" an enthusiastic Bryce screamed from the front porch.

"Hey, Miss Thang!" Tracy said as Graye watched him prissily trot up the steps. "What is this adorable little bundle of precious?" the man asked as he squatted down to pick up the puppy. Tracy was short, stocky, had red hair, a red mustache, and was pasty white. He was wearing baby blue slacks and a white silk button up shirt that almost looked like a blouse.

The man came through the front door holding Bitty while the puppy licked all over his face as Bryce was right behind him. "And why, may I ask, can she have one but I can't?" Tracy asked as he kissed the licking puppy, much to Graye's disgust.

"Because she won't grow tired of her and toss her in the back yard to stay after the first week," Brian said. Graye was excited to get Johnny the help he needed. If anything, this conversation strengthened and reconfirmed the stance she had regarding Johnny's situation.

As Tracy made his way to the couch to greet the family, Bryce followed him closely, hoping he would soon release her playmate. Johnny and Jared entered the living room with the basketball.

"Hello, handsome!" Tracy squeaked at Jared as he

sat Bitty down.

"Hi, Tracy," Jared said lowly.

Graye watched the interaction closely as she knew her son was not fond of Tracy, not because of his flamboyant nature, but because Jared had witnessed a few of Tracy's dramatic tirades when he didn't get his way. The only Everett that seemed to truly like the man was little Bryce.

Jared continued to the front door, but Johnny appeared frozen still, staring at Tracy.

Johnny's cheeks became red, his fists were clenched, and he began breathing rapidly.

Graye, as well as the rest of the room, seemed to notice Johnny's strange behavior.

Tracy had a very strange look on his face as he approached Johnny and stuck out his hand. "You must be what all the fuss is about. I'm Tracy," the man said coldly.

"Just what the hell are you doing here?" Johnny snapped at the man. His eyes were wide with anger, and he looked as though he could kill the man.

Tracy had retracted his hand and had placed it on his chest in a dramatic fashion. He had a look of extreme shock on his face.

"I was invited," the man said as Graye watched from the couch in shock, unsure if she should intervene.

"What do you want? How, how did you find me? Does he know where I am?" Johnny asked as he turned from the man and placed both hands on his head, squeezing it as Graye arose from the couch.

"What the hell are you talking about? I don't know you from Adam, you little asshole," Tracy said in a sassy tone as he placed his hand on his hip.

"Tracy," Brian said sternly as he rose from the coffee table.

Johnny continued to squeeze his head as Graye watched him retreat through the kitchen toward the laundry room.

Brian quickly followed Graye from the living room.

"I'll tell you all right now, that there is a vicious brat!" Tracy said, looking at the family from the doorway, as he was obviously offended.

Graye felt badly for the man, but her attention was on the well-being on Johnny, not Tracy's hurt feelings.

"Why don't you shut the hell up and leave?" she heard her son demand as he looked at the enraged, prissy man.

"Jared!" Graye yelled at her son. "Tracy, I am so sorry," the woman apologized as she walked toward the outraged guest, but Tracy held his hand up to silence her.

"Graye, your unruly brood has more than once offended me, and now you bring in this hateful hooligan and allow him to belittle me without mercy. No, ma'am. I will wish you and yours a lovely evening, and you can tell the miracle worker I'll be at my sister's," Tracy said as he stormed out of the house in a heated tirade.

As soon as Tracy was out the door, Graye turned and walked back to situation 1n the laundry room. Johnny was tucked in the corner, between the wall and the washing machine. He had his back to Brian, who was crouched down and had his hand on Johnny's shoulder as Graye and Jackson looked in from the kitchen.

"Jared, take your sister upstairs, now," Jackson said to his son as Jared tried to enter the kitchen.

Jared seemed unhappy about the demand, but he offered no resistance.

"Who do you believe that was, Johnny?" Brian asked in a soothing tone.

Johnny was breathing heavily and appeared on the verge of tears as Graye felt a lump developing in her throat.

"Doug. Uncle Doug," Johnny said in a shaky, cracking voice.

"And why do think Doug is here?" Brian asked. He was now touching Johnny's shoulder.

"For money. He gave my dad money." Johnny's voice was so soft it was difficult for Graye to hear.

"Why did he give your dad money, Johnny?" Brian asked in a monotone voice.

"He won't anymore. I'm too old, I got too old." Johnny began to sob as Brian developed a look of disgust on his face.

"Doug isn't here, Johnny. You may have thought that Tracy looked or acted similar to Uncle Doug, but that was not him," Brian said, trying to calm Johnny.

Johnny continued to sob as did Graye while she watched from the kitchen. She knew it was necessary for Brian to talk to Johnny, but at this point she wanted to push him aside and comfort the crying teen. "Would you like to come out of here? Tracy is gone, and there is no one here by the name of Doug, I promise," Brian asked as he patted Johnny on the back.

Johnny turned and looked at Brian over his shoulder, giving him a simple nod as Brian rose to his feet, offering Johnny a hand to help him up. As

Johnny stood, he noticed Graye and Jackson in the kitchen.

"I'm sorry."

"Hey, Johnny, you're okay," the woman said in a comforting tone while she hugged him.

"You have nothing to be sorry about. I need you to wait here and I'll be right back, okay," Graye said. She then turned from the laundry room to investigate Brian's opinion.

"It appears that his father allowed this Doug character to violate this young man in exchange for money. The pedophile stopped paying once Johnny entered puberty," Brian explained to Graye and Jackson, who both seemed in a state of shock.

"That's why his mother left. That's why she took his little brother from the house," Graye proclaimed as she stared at the wall.

"You need to contact the authorities. There is a statute of limitation on sexual assault. He needs to be seen by a proper physician, and speak with the police," Brian said as he looked at Graye and Jackson.

Jackson said nothing; Graye noticed he too had tears in his eyes.

"I am going to call a dear friend of mine. She deals exclusively with patients that are afflicted with post-traumatic stress disorder associated with sexual trauma. I will convene with you at the gathering this Friday. I would highly recommend Johnny not be present at this party."

"We already said he isn't going anywhere," Graye heard her husband say as she turned to return to Johnny.

CHAPTER THIRTY

Vile

Johnny

He was alone on his mother and father's bed, waiting. He knew it wouldn't be long. His mother was gone; she always left on these days. She hated these days. His father was talking to Uncle Doug in the kitchen. The sound of Doug's voice was disgusting. He was disgusting. Johnny absolutely hated the man. His breath was hideous, his mustache was nauseating, and there was nothing about the man that was even remotely desirable.

Johnny often wished a horrible death on him.

He hated his father for allowing this to happen. He was disgusted with his mother for leaving the house and not protecting him. He knew the woman had protested the night before, he heard her begging his father to stop hitting her in retaliation of her resistance.

One hundred dollars. It was always a one-hundred-dollar bill, folded nicely in Uncle Doug's pocket. Doug was short, balding, and had dirty blond hair. His mustache was a dirty blond as well. He was portly, and always wore very tight t-shirts and very short shorts. He was vile in every sense of the word. As Johnny lay on the bed, he wanted to run through the kitchen and out the door. He wanted to escape the clutches of Doug. He hated when Doug touched him, and he hated it even more when Doug made Johnny touch him back.

The bedroom door opened. "Well, there is my little buddy!" the flamboyant man said as he happily walked to the bed with a tin Batman lunch box in his hand. "It has just been too long!" the man exclaimed happily. Uncle Doug used to visit Johnny once a week, sometimes more, but he hadn't been to see Johnny in nearly six months, as he was out of state.

"Tell your Uncle Doug hi, Johnny," Johnny's father demanded politely.

"Hello," Johnny said as he turned and looked at the wall.

"Thomas, his voice is cracking. Is he going through the change? You know the arrangement," Doug said as he put his hands on his hips and turned to Thomas, looking panicked.

"He ain't got no hair on his nuts," Johnny's father said reassuringly as he looked anxiously at Doug.

"Well, then how about you leave us to our little play date. Now," Doug said in an irritated voice. "I brought our little box of fun!" the man said with a squeaking voice, smiling largely as he looked down at Johnny.

As Thomas left the room, Doug made his way to the bed and happily held up the tin lunch box. Doug sat down on the bed and ran his fingers through

Johnny's hair. "I need you to take these off. Now, Johnny," Doug said as he pulled on the bottom of Johnny's shorts.

Johnny offered no resistance. He knew it was pointless. Doug's face was bright red with anticipation as Johnny unbuttoned his corduroy shorts and began to pull them down.

"Wait. What the fuck is this?" Doug asked angrily. He slapped the boy's hands away from his shorts and grabbed the top of them, yanking them violently further down, exposing the top of Johnny's pubic area. "That lying motherfucker!" Doug screeched as he reached down and open handedly slapped Johnny across the face extremely hard. "Put your goddamned shorts back on, I refuse to touch that nasty shit!" Doug said as he stood from the bed with his hands on his hips. He began nervously pacing the room. "Thomas! Thomas Tregalis, get your fucking ass back here, now!" Doug screamed in a heated fit of rage. Within seconds, Thomas opened the door.

"What the fuck are you screaming about?" Thomas asked as he entered the room.

"He has hair! He's already changing!" Doug screamed as tears began to stream down his face. "You know our arrangement! And now my erection is gone! I have looked forward to this day for a very long time, and you have betrayed me!" Doug screamed dramatically, pointing at Thomas as he began to shake.

"He ain't but twelve or thirteen. We can shave 'em," Thomas suggested as he put his hands out, attempting to calm the belligerent molester.

"Fuck you!" Doug screamed as he began crying violently, and ran from the room.

Thomas followed the crying man from the room and out the kitchen door.

Johnny began to button his pants back as he heard Doug and his father in the front yard.

"I can't deal with this, Thomas! You know how fragile I am right now! You can take this shitty hundred-dollar bill and shove it up your white trash ass! Don't you dare call me ever again!" Doug screamed as Johnny heard a car door slam. He then heard the car start and the sound of tires spinning wildly in the front yard.

Johnny was thankful to know that Uncle Doug's visits wouldn't be happening anymore. He was also pleased that Doug gave his father the money anyways, he knew they needed groceries. He felt horrible that he let his family down. He felt like it was his fault that they wouldn't be getting the extra grocery money in the future.

He heard his father come back in the house; his boots pounded the tattered floor as he the man made his way to the bedroom at a quick pace. Johnny looked at his father as the man flew through the door in a wild rage.

"I'm sorry, Dad," Johnny said in a pathetic voice as he looked at his father.

"Don't you fuckin' apologize to me. You wanna be a motherfuckin' man? Well it's about time you start gettin' treated like a man!" Johnny was horrified, he had seen his father beat his mother relentlessly, but he had not beaten him before. Thomas grabbed a large belt from the floor.

Johnny looked at the enraged man and the large belt as he began to tremble. He moved backward on the bed and began to cry.

"Please don't! I'm sorry. Please don't hurt me!"

***

"Johnny! Johnny, wake up!" Johnny awoke to a yelling Jared shaking him. Johnny had made a pallet in Jared's room and decided to sleep in there after the incident in the laundry room. As Johnny opened his eyes, he looked about the room, completely horrified.

"Dude, wake up. It's just a bad dream! It's me, Jared!" Johnny sprang from the floor and backed up against the wall.

Jared quickly jumped up and turned the light on.

Johnny touched his shorts, assuring himself he was fully clothed. He found he had wet himself in his sleep.

"Johnny, dude. It's Jared. You were just havin' another nightmare. You're good, dude." Johnny watched his friend as Jared slowly made his way to where Johnny was standing, holding his hand out and slightly crouching.

"I was asleep? I've been here and asleep?" Johnny asked, shaking and attempting to make sense of what had just happened.

"Yea, man. It's five in the morning and you been in here since we crashed around ten. You're totally fine, dude."

Johnny knew there was no way Jared could understand what was going on in Johnny's mind, but every time Johnny suffered an episode, it seemed to upset his friend. As Johnny stared at the floor in confusion, he felt Jared's hand on his shoulder.

"Dude, you're fine," Jared said again as he looked at Johnny square in the eyes. "I'm gonna get you some dry boxers and some new blankets while you go get cleaned up in the bathroom. And don't sweat it, dude. I've pissed the bed a few times too." Jared headed to his drawer to get Johnny some new boxers and a shirt to sleep in.

Johnny continued to stand with his back to the wall. As his fears began to subside, his humiliation and disheartenment began to increase tenfold. The events that continued to take place, the uncontrollable breakdowns and secrets disclosed during sleep, Johnny just knew they must be weighing heavily against his future at the at the Everett place. As Jared handed Johnny the dry clothing, Johnny simply exited the room and went directly to the bathroom.

As he changed from his wet clothes, he imagined what the Everetts thought of his actions. He wondered what that poor man, Tracy, thought of his outburst. He had an overwhelming sense that his time on the Everett farm with the family would soon be coming to an end. He felt the need to run, to leave this place and seek lower life. He felt the need to seek out his own kind, damaged and ruined souls that find comfort in each other's damaged lives and minds.

Looking at the wet clothes on the floor, Johnny felt disgusted with himself. He knew Jared was a patient and kind person, but he also imagined the boy was growing tired of the constant antics and unexplainable actions that Johnny continuously subjected him to. Johnny decided he was going to slip down the hall to his own room with his wet clothing, hopefully undetected. He picked up his wet clothing and headed for the door.

As soon as he opened the bathroom door and stepped into the hall, Jared stuck his head out of his bedroom door. "Hey man, I got you some new blankets in here," Jared said in a light tone as he stepped into the hall. Johnny kept his gaze toward the floor, holding his clothes far enough away that he wouldn't get his new clothes damp. "Man, just throw that in my hamper." Jared pointed to his clothes hamper inside the bedroom door.

"I think I'm just gonna go to my room and hang out until everyone gets up and around," Johnny said with a defeated tone to his voice while he avoided eye contact with his friend.

"Well, dude. I'm wide awake now. You wanna go chill in the basement?"

"Nah, man. Thanks anyways. I think I'm just gonna go hang out by myself for a bit," Johnny replied as he slowly walked past Jared.

"Man, you're seriously not the only person on Earth that has a few issues. Don't sweat it, man. Just let it go," Johnny heard Jared say behind him.

Johnny stood still a moment with his back to Jared. "Dude. I know you're just being nice to me cause you feel bad for me. Thanks for the clothes, man."

Johnny reached for his doorknob as he heard Jared respond in with a defensive tone.

"And just what's that supposed to mean? Why the hell would I feel sorry for you?" Jared asked. His sharp tone caught Johnny off guard as he turned and faced him.

"I know you gotta be sick of havin' me around, dude. I'm sick of myself," Johnny replied.

"Sick of having you around? I've actually been pretty pumped about having you around to hang out with," Jared said as his feet occasionally moved somewhat nervously in place.

"Yea, I don't have many friends, none really. I don't really try to text anyone because I'm afraid I'm gonna send a fucked up, misspelled, bullshit message. Yea, it's awesome having a…a mom that's an English teacher, and to not be able to read out loud in class. Most people just think I'm a fuckin' idiot, and don't take the time to get to know me. Then when I do make a friend, he goes and puts all my shit up on the blackboard for everyone to see, like they didn't already know," Jared exclaimed with his arms still crossed, and his face red with obvious anger and hurt feelings.

"The only person I've had to talk to, or hang out, with has been my mom, or Pops, or a four-year-old, even when school was going. And then you got here. Why the hell would I feel sorry for you? I don't feel sorry for myself, so why feel sorry for you? I'm nice to you because you're my bro and that's how friends treat each other," Jared's voice was shaky as he started stepping backward to his room.

Johnny was completely shocked that this had transpired. This moment offered a small epiphany as he realized everyone had their own discouragements and hardships in life. Jared came from a wealthy, loving family, and had just about every material possession a seventeen-year-old boy could want, yet he had no friends, no one to confide in, and there was nothing that could mend his learning disability. Johnny knew Jared must have been miserable without anyone his age to talk to. He also realized that Jared wouldn't have confided in him if he didn't trust him. As Johnny entered his room and closed the door, the teen felt ungrateful because of his comments.

Johnny tossed the clothes into the laundry hamper

and walked to his bed to sit down. Other than Bobby, Johnny had never had a friend like Jared. He didn't understand what was going on with his inability to maintain mental clarity, but he did understand that true friends were hard to come by, and Jared had been an awesome friend thus far. Johnny looked at his bed and contemplated another attempt at sleep, but the sickening feeling of guilt brewing in his gut prompted him to stand. He didn't want his friend to be upset with him; he wanted to make things right.

Johnny rose from his bed and walked to his bedroom door. As he opened it and entered the hall, he noticed Jared's bedroom light was shining under the door. He walked slowly to Jared's bedroom door and stood in front of it for a few seconds. He wasn't quite sure how he would go about apologizing, and he was hoping Jared wouldn't tell him to get lost. Nervously, he knocked lightly.

"Yea," he heard from the other side, almost instantaneously. As he opened the door and walked in, he kept his gaze on the floor.

"Man, I'm…I didn't mean. I didn't mean to piss you off—" Johnny fumbled for the words to say.

Jared stood from his bed and lightly hit Johnny in the arm.

"No worries, man. My bad for getting all dramatic."

"Dude, you've been awesome. Your whole family has been awesome," Johnny said as he continued to look downward. This was basically the best apology Johnny could formulate. Johnny finally looked to his friend studying his expression.

"You're good, dude. The whole thing was seriously fuckin' stupid."

"Man, I'm wide awake now too. You still up for headin' to the basement 'til everyone else gets up and around?" Johnny asked.

"Well, hell yea," Jared replied in a chipper tone of voice.

Johnny made his way to the basement with Jared as if nothing had happened.

CHAPTER THIRTY-ONE

Redemption

"Dude, we're basically both adults. I think we'll be okay," Jared said as his father stalled near the curb in front of the large basketball court.

"Dude? Try Dad. And all I said was stay here until I get back, as in no chasing girls or looking for crack cocaine," Jackson replied with a sarcastic smile as Johnny and Jared exited the large, black truck.

"Please. We don't gotta chase girls, they come to us," Jared said as he retrieved his basketball from the front passenger floorboard.

"Yea, I think you have better chances scoring some blow," Jackson said as Jared closed his door.

"Ha, whatever Pops…dude," Jared said as his father waved at both the guys and began pulling away.

Johnny smiled and waved, he thought the entire conversation was amusing, yet didn't quite know where to chime in. He loved the way the two reacted with each other, but it was obviously something he was not accustomed to. Although Jared made no other mention of the small fallout in the early morning hours, Johnny still felt somewhat remorseful for saying what he said. Johnny knew Jared was a nice guy in general, everyone who took the time to know Jared knew that. Johnny was naturally paranoid.

He recognized his paranoia wasn't limited to strange, anxiety-filled episodes where he convinced himself his father would be pulling in the Everetts' driveway at any hour of the night. Johnny had a tendency to think and assume the worst. In regard to his current predicament, however, he hoped Jared might understand his paranoia. His current living quarters were, in fact, much greater than anything Johnny could have imagined. The possibility of it being potentially taken was always lingering on the back of Johnny's mind.

The basketball court included four large courts surrounded by twenty-foot-high, black, chain-link fencing. The fence was surrounded by large trees. It seemed a good majority of structures were surrounded by large trees. The trees appeared uninhabited. Tiny creatures must have sought sanctuary from the tormenting temperatures, as the higher species gathered to exert themselves in the ridiculous heat.

"Dude, those guys look ridiculously bad-ass," Jared said as Johnny looked toward the adjoining basketball court to see who he was talking about. There were several young men that appeared to be in their twenties. They were basically showing off with nearly every move they made. It seemed impossible for the guys to make a simple shot; rather, they would partake in ridiculous displays in an effort to reach the goal. Surprisingly, the majority of these displays looked incredible.

Johnny and Jared began to shoot around, taking

turns taking shots. Johnny noticed Jared continuously looking at the neighboring group of guys. It was apparent that neither of the boys wanted to draw too much attention to their mediocre abilities as they were in the presence of such a talented group in the neighboring court.

"Horse?" Jared suggested as he clumsily dribbled the ball. Johnny felt he was starting to sweat already, although it was only ten in the morning, the heat was already bearing down on him.

"Yea, man. I'm down," Johnny replied as he watched Jared heave the ball from the three-point line. Although the yellow paint was highly degraded on the cement ball court, they were still able to make out the shot line. As the ball bounced loudly from the backboard, Johnny was quick to retrieve it. The neighboring court had a great deal of noise coming from the guys as they competitively played.

Jared watched and seemed in awe, and then he quickly turned his face from the group, as if he'd noticed something or someone.

"Man, what's up? You know those guys?" Johnny asked as he studied Jared's actions. Jared held his hands up, suggesting he wanted the ball passed to him.

"Just one," he said as Johnny passed him the ball. "Man, I know Pops said not to leave, but I wanna run across the street to the C-mart and grab some water. Maybe just wait there 'til Pops gets back. I'm hot," Jared said as he lightly dribbled the ball.

Johnny thought Jared was acting peculiar, so against his better judgment he decided to agree to leave.

Just as Johnny was about to speak, the boys heard

an arrogant voice approaching them.

"How goes it, Mr. Everett?" a boy asked as he made his way across the court. He had chin-length hair. He was shirtless and appeared to have zero body fat and outstanding muscle definition, and looked like he lived on the track. Johnny immediately sensed the tension as the guy got closer. "Hey, Jared, you gotta minute? I need to holler atcha," he said as he approached.

Jared submissively put his head down.

"We were just leaving, Erick," Jared said as he began walking toward the street.

"Whoa, dude, you just got here. Hold up, man," Erick said as he swiftly ran in front of the teen and began walking backward in pace with Jared. "Man, Jared. I really just wanted to talk to you real quick, dude," Erick said as he stopped walking.

Jared stopped walking too, keeping his head down. "What, Erick, do you want?" Jared asked, in an irritated voice.

"Man," Erick continued, "I was just gonna see if maybe you wanted to keep score for us, but uh, then I forgot you might get that all fucked up. Maybe your new boyfriend here could do us a solid." Erick had a cold smile on his face and seemed delighted with the submissive reaction he was getting from Jared.

"I'm fine with numbers, asshole," Jared said, continuing to divert eye contact.

As Johnny heard his friend being abashed, a rage took over him that he hadn't necessarily felt before. "Hey!" Johnny yelled. "Yea you, asshole. I'm fuckin' talkin' to you, you motherfuckin' piece of dog shit, pussy!" Johnny walked fiercely at Erick, yelling obscenities.

Erick at first seemed amused, but his demeanor rapidly changed in a matter of seconds as Johnny approached.

Johnny was now in the boy's face; his voice resounded with rage. "What the fuck did you just say, asshole?" Johnny yelled, he noticed he had attracted the attention of the crowd Erick had left seconds before.

"I…I was talking to—"

"I didn't ask who you were talking to, I asked what the fuck you said!" Johnny yelled in a deep, belligerent tone.

"Dude, I'm out. I was just…I was just fuckin' around," Erick nervously said as he began slowly retreating backward. His face was flushed, and there was no sign of his larger party attempting to offer assistance.

Johnny continued to follow the boy, harassing him as Erick began walking faster.

"Hey! Hey!" Johnny yelled, pursuing the kid.

Erick continued to walk toward the safety of his group, but as he got closer to the crowd, he stopped.

"What, dude?" Erick asked. He appeared frightened by Johnny's actions.

"Look at me, faggot," Johnny said in low menacing voice as he approached Erick. "You ever talk to my friend like that again and I'll beat the fuckin' shit out of you. You piss-ignorant, cock suckin' piece of shit. I'll leave the fuckin' buckle on," Johnny said as he inched closer to the stunned Erick.

"What, dude? All right, man. Back off, I get it," Erick said frightfully as he began a full retreat in his party's direction.

Johnny stood his ground, watching Erick walk to

his crowd.

"Man, when are you gonna learn to keep your mouth shut? You're gonna get your ass whooped someday," Johnny heard another of the guys scold as Erick rejoined them.

Johnny watched Erick walk to the red, wooden bench on the side of the court and sit. Briefly, Erick looked up in Johnny's direction, but looked away as soon as he realized Johnny was still standing there. Satisfied that Erick was no longer a threat, Johnny turned to walk back to where he had left Jared.

Jared had a look of both gratitude as well as shock on his face. Johnny was still visibly angered as he approached his friend. Jared was now holding his hand upside down, insinuating he would like to offer a discrete high five.

Johnny obliged. "Let's go get that water," he said in a much calmer tone.

"Dude! That was freakin' awesome! Did you see his face?" Jared asked as he looked at Johnny with his mouth gaping in admiration. Jared continued to smile at Johnny as they both walked toward the street. "Man, seriously. That was phenomenal!" Jared continued as the two boys reached the curb. "Dude, I hate that word."

"What word?" Jared asked curiously.

"The 'f' word. I hate the word fag or faggot," Johnny said with a look of regret on his face.

"Well, man. I don't like it either, but you were just pissed the hell off. You went off, dude, and it was fan-fuckin-tastic," Jared said, smiling.

"Yea, it was pretty awesome to watch him take off like that," he confessed as they began walking toward the store across the street. "But I like Brian," Johnny continued, "I would never say that to him, and I would never want him to hear me say it." The boys walked hastily across the empty street until they reached the other side.

"Man, I know that, you were just mad as hell. It's pretty awesome," Jared said, still smiling.

"My dad always called me that," Johnny said, offering Jared a small piece of his pain.

"Called you what? Mad as hell?" Jared enquired. "Nah, a faggot," Johnny opened the door to the C-mart, letting Jared enter before him. The rush of cool air was almost too much as Johnny's sweat began to cool rapidly.

"Man, that's messed up," Jared said as he looked at Johnny.

"Well, I don't guess I gotta worry about that anytime too soon," Johnny said as he walked toward the refrigerated 20 oz. bottles.

"Drinks are on me, man," Jared said, obviously still appreciative as he opened the glass door.

CHAPTER THIRTY-TWO

Reflection

The day had been long and the evening had brought with it a welcoming transition. The air was calm, and yet the atmosphere offered a grudging sense of irony. The wildlife was ever present as the last piece of sunlight was slowly melting into the treetops.

Watching a few hundred tiny black ants dismember a dead cricket, Johnny paused momentarily from his ritualistic analysis of the day's events to merely admire the efficiency and effectiveness the colony operated with. Every ant had a purpose; each one had a reason for its existence and knew exactly what it was supposed to be doing at that very second. The thought couldn't escape him; he felt smaller than even the weakest ant. They all had a purpose, they understood their meaning in life, and Johnny could say neither of those things.

His back was becoming uncomfortable. He had been sitting on the ground with his back leaning against the west side of the horse stables. While chewing on random blades of grass, Johnny had repeatedly reassessed his actions that day. There was no getting around the empty feeling of disgust that lingered deep in his gut. He was still angered by Erick's comments and harassment toward his friend, but Johnny knew wholeheartedly that the way he defended Jared was, without a doubt, deplorable. Every fiber in Johnny's body despised the degrading methods of mind control Johnny's father unleashed on him throughout the years, yet he mirrored the man's technique quite effectively on a complete stranger. As Johnny looked at the ants once more, he made a pact with himself. He had little control over the shampoo he used, the food he ate, or any of the trivial matters associated with his current state of existence; however, he knew he had to acquire as much control over his reactions as he possibly could.

He had questioned whether or not his lashing out was voluntary or not. In his mind, he had the optimistic idea that perhaps he had been in control, and perhaps he had merely made a bad judgment call in regard to the language he used.

He wouldn't allow himself to become absorbed, which was why he ran that night. His escape was the ultimate prophylactic move in regard to greatly reducing his chances of becoming all he despised. Now, it was time to embrace the fact that a healthy mind requires rigorous maintenance. He knew he would never have a fresh start, but he was ready to embrace the challenges associated with obtaining healthy mental hygiene.

The sound of approaching footsteps startled the pondering boy. Although the sound and pace were undeniably human, Johnny found himself increasingly jumpy while outdoors on the farm after the coyote incident. The thought of his father walking around the corner of the stable also briefly violated his imagination, but he pushed it back. He was becoming increasingly appreciative of the times when he could push memories and thoughts of his father to a place where they were no longer a threat to his current state of mind. He could never physically push the man away, so a slight amount of gratitude came with each minor mental victory.

"What is up, my buddy?" Jared asked loudly and happily as he came around the corner in his pajama bottoms, a ridiculously huge white t-shirt, and his father's work boots. His hair was extremely wet. It was obvious that he had just showered.

"Not a hell of a lot, just thinkin'," Johnny said with a welcoming smile. Jared stood in front of Johnny and extended a hand to help him up.

"Well, man, that's never done anyone a damn bit of good. Let's go in," Jared said excitedly as Johnny accepted his assistance. "Mom and Pops are taking Bryce to the sitters' and going out with friends," Jared said happily.

"So, we got the ice cream stash to ourselves?" Johnny asked sarcastically as he dusted himself off.

"Dude, we got a lot more than that. The night is ours, my man," Jared replied as the two headed for the house.

CHAPTER THIRTY-THREE

To Hate

The boys embarked on their night of innocent antics by first cooking a frozen pepperoni pizza and retreating to the basement to play video games. The entire pizza and the majority of a large bag of potato chips were both devoured in a matter of minutes as the boys frequently paused their game to enjoy ridiculously large bites of greasy pepperoni and melted cheese.

"Dude, we're totally gonna raid Pops' whiskey cabinet tonight," Jared said, smiling as he virtually assassinated a fictional terrorist on the large flat screen television. Johnny, looking quite confused, had no idea why they would do such a thing. His father kept a liquor stash and money for booze in the kitchen cabinet by the refrigerator, but the only thing Johnny had ever taken from it was the stash of money on the night he left.

"What d'you mean, raid it?" Johnny asked innocently. Jared paused his game, and looked at his friend.

"I mean, we're gonna get a little bit tipsy this evening, my good sir." Johnny looked at Jared with a look that could arguably be that of disgust.

"Well, you have fun with that. I've never touched that stuff, and I don't plan to start anytime soon," Johnny said as he looked at the empty porcelain plate in his lap.

Jared paused his game, glancing toward Johnny, "Yea, man. It was just a suggestion," he said with a disappointed look on his face as he turned his attention back to the game.

Johnny continued to stare at his plate. The excess pizza sauce and tiny pieces of potato chips briefly offered a captivating escape as Johnny thought they resembled tiny pieces of eggshell. Johnny remembered gathering the eggs from his father's chicken coop. Some days Johnny would gather an egg or two from the coop, scramble them in a plastic bowl and cook them in the disgustingly filthy microwave. He could never seem to get all the pieces of shell out of the mixture.

"My dad drinks," Johnny said solemnly as he continued to look at the greasy plate. This comment seemed to catch his friend off guard. "He drinks every night. As soon as he gets home from work he sits at the table and drinks. Glass after glass of ice and this Wild Turkey bullshit," Johnny continued as Jared looked at him with concern.

"Is that why your mom and brother left?" Jared asked quietly as Johnny looked at him.

"Partly," Johnny said as he broke eye contact.

"She shouldn't have left you there if your dad drank every night," Jared proclaimed.

As he said this, Johnny realized that Jared had no

idea of the extent of the turmoil that Johnny had been subjected to. Johnny's idea of normality had been drastically transformed in a very short time. However, his grasp on how desperate his pathetic situation actually was had yet to fully sink in.

"Well, Pops has a stash of licorice too, we can always hit that up," Jared said playfully.

"I don't wanna ever be like that. I don't wanna be him. I can't be like him because I fuckin' hate him. I hate everything about him and I wish he'd just die and burn in hell," Johnny said in a vengeful, tortured tone. Jared stared at Johnny with his mouth open in shock. "Johnny, man did your dad beat you?" As Jared asked the question, Johnny found himself feeling increasingly uneasy. He sat silent for a few seconds, staring at the large television.

"We got this whole night to chill and have fun. Let's talk about something else," Johnny replied without eye movement or change in tone. Johnny knew his father had a heavy hand, yet he was unsure of the line between discipline and torturous, violent abuse. It had never been clearly defined for Johnny. Part of him felt he was deserving of his father's rage, but he hated the man just the same.

"Sure thing, man, I hate the taste of whiskey anyways," Jared said softly as Johnny looked at him in a peculiar manner.

"So, rocky road or plain vanilla?" Johnny asked with a smirk, totally changing the stale mood.

"Dude, rocky road for sure," Jared replied as he jumped up from his chair.

Johnny's mind was still a collage of commotion, yet he was realizing he was gaining ground in this healthy environment. He was even more optimistic about talking to Brian, as he was certainly making progress by slowly opening up to his friend, Jared.

Johnny arose from his recliner with plate in hand, and the boys made their way up the stairs and into the immaculate kitchen.

"Man, we gotta make sure we leave this place spotless, Mom busted her ass cleaning this place today," Jared said as he made his way to the refrigerator.

"Yea, for sure, dude," Johnny replied has he grabbed two bowls from the cabinet.

"Dude, let's forget the bowls and just eat it out of the container," Jared suggested as he peeled the flimsy plastic lid from the half-eaten gallon of rocky road ice cream. Johnny shot Jared a look as he sat the bowls on the kitchen countertop. "Just grab spoons," Jared said with a mouth full of ice cream that he had scooped out with two fingers.

The intrusively loud ring of the landline phone rang from the kitchen. Jared swallowed what he had in his mouth and went for the phone, which was a 1960s rotary dial that was more for show and telemarketers than anything.

"Hello," Jared said as he picked up the black receiver. "Oh hey, Pops. Everything is great, just about to load up some syringes."

Johnny looked curiously at the sarcastic Jared. He found no humor in drug abuse and wondered why Jared and Jackson joked about it so randomly, especially after what Jackson had told him about his mother.

"Yea, yea. Love you too, Pops," Jared said to his father as he hung up the phone and returned to the table.

Johnny walked to the table and stood next to Jared, handing him a spoon. Johnny watched Jared curiously as the boy began eating the ice cream in a ravenous fashion, as if he hadn't eaten in days. He decided to make at least some effort to keep up with him, dipping his spoon into the container. The two were moving through the remainder of the ice cream at an impressive speed.

"Dude, you wanna go walk the dirt road when we're done?" Jared asked as squinted his eyes, seemingly due to the frigid cold of the ice cream.

Johnny sat his spoon down and swallowed the last bite he was able to stomach.

"Sure, dude, if I can freakin' walk," Johnny replied as he patted his belly.

"Pick that damn spoon up, we gotta bit more to go," Jared brought a heaping spoonful to his open mouth.

"That's all you, man. I'm stuffed," Johnny replied, looking at Jared and thinking he was crazy for attempting to eat even more. Johnny wasn't used to having a full stomach and regular, nutritiously prepared meals. The pain of hunger was certainly something he didn't miss, however, he was now realizing there was another end of the spectrum as well. Gluttony could be painful too.

As Jared polished off the container, Johnny made his way to the living room, staring out the front door. The night seemed peaceful. All that seemed to be stirring were the hundreds of tiny flying insects and moths drawn to the porch light. Johnny thought a walk sounded settling, and was happy to be going on one.

"Man, I'm gonna run upstairs to the bathroom,

then we can catch them fireflies," Jared said as he passed through the living room to the stairs.

Johnny gave him an affirming nod, and then returned his attention to the determination of the relentless mob of insects patronizing the glass fixture.

Turning the doorknob, Johnny opened the front door and exited the house. As he stepped on the front porch, he walked passively to the porch swing and carefully sat down. The white-painted chains supporting the swing made a creaking sound with every slight movement Johnny made. Johnny leaned his head back and rested it on the back of the seat, staring at the ceiling of the porch. He heard his stomach rumbling and was beginning to wonder if pizza, ice cream, and potato chips were a good combination.

As he looked to the right, he noticed the pillar closest to him had tiny marks on it, with a year next to each mark and Jared's name. They were displaying the growth of the boy throughout the years. Johnny began to wonder if Bryce had her own until he noticed small markings on the next pillar down.

Johnny began to imagine how tall his brother was, if he was in preschool, and most importantly, if he was happy. Johnny tried to imagine his mother, brother, and him living in a house like this. For some reason or another it didn't fit, and something about it didn't make sense. He hoped his mother had found another husband, and that he was taking care of her and Jacob. He wondered if she ever thought of him, or if she was forgetting his face the way he thought he was forgetting hers. He knew, at best, the woman was in a nicer house, with a decent man, and free of bruises, both from fists and needles alike. Johnny remembered the way she would always attempt to hide her mouth when she smiled, he wondered if she was ever able to get her teeth fixed.

The bark of one of the quarantined dogs startled Johnny as he turned his attention to the barn. The dog continued barking, so Johnny thought he would investigate the situation. As he rose to his feet, the barking got louder, and it sounded like the other two dogs had joined in too. Johnny walked down the stairs and started heading toward the barn. He got about fifteen feet from the house when he felt a cold chill of fear run up and down his spine. He envisioned the coyote, maddened and charging, and instantly turned and ran back the safety of the lit front porch. As Johnny walked cautiously back to his seat, the barking seemed to gradually subside. As he sat down again, waiting patiently for Jared, he rested his head once more. He then heard the whimpering of Bitty and wondered if taking the pup on the walk with them would be a good idea.

He imagined what the house and yard would look like the next night with large serving tables, nice music, and several conversing guests. The thought of crawfish, or any food for that matter, made him want to gag. He was hopefully going to sleep well tonight, but he was hoping this walk would settle his grumbling belly.

As the front door opened, Jared exited. "Bout ready, man?" he asked as he closed the door behind him.

"Just waiting on you, sir," Johnny replied as he stood from the swing.

Jared jumped from the front porch in his typical fashion as Johnny calmly followed down the stairs.

Both boys instinctively walked toward the dirt road at the end of the driveway.

"The dogs were barking their heads off a minute ago," Johnny said as he casually kicked loose rocks from the driveway.

"Dude, they bark nonstop all night." Jared placed his hands behind his head and walked with his elbows in the air.

"Do you think we should take the pup?" Johnny asked.

"Nah, man. It's at the sitter's with Bryce." "But I…she's really not here?"

"Nope."

"Why did they take Bitty to the sitter too? She's probably gonna shit all over that lady's house," Johnny asked as they came closer to the dirt road. He instantly knew the whining puppy he'd heard on the porch was merely his mind playing yet another cruel trick on him.

"Well, hell, I guess they just wanted us to have a carefree night, no Barbies, and no puppy piles," Jared replied.

The night was still, the air was lifeless and absent of even the slightest breeze as the boys reached the dirt road at the end of the drive. Going east would have put them walking next to the cornfield, going west would put them walking down a road lined with trees and other vegetation.

"So, left or right?" Jared asked as he stretched his arms out and let out a loud sleepy yawn.

"Let's go left," Johnny said as he turned in that direction, kicking more rocks from the road. "There was a big cornfield where I used to live too," Johnny said as he stared at the stalks of corn, glistening in the moonlight.

Jared merely looked at him, acknowledging that he heard what he had said, but asking no further details.

The two boys began walking side by side, looking at the clear, bright sky completely full of millions of stars. The two were somewhat silent as they slowly walked, admiring the calm, hot night. The moon was just bright enough that it illuminated the only visible cloud in the sky, scattered and nearly transparent.

"How far out is your house from town?" Johnny asked. The question was an attempt to start a conversation.

"Um, from city limits I think we're technically only about five miles out, but to actually get into town—"

"Do you hear that?" Johnny interrupted Jared as he held the back of his hand to his friend's chest, gesturing him to stop. The grumbling sound of a very familiar motor could be heard from a mile or two away. Jared looked at Johnny, somewhat confused, as two dim headlights appeared at the end of the dirt road, heading for the two teens.

"Fuck! Get in the corn, now!" Johnny yelled out as he grabbed his friend's forearm and began pulling himin the direction of the cornfield.

"Dude, what the hell?" Jared asked in an irritated and confused tone as Johnny pulled him to the ditch.

"Jared! Dammit, we need to get hidden, now!" Johnny yelled sternly at Jared. Johnny understood that Jared was unsure what was going on, but Johnny felt he hadn't the time to explain before they took cover.

The two teens leapt over the ditch and into the cornfield, but Johnny feared it was too late. He knew for certain this vehicle was his father's shitty old truck, and he was convinced the man had spotted them. As Johnny watched from a few feet within the cornfield, he pushed Jared behind him and stood shaking in front of him. He knew if his father had in fact seen them that the man would undoubtedly hurt him beyond anything he had yet experienced, if not kill him. Johnny had already made up his mind that he would tell Jared to run, he would make his friend run away, no matter what happened. Johnny's nightmares seemed to be coming alive as the old truck began to slow drastically and came to an abrupt stop.

"Run, Jared!" Johnny said wildly as he turned and pushed his frightened friend a few feet further into the field.

Jared's eyes were wide with fear; he seemed as though he wanted to run for simply not understanding what the danger was.

The truck was idling in the middle of the road as the boys heard one of the doors open and someone step out onto the gravel.

"Who's there? Who the hell is in my corn! Show yourself," an aged, male voice said. A sudden look of relief came across Jared's face as inhaled deeply and stepped around Johnny.

"Mr. Morris, it's Jared." Jared made his way to the ditch as Johnny stood frozen in place, completely overtaken with fear.

"Jared? Jared, boy, what are you doing out here, son?" Johnny heard a kind, weathered voice ask of his friend.

"Sorry, Mr. Morris, I guess we must have thought you were somebody else," Jared replied nervously as he jumped back to the road.

"We? Who you got with you? A lady friend?" the

old farmer asked with a smile as he looked curiously into the field just as Johnny had mustered the courage to show himself. "Jared, son, just what are you doing hiding in my cornfield with another man?" the smiling man asked sarcastically.

"This is my buddy, Johnny. He stays with us at our house," Jared said as he looked back at Johnny, who was about to leap over the ditch, as well.

"Stays at your house? Is this boy family?" Mr. Morris asked as Johnny felt he fell in the stereotypical character of nosy neighbor quite fantastically. As Johnny jumped over the ditch and walked over to Jared, Mr. Morris looked at him in a peculiar manner.

"Yes, sir. He's family," Jared proclaimed as Mr. Morris extended a handshake to Johnny.

"Well, there's nothing wrong with more Everett blood. It's nice to meet you, young man."

"Nice to meet you too, sir," Johnny said as his heart rate was slowly beginning to decrease. Johnny could feel several beads of sweat falling his forehead and his face felt flushed.

"I'll be cuttin' this shit here soon and you little bastards will have to find someplace else to hide out at," the old man said as he loaded back in the seat of his truck, slamming the door loudly. "You boys stay outta trouble and outta my fields, ya hear?"

"Yes, sir," Jared replied as the truck began pulling off. As Johnny watched the truck depart in a cloud of dust illuminated by red taillights, Jared turned to Johnny with an inquisitive look on his face. "Dude, what the hell was that? Mr. Morris is one of my parents' good friends. Why did you feel the need to hide from him?"

Jared appeared irritated as Johnny looked at the

boy. Johnny knew this wouldn't be something he could get out of without providing some sort of explanation.

Jared stared at him, waiting in the dark for an answer, his expression indicated that he was upset about being frightened and drug into his neighbor's cornfield.

"I thought…I thought it was my dad's truck. It sounds just like the damn thing and even looks like it in the dark," Johnny said as he put his hands behind his head and turned his back on Jared.

"Dude, you're my best friend, just tell me why the hell you're so damn scared of your dad finding you," Johnny heard Jared say from behind him. The two boys stood silent for a few seconds, until finally Johnny put his hands down and turned to Jared.

"I don't want him hurting…I don't want him hurting you guys if he finds me here," Johnny said with a shaky voice as he studied Jared's face for a reaction.

"Hurting us? What do you mean, hurting us? Pops has about six or seven guns, and I'm pretty sure he could beat some ass," Jared said in a much calmer tone. "Dude, he's not going to find you here, and even if he does there's not a damn thing he can do about you being here. You're eighteen years old; you're here on your own free will, and there's nothing he can do to you. Did he beat you, man? Did your dad beat you or something?" Jared asked yet again.

"I don't know," Johnny said as he turned from Jared and began walking back to the house.

"What you mean you don't know?" Jared demanded in a calm, yet stern, voice as Johnny continued to walk, hoping the question would fade like a bruise. "Dude, why won't you just talk to me? What do you mean you don't know?" Jared repeated the question in a more demanding tone of voice as he began walking to keep up with Johnny.

"He used cigarettes and belts and sometimes nothing," Johnny said softly as his pace began to increase, Jared who was now close behind him.

"What do you mean? He smoked? What do you mean he used nothing?" Jared continued as Johnny stopped walking and put his hands back behind his head, turning to face his friend. He stared blankly at the ground, eyes fixed, with a statue like composure. Without making eye contact, he stood motionless for a few more seconds.

"He would wake me up for school with cigarettes on my back when I was sleepin'. He used the belt a lot, and sometimes he would leave his belt buckle on if I had been really outta line. Sometimes he was just too mad to take the belt off so he'd just start punching me; he didn't use anything else, just his hands."

Johnny put his hands down and briefly made eye contact with Jared, whose mouth was hanging open in disbelief.

Johnny turned from his speechless friend and began walking again. The confessing teen was surprised that he didn't have the oppressive sense of guilt that usually accompanied any slight disclosures. This was more than a slight disclosure; this was the first time Johnny had said out loud what had taken place in his father's house. The black eyes, busted and fat lips, and bruises in every stage of healing spoke for themselves to several classmates, teachers, and other people in Johnny's life who chose to look the other way.

This, however, was more than that; this was the first time Johnny had told anyone what his father had done to him. He didn't feel guilty, he didn't feel relieved, he merely felt numb and empty as he walked on the Louisiana dirt road. He walked a bit further before he heard Jared run up behind him.

Jared ran in front of Johnny and placed his hand up to stop Johnny from walking any further.

Johnny looked at Jared as his friend's eyes glistened with tears in the moonlight.

"Dude, I'm not sure…I don't even know what to say. But, dude, I meant what I said, you really are my best friend. I don't think you're a freak, and if that motherfucker shows up anywhere in this parish I swear to God he's gonna regret it," Jared said as he put his hand down and stepped back.

Before Johnny could respond, two more headlights appeared behind them.

"Aww, shit, I bet that's Mom and Pops. They said they were heading home."

As Jared stared up at the lights, Johnny grabbed his arm and looked at him as desperation made its way up trachea and tightened in his throat.

"Please, don't tell your folks about this. I don't wanna talk about it anymore tonight," Johnny pleaded with his friend.

"No worries," Jared replied, "it's been a long day, I say we just catch a ride home and get some shut eye."

CHAPTER THIRTY-FOUR

Preparation

Johnny woke up at nearly nine to the sound of slamming metal in the front yard. A horse trailer full of round fold-up tables and chairs was Johnny's wake-up call. After Johnny finished rinsing the toothpaste out of his mouth, he headed to Jared's room to see if he was awake or not. Johnny felt rested, like he could do a little heavy lifting, so he was hoping Jared would be up for it as well. As he knocked lightly on the door, he heard someone coming up the stairs.

"Good morning, sunshine," Graye said as she appeared at the top of the stairs. "Sweetie, if you're looking for Jared, he's on the couch with a wet rag on his head, and a trash can beside him. I hear you two wild men had quite a night of pizza and ice cream," the woman said as she smiled and kissed Johnny on the forehead.

"Is he okay?" Johnny asked with concern in his voice as he headed toward the stairs to see his friend.

"Oh, he's just suffering from the friendly symptoms that come with being a little lactose intolerant," the woman replied as Johnny headed down the stairs.

"Man, are you okay? You look like hell," Johnny asked as he stepped off the staircase and approached the couch. Jared was in a white tank-top undershirt and old shorts with a rag on his forehead. His stomach looked swollen and bloated as he held it with both hands.

"Man that looks painful. You look kinda like you're pregnant," Johnny said as he glanced at Jared's swollen belly.

Jared began to chuckle a little as Johnny sat down on the coffee table across from him.

"Do you think you'll be okay by tonight?" Johnny asked, concerned as he watched Jared grimace in discomfort.

"Oh, yea, dude. It happens sometimes, I'll be good to go for some serious eats tonight," Jared replied, however, his facial expression and the way he was rubbing his stomach made his proclamation less than convincing.

"I'm gonna go and ask your dad if he wants some help setting up, you want anything?" Johnny stood from the coffee table, stretching and yawning.

"Nah, man. Pops will probably appreciate the help though."

"Johnny!" an excited Bryce came running through the front door with her rambunctious sidekick, Bitty, not far behind her. The little girl smiled as she ran to Johnny and hugged him, "Come see the lights me and Momma hung up!" Bryce grabbed Johnny's hand and led him to the front porch as Graye began descending the staircase. As they exited the house, Johnny saw the hanging orange and white string lanterns draped across the front of the porch awning. There were already several serving tables either set up, or leaning against the north end of the house. Most of the chairs were still folded at the end of the house too.

"They're beautiful, you and your momma did a great job!" Johnny praised the little girl as Graye appeared at the screen door, watching the two interact. "Where's your daddy at?" Johnny asked the girl as she stared proudly at her work.

"He's in the barn, getting the game stuff. Where is your daddy, Johnny?" the little girl asked innocently as she looked at him with a smile. As Johnny looked at her, his mind immediately went back to the previous night's events. He was somewhat embarrassed at the mistaken identity, but he had yet to acquire the normal sense of guilt he was so accustomed to when he disclosed details of his past.

"I'm gonna go help your dad, Bryce," the teen said, smiling at the little girl who had messy hair and a big smile across her face.

"Well, then I'm gonna go with you!" the little girl proclaimed happily.

"B, Momma needs your help up here," Graye chimed in from behind the screen door. The little girl looked disappointed at her mom.

"Aww, man. Okay, Momma. I'll help you."

The day was beautiful, and there was even a slight breeze, which seemed to carry the lingering scent of skunk from the penned dogs. As Johnny reached the barn, he saw a filthy, dusty Jackson pulling items out of a large plywood crate. He imagined this was the stuff that little Bryce was talking about. The three dogs were sleeping lazily in their crates, more than likely out of extreme boredom.

"Hey there, bud. You come to get dirty?" Jackson asked as he held a croquet mallet up proudly.

"Yes, sir," Johnny replied as he walked in to examine the equipment more closely.

"Your buddy still gassed up?" Jackson asked, smiling at Johnny as he dusted his dark blue jeans off with his free hand.

"He spared me the details, but he looks like he's about to pop." Johnny continued to look at the game pieces and was growing increasingly interested in the concept.

"I don't know what that boy was thinking. Ice cream will tear him up every time, and he ate almost half a gallon," Jackson said as he picked up one of the croquet pieces. "Have you ever played?" Jackson asked Johnny as he set the mallet down and walked toward the lowered tailgate of the truck, grabbing the large glass of iced sweet tea. The condensation on the glass made Johnny's mouth water.

"Nope. It looks kinda cool though, do you play a lot?" Johnny squatted down and picked up the large wooden red ball. It looked weathered, as there were several scuff marks and large chips of paint were missing.

"I used to. It's more for the kiddos than anything. You know, bud, there's gonna be quite a few people here tonight. I just want you to know that if at any time you don't feel comfortable, you and Jared can leave the scene and go game in the basement."

"I'm sorry about Tracy," Johnny said as his thoughts transitioned from intrigue to shame in a matter of a few seconds.

"No. You've got nothing to apologize for. That's

not even what I'm getting at, bud. I just want you to know that you don't have to feel obligated to be around a bunch of people you don't know if you aren't up for it." Jackson took a huge gulp from his tea and sat the glass back down on the tailgate.

"Graye's taken care of your school records request, we just need to get your medical records, and you'll be good to go in a few weeks. Are you excited about starting school with Jared?" Jackson asked.

"Yea, I'm nervous as all hell, but I'm excited to get this year done with," Johnny replied as he offered a slight smile.

"Well, we need to sit down with you and Jared and talk about college. I know Jared wants to go to school in town so he can stay out here—he really liked the tour of McNeese. What were you thinking?" Jackson asked as Johnny had no clue how to respond. College had never been a valid option for him.

"Oh, I don't think I'm gonna go to college. Not yet, anyways," Johnny said as he put his head down, kicking up dirt. This was a sore subject for Johnny. He was naturally intelligent, and despite the extreme adversity he had endured, he did surprisingly well in school, and even enjoyed his studies.

"Why are you wanting to wait, bud?"

"I think I'm going to get a good paying job and save a year or two, and then I'll probably go." Johnny wasn't necessarily comfortable talking about furthering his education after high school, but there was really no way of getting out of it.

"So, you're gonna get this great job right out of high school, huh?" Jackson asked, smiling at Johnny as he looked up at the man. "What are you wanting to be when you're all grown up?" Jackson asked with a playful tone to his voice.

Johnny didn't take long to respond, this question he could answer confidently, "I think I wanna be like Brian; I mean, I don't wanna be gay, I wanna help people by talking to 'em."

Jackson began to chuckle. "Well," the man said, smiling, "I think you're gonna do great at helping people. I do, however, think it would be a better idea if you start as soon as you're done with high school. I know Jared would be thrilled if you went to McNeese with him."

Johnny thought that surely Jackson could understand that he didn't have the money to pay for a college education. He didn't understand why the man was being so persistent.

"Listen, Johnny. If you are serious about going to school next year, then we're gonna make sure you go to school. My wife and I have been very blessed, and we have already decided we'd love to help you through school if that's what you're wanting to do, and you don't need to worry about paying for it, just concentrate on getting the grades, and not letting those girls get in the way."

Johnny stared at Jackson; he remained completely speechless—his jaw lifelessly agape. There were no words to thank someone for such selfless generosity. Johnny felt his mouth form an uncontrollable smile, his insides tingling as he placed his hands behind his head, drawing in a deep breath.

Jackson took a few steps in his direction,

"I haven't seen my boy this happy and carefree in a while, he absolutely loves having you here. My wife loves you to death, and is thrilled with your decision to stick around. Bryce talks about the new boy nonstop, and even Daryl Morris spoke very highly of you during our thirty-minute phone call this morning, that nosey bastard. We're all glad you're here, bud, and I'd personally like to see you stick around. You boys can stay at the house while you get your degrees, that way you're not worrying about paying bills and recovering from hangovers. Paying for school is something I refer to as seed money. We help you out, and in turn you take what we've given and do something awesome for yourself and others around you. It's all about growing something great, something to be proud of. I know…I know that sounds cheesy as hell, but the greatest man I've ever known, my father-in-law, told me the same thing once when I was just a bit older than you."

Johnny may have been looking at the ground, but the kid could feel his excitement beaming, and he couldn't hide it. The idea that a college education could actually be in his future sent a euphoric surge through him that he couldn't contain.

"So, does that sound like something we can shake on?" Jackson asked, smiling as he walked toward Johnny with his hand extended.

Johnny, somewhat embarrassed by his uncontrollable smile, shook the man's hand.

"I don't…I don't even know what to say, sir." Johnny said as Jackson put his large hand on top of his head, gently shaking it.

"You don't need to say anything. I think that smile says it all. I love ya, bud, and I'm thankful you've decided to stay here with this family."

Jackson's words were almost foreign to Johnny. Johnny couldn't remember a single time that his father ever told him that he loved him. To Thomas

Tregalis, the word love meant weakness, and was to be ridiculed and disgraced and beaten into something unrecognizable. Johnny did love this family, more than they could imagine, but he wasn't nearly ready to make that proclamation. Johnny briefly looked up at Jackson, making split-second eye contact.

"So, you wanna help me set up all those damn tables? I think that's gonna take a bit of time, and that damn party tent gives me hell every year," Jackson said as he turned from Johnny and began walking to the door.

"Yea, of course, whatever you need me to do," Johnny said graciously. The boy didn't have the emotional capacity to process everything all at once, and he felt like he was almost in a state of shock. He understood that, to the Everetts, displays of affection were a daily activity that strengthened the bond of the family. To Johnny, although it wasn't necessarily unwelcome, it was something he was going to need to adjust to, and coupled with the idea of going to college, it was almost overbearing. An uncontrollable smile etched its way across Johnny's face as they exited the barn.

CHAPTER THIRTY-FIVE

Shirts And Skins

Johnny had never seen so many nice people in his life. Graye had done a spectacular job keeping the visitors occupied on the front porch and under the party tent, with the exception of bathroom visitors. A song by D.L. Menard was playing through the loudspeakers by the barn.

People were dressed casually, mostly in khaki shorts and sundresses, and they drank champagne, wine, and an assortment of imported beers. The tables, all nine of them, were covered in old newspapers and pounds of crawfish shells and remains. People surrounded the tables and continued to ravage the feast as the smell of the Cajun spices and crawfish was thick and hung heavily in the muggy air. The evening was saturated with alcohol and laughter. Neighbors and clients drove from miles around to trample the Everetts' beautiful front lawn and converse loudly. The dark of night was fast approaching, and the evening had brought old friends, old clients, new faces, and Tyler Jenkins to the

Everett residence.

Jared initially seemed totally put off by Tyler's repeated attempts of apology.

Johnny stuck close to Graye and allowed Jared and Tyler a chance to talk. Johnny wanted nothing more than to punch the shit out of Tyler, but he knew that in order to be true to the promise he made to himself, he would need to avoid Tyler all together.

Jared had retreated from Tyler several times in an effort to collect Johnny to join them, shooting the basketball out by the barn. Johnny would simply decline and tell his friend maybe later. There were a few other young men there as well that Jared had introduced Johnny to. The fourteen-year-old grandson of Mr. Morris and two fifteen-year-old nephews of Phil and Ivy Emhoff, from about fifteen miles south of the Everett farm, were at the party.

Johnny watched from the front porch as the boys shot around. He could gauge by Jared's body language that he was still angry at Tyler to some degree. Johnny imagined that Jared would never fully forgive Tyler, but given the circumstances, it likely made more sense to be cordial to the guy rather than awkwardly avoid him all night.

Johnny tried to eat some crawfish, but his insides were a bundle of nerves. He was still ecstatic about the idea of going to college and had actually made his own first appointment with Brian Mulberry, who was without his dramatic other half while at the party. There were a few girls around Johnny's age at the party, but they seemed to be only interested in talking to each other about the upcoming school year. Johnny made no attempt to converse with them. He was, however, growing increasingly nervous about allowing Graye to send for his school records as he still had this strange idea that his father would somehow find out where he was. He feared that if his father had reported him missing, the records request would lead the man straight to him and the family.

Johnny left the safety of the Everett couple to retrieve a Dr. Pepper from one of the several coolers. The humidity was relentless as the sun's rays were giving way to an endless blanket of stars. The coolers were near the tent, and Johnny was well in route to them when he noticed a small child.

He was three years old at the most; he had dark brown, thick curly hair, and dark brown, beautiful eyes. The little boy was happy, smiling, and jumping around, seemingly without a care in the world. His parents were beautiful too; both were young, vibrant, and ever watchful. As Johnny looked at the little boy he felt his heart ache; he longed to see Jacob and to know if he was happy. He wanted to know if Jacob was smiling like this little boy, he wanted to know if he was safe.

Watching the boy jump around under the safety of his loving parents' watchful eye was simply too much for Johnny. Going from one end of the spectrum to the other in such a short time had left holes in Johnny's psyche, and now witnessing a small boy laugh and play happily almost seemed to anger Johnny. Why didn't Jacob have this? Why couldn't Jacob have two parents like these? Johnny decided to hell with the can of Dr. Pepper and headed toward the house. It had been a long day, and he was tired from the countless introductions, and had felt like a wallflower for the past few hours. Placing his hands in his pockets, he was almost to the stairs when he heard his name called.

"Johnny," Jared said from behind him. "Dude, please come shoot some hoops. We're short one man and I'm done being around these douchebags with no one to talk to."

It was clear that Jared genuinely wanted Johnny's attendance. Without saying a word, Johnny simply removed his hands from his pockets and nodded his head.

"'Atta boy!" Jared exclaimed as the two guys headed back to the barn.

As they walked, Johnny heard the little boy laughing.

He couldn't understand how laughter could hurt so bad, it was more excruciating than the slow burn of his father's Pall Mall. Johnny felt the gut-wrenching truth course through his veins, he felt guilty and selfish. Now that he had been safe, fed, and loved, he was able to focus his attention on things other than merely surviving. Johnny had no idea if Jacob was eating regularly, or if he had someone there when he was scared.

"Tyler Jenkins," the boy said as he put his hand out to shake Johnny's, completely derailing his train of thought. Tyler was broad, with big shoulders and biceps. He had piercing blue eyes and large nose. Johnny thought the boy could easily pass for twenty-five, yet he was going into his senior year.

"I know," Johnny muttered, staring him down. Just as Tyler began retracting his hand, Johnny reached out to shake it, "Johnny. Johnny Tregalis."

"You goin' to school here next year, man?" Tyler asked.

"That's what I hear," Johnny said in a cocky tone

of voice. Johnny understood he was smaller in size than Tyler, but wasn't intimidated by him in the least.

"Well, hell yea. We need another baller," Tyler said as he flashed a smile and threw the ball to Johnny. "Dude, you're on my team, and we got Jasper too," Tyler said as he removed his polo shirt. "We're skins, you three fags are shirts," Tyler pointed and smiled at Jared and the Emhoff cousins.

Regardless of what Tyler said Johnny knew this was merely a ploy to assert dominance and intimidation as the bigger boy flexed his pecs and paraded around like a caveman.

"I'm not taking my shirt off," Johnny said as he shot the ball, sinking the shot from about twenty feet away.

"Dude, we're skins. They're shirts, you wanna be on their team?" Tyler asked as he went to retrieve the ball which had rolled a few feet away from the barn.

Johnny looked at Tyler, wondering what it would be like to sock him right in his mouth.

"Yea, man. I don't gotta problem not being on your team, probably sucks to be on your team anyways," Johnny said as Jared gave him a half smirk.

Tyler didn't seem find the comment too funny as his demeanor and facial expression hardened with seriousness.

"What's the matter, pussy? You a fag or something? Just take your fuckin' shirt off," Tyler said as he began dribbling the ball, moving closer to Johnny.

Johnny immediately broke eye contact, looking toward his mismatched shoelaces and attempting to block the boy's words.

"Hey, asswipe, I said take your fuckin' shirt off!"

As Tyler made the demand again, Jared noticed Johnny's eyes become large, and he began breathing heavily as he nodded his head in submission.

"Tyler, dude, chill the fuck out," Jared said as he approached Tyler, who was watching Johnny with a strange look on his face.

"Hey, douche!" Tyler yelled at Johnny as he threw the ball at him, striking him hard in the chest.

Johnny had made no effort to catch the ball or even divert it, as he stared at the ground. He had wide eyes, flared nostrils, and was breathing rapidly.

"Dude, what the fuck is wrong with your friend? Your folks runnin' a retard ranch out here or something?" Tyler asked hatefully.

"Johnny, dude, don't mind that stupid piece of shit. He was just about to leave," Jared said in a concerned voice as he watched Johnny's strange behavior, stepping closer to him.

"Okay!" Johnny said sternly, catching the attention of some of the adults who were socializing near the barn.

Jared and the group of boys watched Johnny, who was still staring at the ground.

The boy grabbed the bottom of his shirt and began pulling it up over his torso and over his head, tossing it to the ground beside him.

"Ja—Jared, man I didn't know! How could I have known?" Tyler yelled from behind Jared, who was speechless.

The adults closest to the barn slowly moved closer to Johnny, who was standing very close to the bright barn light. The Emhoff cousins left the barn, running back to the adults.

"Jared, dude! What happened? What happened to

him!" Tyler yelled loudly as they stared at Johnny's scarred chest and abdomen.

Johnny had well-defined pectoral muscles, and nearly all his abdominal muscles were defined. He had nearly fifty circular scars from his father's cigarettes and cigars, some large, some a little smaller, and a long thick scar running horizontally over his left pectoral, down his sternum, stopping just shy of the boy's upper abdomen.

Jared approached his friend, who appeared to be in some sort of horrified trance. "Johnny, dude, you can put your shirt back on."

"Okay!" Johnny yelled out again. His tone wasn't one of anger; rather, it was the submissive tone of someone who was completely petrified with fear as he continued to stare at the ground, avoiding eye contact at all cost.

Jared jumped back in a startled manner as he watched as his friend put his hands behind his head and turn around, exposing his back to Jared. As he did, Tyler ran past both the boys, back to his parents near the house.

"Pops!" Jared yelled out, "Pops! Come here!" Jared stared in horror as he saw several of the party goers rushing to his aid. Jared felt the tears streaming from his eyes as he looked at Johnny. The fading sunlight set upon the thick, discolored, and layered scarring all about Johnny's back. Not one or two scars. His entire back, from near his shoulders to where the boy's shorts covered his buttocks, was covered with horrific scarring. The boy looked like he had been whipped a series of times.

As several adults began to gather, some covering their mouths in horror, Jared searched the crowd for his parents, "Pops!" he called out again, startling Johnny who had turned to face him.

"Jared?" Johnny asked in a surprised, almost relieved voice as he looked at his friend.

"Johnny, who the fuck did this? Your dad did this, didn't he? That motherfucker!"

As Jared yelled in anger, Johnny looked down to see his shirt was off, and all his secrets were on display in front of a crowd of people he didn't know, yet he didn't understand what had just happened.

Johnny looked to see Jackson running through the crowd to the sound of his yelling son, but the man stopped suddenly as soon as Johnny was in his sight. His hands covered his mouth, his eyes widened, and it appeared to Johnny as though he were crying in the twilight.

As Johnny turned from Jackson, his eyes met Jared's, the two stared at each other momentarily, and then Johnny realized he couldn't be saved, he didn't want to be saved, not tonight; tonight, he wanted to run.

Johnny wasted no time, he ran from the stunned and silent crowd, many of whom were shocked and on the verge of tears. He ran past the porch; he ran from Tyler and from the Everetts' home and all he had grown to love. He ran from the gasps of the tearful, wealthy, southern socialites. He ran past the horse stable and into the night. He ran through the pasture and toward the pond Jared had spoken of, the one that was so difficult to reach, and had sinister beings residing in its swampy waters. He felt he needed to join them, to join his lowly fellow creatures that resided in the scum and muck, and never again have to look on the faces that looked upon him—horrified and sympathetic to the plight of the poor punching bag, Johnny Tregalis.

CHAPTER THIRTY-SIX

Donny

The musky smell of mildew coupled with the hanging cloud of smoke left a heavy, pungently nauseating smell throughout the entire house. He watched as the heavy rain ran down his window. The inner part of his wooden windowsill, which was rotting away, was completely saturated, and had standing water and roach remains all along the bottom. The rains had been constant for days, and there was no means of comfort as the swamp cooler wasn't working. The sweltering house was sticky and inescapably miserable.

As he watched his brother sleeping, he couldn't help but wonder if it would be better if he never woke up and continued his slumber into eternity. He looked at the pillow the little boy was sleeping on and, for but a brief second, he questioned how long it would take to end the boy's suffering, and more importantly, to prevent the suffering that was soon to take place.

Instantly, he felt like a miserable wretch for even thinking such a thought. He loved this little boy so much, and the thought of Jacob being hurt to the degree that Johnny had been beyond unfathomable.

He knew the rains were supposed to be reviving and reinvigorating as they fell heavily on the decrepit domicile and the surrounding area. These rains, however, were restricting and suffocating and had brought with them a familiar face of disgust.

As Jacob slept heavily, Johnny looked at the boy's dirty little fingernails, and filthy feet. The two boys had been locked in the bedroom the majority of the morning as their father had been working in the kitchen. Johnny's mother had left the house around eight in the morning, which was highly unlike her, so Johnny knew something was going to happen even before the disgusting bastard showed up with his box of fun. It would only be a matter of minutes and Jacob's life would be drastically changed forever, and he would be forever ruined to some degree or another.

The tears swelled in Johnny's eyes as he watched his defenseless baby brother sleeping. Loud laughter from the kitchen startled Johnny as his little brother opened his eyes and instantly began crying. His little cheeks were red and his thick brown hair was wet from perspiration. As Jacob looked around the room, he saw his older brother and instantly laid his head back down. Johnny knew he was a constant source of comfort for the little boy.

Jacob put his arms out for Johnny to hold him, "Hold you, Donny," the little boy said as Johnny stretched over to pick him up. As he did, the bedroom door opened.

"Hey, boys!" Doug shrieked as he entered the room with the same tin lunch box of atrocious gadgets

that Johnny had grown to hate. Doug was even fatter and had basically no hair now. This was the first Johnny had seen of him since the man stormed out of his room at the sight of Johnny's body hair a few years earlier.

"Johnny, I need you to leave me and this handsome little devil alone, and I need you to leave now," Doug said as he walked into the room, salivating at the sight of the toddler.

Johnny stood from his brother with tears in his eyes and a vengeance in his heart. As he walked past Doug, he wanted to gouge the man's eyes out and watch him scream in agony.

"Move!" Johnny demanded as he headed out the door.

Doug paid no mind to the boy, his attention was focused elsewhere. As the bedroom door closed, Johnny could hear his little brother scream loudly, "Donny! C'mere! Donny!"

Johnny walked to the kitchen to exit the house, hoping the rain would silence his brother's screams, but Jacob continued to scream louder.

"Donny!"

***

"Johnny!"

"Johnny!"

The boy's eyes, puffy and swollen from crying during his sleep, opened as he heard his name being called out in the distance. He didn't know where he was, only that it was still dark and he was wet, not completely soaked, but damp as a result of lying down on the saturated earth. The ground was soft, and every step left a two-inch indention when Johnny was walking through the soggy backwoods.

The evening's events came back to him rather uneventfully as his mental efforts were being devoted largely to maintaining the vivid image of Jacob, which was fading rapidly. Although he never found the pond he was searching for, the boggy landscape seemed just as treacherous, as there was no telling how many menacing moccasins and other unruly foes were within close proximity to him.

As he sat up and attempted to wipe his eyes clean, he noticed a glimmering light several yards away through the thickly wooded area. Johnny knew he was more than likely covered in ticks and possibly even had leeches on his person somewhere, as he had traveled foolishly through ankle deep waters to reach this undisclosed and meaningless location. His legs and shoes were completely covered in smelly sludge. His skin had a sticky, dewy dampness that made Johnny even more uncomfortable.

Johnny knew he had traveled for miles after he ran from the Everetts' party, and the crowd was privileged to everything Johnny had worked so hard to conceal. The pasture leading away from the house was easy to overcome, as Johnny was a natural sprinter. Once he reached the trees, however, the vegetation and soggy earth hindered his escape method greatly. There was no specific path, only random tree trunks, thick vinery, thousands of trees, and startling noises of frightened animals as they fled to safety from the clumsy teenager.

Johnny was now beginning to question the amount of space he had put in between himself and the house. If whoever was looking for him had almost reached him, perhaps he was closer than he originally anticipated. Johnny had no clue how long he had dosed off. Although an impromptu rest wasn't in the original escape plan, Johnny had rested near a large log momentarily to catch his breath and regain his thoughts. He then replayed what had transpired by the barn over and over again in his head as he closed his eyes. Johnny had actually been sleeping for nearly two and a half hours on the boggy floor of the dark and highly inhabited wooded area. The combination of the previous day's labor, coupled with a lack of food intake and an extensive hike, had left Johnny extremely exhausted.

Although his exhaustion was nowhere near quelled by the lengthy nap, Johnny knew he needed to rise to his feet and continue on his route to nothingness. There was indeed a large part of him that wanted to run to the lights and the comfort of the family he had so grown to love, but the larger part couldn't face the questions, and more importantly, the answers. He had no plan other than getting the hell away from everyone, and he was at the level of mental and physical defeat where he didn't feel an extensive plan of action was necessary. He felt he only needed a calm place to merely fade, and to stop being.

"Johnny!" Johnny heard again, this time the voice seemed further away. He thought perhaps whoever it was was walking in the wrong direction. As he looked again for the lights, he saw only a small glimmer, he was right; whoever was looking for him was moving in the opposite direction.

As Johnny looked to the black sky for some source of guidance, he heard his name called out once more in a desperate cry through the darkness. It was the voice of Jared, and Johnny knew instantly by his distressed call that Jared was upset and more than likely sick with worry. Johnny quickly compared his friend's potential sense of despair to his own situation with Jacob. Although time had softened the harsh void that plagued Johnny's soul, the reality was that Johnny was deeply burdened by the lack of knowledge surrounding Jacob's well-being.

As a deep sense of empathy overtook Johnny's emotions, he knew he couldn't allow his friend to spend the rest of his life wondering what happened to him. He knew that Jared would need answers, and those answers would only be made available through Johnny himself. Completely filthy, Johnny turned back to the fading lights and began to reluctantly move in their direction.

"Johnny!" He heard Jared call out his name again in a pathetic manner that indicated to Johnny that his friend was beginning to lose hope. Johnny heard other people talking as well, and he knew that there must be a search party looking for him. Again, Johnny wondered what time it was, and how far he was from the house. His mind was gradually becoming as boggy as the surrounding woodland, saturated with confusion. His lips were dry and cracked, and his tongue continuously stuck to the roof of his mouth. His voice was shaky, but he knew that the party would more than likely be moving faster than he would, he knew he needed to cry out to announce his location.

He sat back down on the ground and covered his face with his grimy hands. As he drew in several deep breaths, he put his head back and yelled loudly, "I'm here!" Johnny's voice cracked, but it carried across through the darkness. Johnny knew the party heard him as he could hear a great deal of commotion coming from the group.

"Johnny! Where are you?" Johnny heard Brian's voice yell out as his thoughts of surrendering to the elements were being rapidly replaced with feelings of humiliation and a great concern in regard to how the party would scorn him for this irresponsible act that had them out trudging through the boggy, dangerous backwoods of deep Louisiana.

"I'm here!" Johnny screamed out again, "I'm here!" Johnny sat, holding his knees with his arms. He had never felt more pathetic in his miserable life. As he looked at the sky, the reality set in and he knew beyond the shadow of a doubt that his time at the Everett house was done, and his future had once again been tossed into the realm just past uncertainty. He didn't want to think about tomorrow, or even five minutes from now. For now, he wanted only to sit and stare into the dark nothing, and push all thoughts away to the back of his psyche.

"Johnny! Dude, where are you!" Jared yelled loudly.

Johnny could hear the renewed hope in his friend's voice and he felt horrible for causing him and the others in the party such distress. Before Johnny could respond, Jared's flashlight was upon him.

"Johnny!" Jared yelled gleefully as he moved quickly over the stumps and knee-high vegetation, frequently losing his footing and having to rely on nearby trees for a counterbalance.

Finally, Jared reached Johnny, who was shirtless and making no efforts to cover his scarred body, as there was no longer a need. "Pops! He's here!" Jared yelled loudly as other lights began to head in their direction.

"Is he okay?" Johnny was shocked to hear Tyler ask as the boy walked up behind Jared.

Jared, who had obviously been upset, was squatted down by Johnny, smiling as silent tears streamed.

"Dude," Jared tried to talk but he couldn't as Tyler kneeled down by Johnny as well.

"Johnny, man, I had no idea, dude. I'm so fucking sorry, man," Tyler said in a deeply genuine tone of voice, placing his hand on Johnny's shoulder.

Johnny was rather confused as to why he was apologizing as he had little recollection of what actually happened; Johnny felt as though he should be the one making apologies for everyone's inconvenience. The entire situation was becoming increasingly confusing to Johnny as he chose to say nothing until Jared grabbed his shoulder. As Johnny looked at Jared, who was still silently shedding tears, Johnny felt horribly guilty, "I'm sorry," Johnny mumbled.

"Jared! Johnny, are you okay?" Jackson had finally reached the boys.

Johnny noticed the man hadn't changed clothes prior to searching; his nice shorts, and even nicer shirt, must have been completely ruined. Johnny slowly rose to his feet as Brian approached with one of the Emhoff nephews.

"I'll call the others to notify them!" Brian said excitedly as he pulled out his phone.

Johnny searched his mind for the words to say, but before he could formulate any form of an apology Jackson hugged Johnny tightly, almost squeezing him. He placed his hand on the back of the boy's head and held it tightly against his chest. "Are you okay, bud?" Jackson asked in a cracking, shaky voice.

Johnny knew he had caused the man much worry, and didn't know how to even begin to ask for forgiveness.

"I'm sorry, Jackson," Johnny muttered into the man's chest, "I'll go. I'll go tonight and get a ticket." As Johnny began to verbally announce this random plan of action, Jackson held him out and made direct eye contact.

"What the hell are you talking about, a ticket? I told you that you're a part of this family, and you're not going anywhere!" Jackson said sternly, yet lovingly, the way a father would speak to his son.

Johnny couldn't understand why, after everything, the family continued to support him.

"Why? I don't understand why," Johnny said as Jackson released him, staring at the sludge covered teen. "My life is fucked, and my head, my mind ain't right, my mind is completely fucked! I got nothing!" Johnny exclaimed as he began to slowly break down. The last several hours were proving too much to bear as everything seemed to be coming to a head.

Jackson looked at Johnny as the boy put his hands on his head again, looking at Jackson for an answer.

"We don't have to know everything right now, Johnny. Life doesn't work that way, and it never will. I can't tell you that it's all gonna be easy, but I can tell you that this family has been through some really tough shit, and we are all gonna get through this too. Do you understand me?"

As Johnny looked at Jackson and then the rest of the group, he noticed that no one appeared angry or irritated with him. He looked at Jackson and gave the man an affirming nod.

Jackson moved toward Johnny again, placing his hand on the boy's shoulder, "Now let's go home."

CHAPTER THIRTY-SEVEN

Decision

His hair was still wet and even dripping somewhat on the kitchen table as he sat, surrounded by his seekers. Johnny was embarrassed to learn that there were actually two parties searching for him, and had he not disclosed his location when he did, the search would have extended to official law enforcement.

The shower was invigorating as it had washed away the muck and grime from Johnny's body. Regardless of how hot and powerful the water was, it hadn't been able to wash away the humiliation and the feelings of devastation as they still lingered heavily on Johnny's mind.

Graye, Jackson, and Brian all sat with the Johnny at the kitchen table, as Jared had reluctantly gone to bed, and the rest of the party had gone home. Tyler was sleeping on Bryce's bed, and the little girl was sound asleep in her parents' room with her puppy.

Johnny stared at the droplets of water that fell from his hair to the table. He had no idea what the three adults were going to say, but he found some comfort in knowing that their basic demeanor was that of concern, rather than anger or irritation. When the party returned, Graye ran to Johnny and hugged him and seemed unconcerned that she had soiled her silk nightgown with the filth that Johnny was covered in. She had even kissed his cheek, which was covered in sludge and muck as well.

Johnny knew without a doubt that Brian genuinely cared for him too. It was after four in the morning, and the man was still there and awake, even after the exhausting search efforts. The walk back to the house had been a walk of deep shame for Johnny. No one said much the entire way home as Johnny and the men found it difficult to navigate and maneuver as a group through the boggy backwoods. Tyler had removed his soiled shirt so that Johnny could wear it to cover his scarred body.

"We have to start somewhere, my friend," Brian said as he looked up from the table at the silent teen. "It is totally natural for you to withdraw when you are questioned about the devastating events that have taken place in your life. All of this can, and will, be worked out with vigilance and due time. I can assure you, that if you dedicate the effort, you will only move forward." Brian's tone was rich and soft, as his British accent and hand gestures were comforting and almost relaxing to Johnny. "First thing is first, Johnny, we need to have you physically examined by a proper physician to assure you are in good operational health. Treat the body, and then we will mend the mind with extensive, effective, and proven therapeutic interventions."

"Nothing good is going to happen overnight, and this process isn't going to be easy, but I need you to trust in yourself and utilize your support system to its fullest, Johnny. These people love you, and wish only for you to excel into the bright, successful, and stable young man that we all know is there. Your potential is limitless, and you have an incredibly bright future ahead of you, we just need to figure out how to take the most advantage of that. Does that make sense, Johnny?" Brian asked with his hands folded and a smile on his face.

Johnny simply nodded as he gave a small smile. "Good!" Brian said happily, "So, is it safe to say

you are open to visiting my personal family physician today?"

As Brian asked, Johnny inhaled deeply and turned his head away from the three sitting at the table. Graye, who had puffy eyes from excessive crying, was now smiling at the thought of Johnny possibly being receptive to the help they so desperately wanted to give him. Jackson had been sitting with his elbows on the table and both thumbs in his mouth, chewing his thumbnails nervously.

"I'll go," Johnny said with a slight sense of relief in his voice, which indicated a genuine willingness to trust the people that had grown to love him so much.

"Excellent, Johnny," Brian exclaimed, "who was your primary care physician back home? What was their name, Johnny?" The question was confusing to Johnny as he broke his gaze from the floor and looked at Brian.

"What?" Johnny asked in a bewildered tone.

"When, Johnny, was your last visit to see your family doctor?" Brian continued as he looked at Johnny curiously.

"I got some shots a long time ago with my mom so

I could go to school, but I don't know that guy's name, or even if he was a doctor," Johnny replied, hoping the response would satisfy Brian.

The three adults all looked at Johnny in a surprised manner. "The last time you went to the doctor was for your immunizations?" Graye asked in a shocked voice as she stared at Johnny with a puzzled look on her face. Johnny couldn't understand why this information came as such a shock to the adults.

"I'm not sure. That's the only time I remember going." As Johnny replied, he yawned loudly with exhaustion. He knew he needed rest for the long day ahead of him.

"Johnny, Dr. Evans is an excellent doctor, and I can assure you she will make the process as comfortable as possible for you today. I do think that it's a good idea for you to go upstairs and try to get some sleep because I feel you should be well rested, and I'm unsure of when she will be able to see you," Brian said as he smiled at Johnny.

As Johnny looked up at the three sitting at the table, hundreds of thoughts ran through his head, and one of them escaped Johnny's mouth. "I don't know how to say thank you, and I suck at talking sometimes, but thank you all and I'm sorry again for tonight," the boy said as his gaze fluctuated between each person at the table.

"You're more than welcome," Jackson replied. "Let's just worry about getting you some rest right now. Today, I'm sure, will prove to be difficult, and the authorities will most certainly be inquiring about the extensive scarring and signs of obvious abuse," Brian said as Johnny stood from the table.

CHAPTER THIRTY-EIGHT

Scarred

"Who the fuck do you think you are? And you sure as hell better not answer that, you little faggot-ass piece of dog shit!" His father paced back and forth behind him as he was standing facing his bed with his head down in his pathetic room, sweltering and sweating in the Louisiana humidity and heat as the sun was still blaring outside.

Johnny would often just stare at the wall when he was in this situation. His father liked to begin the punishment by first saying horrendous things to Johnny. He liked to belittle him, humiliate him, and let him know just how bad it was going to hurt. A few times Johnny wet himself during a beating, and this only angered Thomas even more. Now, Johnny would try his hardest to mentally block out what his father was saying. He knew this time the buckle was going to be left on.

"You think you can just walk up in this motherfuckin' house any goddamned time of the day, and it's cool? Oh you're so fuckin' cool, ain't ya,

faggot?" Johnny felt the man's fingertips abrasively push the back of his head. "What the fuck would you had done if them fuckin' chickens had been outta water in this goddamned heat? Huh? I fuckin' hate you. I wish to God every day I woulda shoved a hanger up your slutty mother's disgusting pussy and scraped you out before she shit you out on the kitchen floor. You're never leavin' this place, fag. Never!"

His father continued to pace, further building anxiety in the trembling teenager. He was the typical alcoholic, swollen belly, stained, white tank-top, and bright red cheeks. To make his appearance even more monstrous, his teeth were yellow and dingy, and his hair was extremely greasy.

"Off with your shirt, boy." Johnny's worst fear. The pain that came with being beaten with a belt buckle was unbearable on bare skin. Shaking, Johnny removed his worn, gray t-shirt and tossed it on his bed. "Pants and skeeters too, fag. You gonna learn better than to piss me off."

Trying his hardest not to give into the temptation to turn and beg, or to cry, Johnny began to unbuckle his jeans. His hands were shaking so bad he was almost unable to get them undone as his fingers kept slipping off the button. Finally, he was able to unfasten them. Quickly, he began to remove both his jeans, and his underpants; once he got them to the floor he used his feet to push them away.

"That'a faggot!" Thomas yelled out.

The force and the pain from the belt almost knocked Johnny over, yet he stood silent, grimacing, and anticipating the next blow. Just then another hit came to his back, the same area. And again, and again.

"Bend over!" Thomas screamed at his son, who could feel blood streaming from where the buckle hit his flesh just right. Thomas continued to beat Johnny on his buttocks, and the backs of his legs. He hit the boy many times before he stopped.

Johnny found it difficult to breathe as the pain seared from his legs and back and was completely unbearable; yet he remained silent.

"Stand up straight!" Thomas yelled as Johnny quickly stood up as straight as he could, shaking and breathing hard as he was on the verge of vomiting. "I hope you's enjoying this as much as me, fag. Look what you make me do." Thomas said in a cold, quiet voice. "Now turn around," Thomas continued as Johnny turned around and faced his father as quickly as he could.

The boy felt dizzy and lightheaded, shaking, and sweating profusely. "Now, put your arms straight out, and I swear to God boy if you try to cover them balls, I'll cut 'em off ya!" Thomas yelled loudly as the veins in his head were bulging. Johnny did as his father said, his hands reluctantly uncovered himself, his arms were shaking as he tried his hardest to straighten them out on either side as if he were about to be crucified, but he could no longer contain the tears as he felt them escaping his eyes.

"What a faggot, what do you think I am? Some sick fuck?" the man smirked, as he tossed the belt to the floor. "I really hope I got my message across to you, you little girly bitch. You're just like your mother, but her balls were bigger. Do you hear me, boy!" The man yelled at the top of his lungs. His face was bright red, and his nose was only about an inch from Johnny's.

"I think I need to throw up. I'm going to throw up."

***

"Okay, I'm going to grab you a trash can, Johnny," Brian said as Johnny jumped from his bed, falling to the floor in a complete state of confusion. Johnny looked wildly around the room from the floor as Brian seemed to remain completely calm and unaffected. Johnny began grabbing the backs of his legs, he was completely certain that he had just been beaten.

"Johnny, do you understand where you are?" Brian asked calmly as Johnny noticed the man observing him. "You are in your room, you just woke from a deep sleep, and you are completely safe. Do you understand that, Johnny?" Brian continued as Johnny watched him, breathing sporadically through his flared nostrils.

Johnny had a slight recollection of the events that had transpired the night before; however, he had no idea how Brian got in his room, or where his father was.

"Johnny, I stayed in your room to sleep this morning on the floor. Do you remember that?" Johnny looked at the blankets and pillow on the floor as if everything began to come back to him. He didn't even ask, he knew his father wasn't there, he hadn't been beaten, and Brian had stayed in his room in case anything strange happened. He felt his gym shorts, and was relieved to find they were dry.

"What time is it, Brian?" Johnny asked as he used his bed to lift himself up off the floor. He then felt his watch snagging the bed sheets and looked for himself.

"It's nearly eleven thirty, Johnny. Our private appointment with Dr. Evans is at three o'clock, sharp."

One thing that hadn't come back to him quite yet was the appointment that Johnny had agreed to go to.

"Are you okay, Johnny?" "Yea, I think so."

"Johnny, there will be an investigating officer there as well, and he will be compiling a report. It will be a slow process, but their job will be to obtain information about what happened, would you like to attempt to discuss what happened with me, prior to talking to Dr. Evans or the officer?"

"What if…what if he finds out where I am?" Johnny asked Brian with fear in his voice.

"Johnny, your case will more than likely result in criminal charges brought against all involved in your abuse. You needn't worry about your father hurting you in any way, now is the time to heal. Focus on healing, Johnny."

"I gotta talk to them today? What if I'm not ready to talk to them today? I'm not ready," Johnny said as he sat down on his bed.

"Johnny, I am unfamiliar with your case, so I'm unsure of a timeline regarding events. I can tell you that there is a limited amount of time that the authorities have to file charges for certain crimes. We need to start this ball rolling if there is to be justice for what has taken place. I need you to understand that you will never be alone in this process because there is always going to be someone there with you."

Brian's words seemed genuine as the man calmly sat back down on the floor, looking up at Johnny.

"I was outta line when my father got on to me, but Uncle Doug. I hate that dude." As Johnny said this, he folded his hands and looked at the floor. He felt belittled even thinking about the atrocities that took place. He understood that he needed to discuss what had happened, but he literally didn't understand how to. "He had a fun box. He brought it over all the time until he stopped coming. Then one day outta nowhere he just showed up to meet Jacob. He hurt Jake pretty bad. Mom left with him the next day." Johnny's words tasted like vile poison as they left his mouth. Hearing himself talk about such business out loud was something he wasn't quite ready for.

"Johnny, if your father is the person responsible for the extensive abuse you have obviously suffered, then he is to be held accountable as well. Disciplinary action and abuse are two entirely different things. Now, let me ask you, when was the last time you remember Uncle Doug visiting you specifically at your father's residence?"

"It feels like it was only a few nights ago, maybe the night before last, but I know that ain't right. I think the last time he came to see only me I was in fifth grade, I think I was twelve," Johnny said as he choked on the confusion stemming from his attempted recollection. Johnny looked at Brian, wondering what he would say. He didn't understand why Doug did what he did, he only knew how it made him feel. He had hated the man for years, and that hate had long been festering in his heart.

"If you were twelve, then there still might be time to file charges and pursue justice. Johnny, what do you mean it seems like only a night or two ago?" As Brian asked, Johnny had a great sense of urgency to acquire at least some insight into why his mind was playing tricks on him, he wanted answers.

"Sometimes it seems like I can't tell if what just happened, just happened, or if it happened before, like a long time before. It happens a lot when I wake up, but sometimes it just happens at any time, I think." Johnny tried his best to explain what he felt was going on, although his description made little sense to him, he hoped Brian could decipher what he meant.

"Johnny, do you ever feel as if you were just recently with your father, even though you know that can't physically be possible?" Johnny looked at Brian, trying to find the right words to offer an effective description.

"Yes."

"Johnny, I believe, from what I have witnessed, that you are suffering from a condition that several people in your position have suffered. The human mind can only handle so much, and then it seems to take its own path. Understand this may not be normal, but it is common in this situation, and it can be treated."

Brian's words were like music to Johnny's ears, even though he didn't seem to understand completely what the man was saying exactly. In Johnny's mind, past and present seemed like a radical mixture that not only overlapped, but intertwined into a mass of absolute confusion.

"Now, Johnny, how about you get showered and dressed, and I will talk with Graye about getting you a healthy breakfast to start your day," Brian said kindly as Johnny continued to sit on his bed. Johnny was obviously nervous by the idea of being examined by a doctor, and not understanding completely what the process entailed was unsettling as well.

"I know you're nervous, Johnny, but in order to

heal properly the human body and mind must first address the underlying issues; otherwise, it's as if we are placing a band-aid over a broken bone. Make sense?" Brian placed his hand on the boy's shoulder in a comforting manner.

"You'll be there the whole time, won't ya?" Johnny asked in a nervous and anxious voice.

"I will not be in the examination room itself, but I will be right outside with both Jackson and Graye. We will all be there. With your permission, the physician will discuss her findings, her medical opinion, and treatment options, if needed. We will also be present when you speak with the investigating officer; you needn't worry about doing this alone. We will all be there to whatever degree you want us to be."

Johnny knew this was only one of many steps he would have to take to understand what was going on with his head. The night before only proved to Johnny how much the Everett family actually loved and cared for him. He knew that if he wanted a shot at maintaining this unity, and becoming a permanent part of the family, he would need to address several painful and traumatizing factors.

"I think I can do it," the boy said as he looked at Brian with a new sense of determination.

"Well, now that's the spirit! And I absolutely know you can do this, Johnny, I have witnessed several clients in my practice overcome despicable obstacles and blossom into productive and healthy individuals, and we are going to make sure yours is a story of success as well, okay?"

Brian's words were certainly motivating, and they resulted in a small smile and a simple nod from the boy.

CHAPTER THIRTY-NINE

Answers

Graye

The office was beautifully crafted with rich, dark wood, a large bookshelf, and gray marble flooring. Graye and Jackson were with Brian in the waiting area of the empty office. Dr. Evans had performed the examination after hours, which was at noon on Saturday, as a courtesy to Johnny and everyone else involved. Officer Brad Stevenson was present as well; however, he had informed Graye that some special agent would be joining them shortly, yet offered no details or further information. The woman imagined it was standard procedure in a case like this.

Graye had been skimming through magazines the entire time they had been there, yet hadn't read a single article as she was completely nervous and terrified to learn what the doctor had to say. Jackson seemed to be staring at the same section of the wall for the past ten minutes, chewing his gum nervously.

The time seemed to be dragging by slowly, and no

one seemed to want to discuss anything or even attempt to engage in casual conversation. As Brian stood from his chair and began walking in the direction of the facilities, the door to Dr. Evan's exam room opened, and the woman exited.

Graye had heard of Dr. Barbara Evans, but had never met the woman prior to this. She wasn't expecting a beautiful Cajun woman with a heavy French accent. She appeared young, fit, and had blonde hair and green eyes.

"Dr. Mulberry, I'm pleased you're still here," the woman said as she approached the four with a halfhearted smile. "I have been given permission to discuss my findings with you from my patient, Mr. Johnny Tregalis," the woman said as she sat down in an empty chair next to Officer Stevenson and directly across from Graye, Jackson, and Brian.

Graye instantaneously developed the lump in her throat. Part of her wanted to exit the scene rather than hear of the forthcoming list of atrocities.

The woman opened the manila file and began reading in a robotic tone. "Radiology reveals healed fractures of the—" Dr. Evans stopped midsentence and turned her head from the file, away from the onlooking group of adults. She drew in several deep breaths and closed the file.

"The boy has several healed fractures. His right wrist, his right ulna, four rib fractures on the left side, two on the right, four metacarpal bones have healed incorrectly, three on the right and one on the left. He has significant scarring to the surface of his entire back, which is consistent with years of traumatic abuse. Significant scarring associated with healed anal fissures is present, which is most certainly consistent with trauma to the area. There are sixty-six noticeable circular scars on the boy's trunk, and legs. The patient confirmed the injuries were inflicted with lit tobacco products. There was a significant scar on the boy's chest consistent with a blade injury, which the patient confirmed. When I instructed the patient remove his gown, he began trembling in a fearful manner. The examination itself was, in my opinion, traumatic for this young man. Officer Stevenson, I will have my report to your office electronically this evening and in a hard copy by close of business day, Monday. In my professional opinion, I feel it would be in the patient's best interest if you conducted questioning at another time."

"Yes, Doctor, of course," Officer Stevenson said as the look of shock was slowly dissolving from his face as the doctor left the waiting room.

"I'll kill him. I'll fu—I'll kill the bastard," Graye heard Jackson say in a low, distressed voice as his face displayed a look of pure rage.

Graye's attention turned to a gray-haired, clean-shaven, tall and slender man who had appeared in front of the four adults dressed in blue jeans, and a navy-blue blazer. "I assume you're referring to Thomas Tregalis?" the man said as he approached the group. "Are you Jackson and Graye Everett?" the man asked as he shook Officer Stevenson's hand. "I'm Special Agent Terrence Boudreaux. I've been looking for Mr. Johnny Tregalis, and I am beyond pleased to learn the young man is in fact breathing," the man said before anyone could answer. "As for wishing death on Thomas Tregalis, that won't be necessary, the sick fuck is already dead."

Graye was beyond shocked as she stared at the

Agent in disbelief, she found herself almost incapable of speech, as if he had just informed her that he was from another planet.

"So, his father is dead? How? How is he, how did he die?" the woman blurted out to the best of her ability.

"His neighbor, Bill Clementine, found the man dead in his house upstate just four days after Bill allegedly gave Johnny a ride to a bus station in Shreveport. The man's blood alcohol level was a point four nine, but that isn't accurate because the man had been dead so long before they found him. But the examiner concluded natural causes," the agent as Graye continued to stare at him, her ears felt as though they were on fire. "I'm gonna need you two and Mr. Tregalis to come to the local precinct with me to answer some questions, and you can plan on being there a while," agent Boudreaux continued.

"Is Johnny in some sort of trouble? Are we?" Graye asked in an irritated and concerned voice as she leaned forward in her seat.

"Mrs. Everett, there was substantial amount of evidence recovered from the Tregalis residence that has led to at least one arrest. We found some of the most disgusting evidence depicting child abuse that I've ever seen in my career, and Johnny's assistance is going to be needed to put the sick fuck away. We also need to question his knowledge regarding the murder of his mother, and the unidentified child found with her."

"What!" Graye shrieked as she began to breathe deeply in disbelief. "That's not right, his mother left when Johnny was, when he was sixteen. She took Jacob—"

"Jacob? Who is Jacob?" Boudreaux asked with a puzzled look on his face.

"Jacob is Johnny's little brother. Are you telling us his mother and little brother are dead as well?" Jackson asked as he stood from his chair.

"We have no record of Irene Tregalis giving birth to a second child. Unless she never sought medical assistance..." he paused and rubbed his chin. "The remains of Irene and a male toddler were found preserved in a padlocked deep freezer inside the old barn on the Tregalis property. The medical examiner confirmed the cause of death for both victims was blunt force trauma to the head, and that the female had been thawed out at least once, and sexually violated postmortem." The agent appeared to have a difficult time even relaying the information as Graye remained silent and disgusted.

"Are you telling me you believe Johnny doesn't know Irene Tregalis is deceased?" the agent asked as he looked at Graye with a desperate look on his face.

"No. He absolutely has no idea, and it's going to be perhaps more than the boy's fragile psychological well-being can handle at this point," Brian chimed in as he appeared just as overwhelmed as the Everetts.

"Are you the boy's doctor?" Boudreaux asked as he looked at Brian.

"I'm his psychologist, Dr. Evan's is in her office toward the back," Brian replied as he pointed toward the back of the office building.

"Well, it might be best if you came along with us. I imagine it to be a long night," Boudreaux said as he turned from the stunned group, shaking his head.

CHAPTER FORTY

The News

Johnny

"Do these photographs look familiar, Johnny? Do you remember these?" Boudreaux asked the silent young man as he sat across from him with several pictures scattered on the table. The room was dark, pale blue, and as cold as the hearts of some of the violators that had been interrogated in it. Johnny glimpsed at the Polaroids, but quickly looked away. Johnny looked at his reflection in the large mirror on the wall, he had no idea how to admit to himself that the kid being violated in the pictures was him, and he certainly had no clue how to tell the agent this.

"Johnny, Doug Davenport is in custody. He's gonna pay for what he did to you, but you've got to help me out here. There may be other boys out there that this man has hurt, and I need your help." Boudreaux's words appeared genuine to Johnny. The thought of other boys suffering the way Johnny had made suddenly made Johnny realize he had to respond somehow, someway.

"That's me," the boy said as he tapped one of the many pictures, "all of 'em." Johnny then turned from the agent and looked at his reflection again. He was surprised that he didn't feel more emotion than he did as he was neither regretful nor relieved that he disclosed his identity in the atrocious photographs.

"You're a brave man, Johnny. I know without a doubt you're gonna get past this and do something absolutely fantastic, but right now we've gotta focus on putting this son of a bitch behind bars for as long as we can. Do you think you would be willing to talk to a jury in a courtroom?"

Johnny looked at Boudreaux with a frightened look on his face. "I can't. If he found out it would be real bad," the boy said as he briefly looked at the pictures again and then looked back at the mirror.

"Johnny, I got to tell you something, and it ain't gonna be easy for you to hear, but you need to hear it just the same. Johnny, your daddy is dead; he was found dead July 22 by a neighbor, a Mr. Bill Clementine."

As Johnny heard these words, he stared at Boudreaux in disbelief as an uncontrollable smile fell across the boy's face.

"You know that for sure? No lie?" the boy asked as he continued to smile, feeling as though years of oppression were being lifted from his psychology.

"Medical examiner confirmed the identity, he's on a slab as we speak, young man," Boudreaux replied happily as Johnny seemed absolutely thrilled by the news.

"He…he gave my dad money almost every week, and sometimes twice a week, just depending.

Sometimes he took the pictures, but if he wanted to be…if he wanted to be in the picture too, then my dad would take it," Johnny explained as he watched Boudreaux's face develop a heavy scowl and a look of disgust. The agent gathered the pictures and placed them back in the folder file.

"That's why my mom took my brother away. Uncle Doug came to see him once, and the next day they left, just disappeared."

"So, Johnny, are you willing to testify to that in an open court?"

"You mean just tell 'em what I just told you? I can do that," the boy said as Boudreaux began to smile, as well.

"I know you can, son, I have no doubt about it. When this is all over you're gonna have no regrets about putting that nasty-ass piece of garbage behind bars for good. You know what happens to men like him in prison, don't ya, Johnny?" Johnny looked at Boudreaux with an intrigued look on his face. "They get everything given right back to 'em, and they usually don't last too long, my friend."

"Can you burn 'em?" Johnny asked randomly.

"The pictures? No, son, they go logged into evidence, but I assure you, you won't have to see any of 'em again after this is all over."

Johnny shook his head slightly as the agent finished his sentence. "Not the pictures, my dad, can you burn my dad? They burned my grandma when she died and let my aunt dump her ashes out on her land," the boy said happily. The thought of his father's body going up in flames brought Johnny a great deal of pleasure; his cheeks ached under the solid grin.

"That's not my department there, son. But I promise you this, come hell or high water, we'll get you your dad's ashes." The agent looked at Johnny for a few seconds and then rose from his seat. "Johnny, there's something else we need to talk about, and I feel it would be best if you take a small break, grab a soda or something, and I'm going to bring in Brian to sit with us, okay?"

CHAPTER FORTY-ONE

Tarnished

Graye

Graye found the office to be uncomfortably small and cramped, and the air was stuffy and stagnant with the Everetts, Brian, and Officer Stevenson all crammed in the tiny quarters.

"It's worthwhile what y'all have done, but the reality is that you don't gotta clue what you're doing. You act like you rescued this boy from the brink and that's final, like there's nothing else to it," Officer Stevenson proclaimed confidently.

Graye's face was bright red, partially from anger, partially from the claustrophobic surroundings she was in. She felt the urge to reach across the desk and slap the shit out of the young officer. "How dare you assume to know what we do and do not know," Graye snapped hatefully as she felt her husband place his hand upon her thigh. The three chairs on the opposite side of the officer's desk were so tightly packed into the office that there was little elbow room at all.

"I've seen these kids, a good deal of 'em pop a round off in their own head by the time they're twenty-one," Officer Stevenson said as he reclined back in his comfortable office chair.

"Excuse me, do you have any specific evidence or data reflecting suicide rates among victimized teenage boys that were linked primarily to you or this agency? Because if you do then you certainly cannot exclude yourself from the equation, my young friend," Brian said in a condescending manner as the door to the office opened slightly.

"Dr. Mulberry, I believe I could use you in the next room," Boudreaux said politely with a smile.

"Is everything okay?" a concerned Graye asked as she leaned over to see the agent.

"Everything is going better than expected. That's a fine young man in that room, and I commend his bravery," Boudreaux replied as Graye looked directly at Officer Stevenson, smiling as she gave him a glare.

She watched as Brian finagled his way from the office, allowing the Everetts to stretch out some and get a bit more comfortable.

"I really just hope you two know what you're gettin' yourselves into is all I'm gonna say," Officer Stevenson said as Jackson leaned forward in his seat.

"I do believe you have said quite enough. If you think for a damn minute that we give a shit what the hell you think, well guess again, asshole. You think just because the kid is a little damaged that he's what, unlovable, unsalvageable?" Jackson snapped at the officer in a harsh tone of voice as Stevenson's face became red, and his eyes widened.

"Now, hold on there, mister. I never used the word damaged, not even once. These kids are tarnished, and if you think that's just gonna disappear, then you got a rude awakening, my friend," Officer Stevenson snapped back.

Graye began to laugh lightly as she looked at the officer in complete disgust. "We are not friends, and I don't believe I can stomach the ignorance that spews from your mouth any longer. Tarnished or not, we are keeping him, he is part of our family, and that's just what families do. If you'll excuse me, I need to use the ladies' room and rid myself of your face." As Graye stood from her chair, she heard her husband laughing as the man stood up as well. The two began to exit the office of the seemingly stunned young officer, who appeared to have been genuinely offended.

Graye and Jackson squeezed their way out of the tiny office and made their way to the hall. There was a bench to the right side of the hallway. Graye simply followed her husband, as claiming the need to use the facilities was merely an excuse to get away from Officer Stevenson. As the couple sat down, Graye's heart rate slowly began to return to normal.

"Are we making the right decision, Jackson? I know in my heart that we are, but I need to know you feel the same way. We don't know everything about him, are we capable?" Graye looked at her husband, placing her hand on his thigh.

"From what we do know, do you really think we could turn him away at this point?" Jackson asked as Graye felt him take her hand. "Our perseverance is going to determine the rest of his life. I'm not looking at this as some sort of pet project, I love that kid, and I'm willing to do whatever it takes to get him the help he needs. I'm two hundred percent positive we are making the right decision. We have Brian, and a wealth of resources, and as of now we know for sure we are the only thing he has. We can't let some two-bit loudmouth discourage us, Graye. This isn't going to get any easier anytime soon so we need to stay strong for our family, all of them." Graye looked at her husband smiling, and hugged him around his waist.

"I seriously don't know what I did to deserve you," the woman said as her emotional moment was cut short by the sound of loud yelling.

"That's Johnny, what the hell is going on?" Jackson asked as the couple jumped from the bench and headed toward the loud shouts.

Officer Stevenson ran past them and through the door that led to the interrogation room.

"I want Graye! I wanna see Graye and Jackson, now!" Johnny yelled as tore through the doors, looking for the couple.

Instantly, Graye knew Johnny had been informed of his mother and brother's passing.

As Johnny spotted Graye, he ran for her, throwing his arms around her and crying loudly.

Graye tried her best to comfort the boy, but she was crying as well. She felt Jackson approach the two as he wrapped his arms around both of them.

As the tears fell, no one knew the words to say, there were none.

Brian approached slowly, placing his hand on Jackson's shoulder, "They want Johnny upstate in two days for questioning and to assist with making arrangements for the deceased. I think it would be best if I came to your house this evening as well."

Graye watched as Agent Boudreaux approached

with his head down and his hands in his pockets. "I'm sorry, son. If there is anything I can do, please let me know. Mr. Everett can you have this young man in Shreveport day after tomorrow? He needs to meet with the prosecutor and make final arrangements for his family."

"Yes, we'll all three be there," Jackson replied as the agent patted his shoulder and walked away.

Graye looked at Johnny, who seemed completely devastated, and instantly thought of the long road the young man had ahead of him. She knew the entire family would need to be as supportive as possible to see him through.

CHAPTER FORTY-TWO

Preparation

Johnny

The bright blue sky was completely clear of clouds. Johnny imagined it was extremely hot as he gazed out the window from his bed while lying on his side. The night had gone by surprisingly uneventfully as everyone turned in early around nine o'clock. Brian decided to sleep on the couch downstairs rather than camp out in Johnny's room, and had already left the Everett house early in the morning.

Although Johnny was absolutely devastated by the news of his mother and Jacob's deaths, he was thankful he hadn't been traumatized by the specific details, and part of him felt a sense of relief as he no longer had to worry of their well-being. What seemed to trouble Johnny most was the fact that they had been there at the residence the entire time and he had no idea.

He never thought to look in the deep freezer, and he wouldn't have, even if it hadn't been padlocked. In his mind, his brother had been growing up, and happy, and to suddenly find out that he would be forever two years old was sickening to Johnny. He hated his father, and part of him wished he would have killed him. The thought of waiting until the man was plastered drunk, and setting the house on fire had often crossed Johnny's mind, had he known the man murdered his family he certainly would have followed through with it.

Johnny found himself plagued with the thoughts of Jacob's last moments on earth; he must have been so scared. Johnny wondered how much the toddler suffered and if he died quickly, or if the little boy cried for him while he was being murdered. The thoughts of guilt circulated in Johnny's head at an uncontrollable rate, like the worst View Master, as the boy continued to stare blankly at the beautiful, clean, clear sky.

"Hey, dude. I know you probably aren't too hungry, but I brought you up some biscuits and gravy," Jared said as he quietly opened the cracked door and walked into Johnny's room.

Johnny was actually glad that Jared had come up. He had been alone for hours and had been unable to sleep throughout the majority of the night because of his nerves.

"Thanks, man. I actually am kinda hungry," Johnny replied as Jared handed him the plate and sat down on the floor. Johnny knew Jared had had a lengthy conversation with his parents about what had actually happened to Johnny's family.

The landline phone rang from downstairs. Jared began to laugh. "Appears you have a new friend. I bet that's Tyler again. That bitch has called twice apologizing and asking if you were all right," Jared said as he smiled and shook his head.

"I guess everyone needs a few second chances," Johnny replied, instantly catching Jared's attention.

"I believe in Heaven," Jared said, changing the subject. "When my grandpa died, I didn't get out of my bed for an entire week, unless I needed to go to the bathroom. I didn't eat, I hardly even drank anything, and all I wanted to do was sleep. Pops told me that I'd see him again someday, and that he wouldn't want me to be all bummed out," as Jared talked to Johnny he had a kind smile on his face, but Johnny didn't necessarily want to hear about God at this point.

"If there is a God, I don't think I'm ready to talk to 'em just yet." Johnny's words were monotone as he took a small bite of his breakfast. "Will you go with us tomorrow?" Johnny asked of Jared as he swallowed a bite and set his plate aside.

"Yea, man. For sure I'll go. I'm sure Pops won't care, but I gotta ask just to be sure."

"I gotta meet Agent Boudreaux tomorrow, and some attorney in the afternoon, but after that your folks said we were gonna stay at this hotel that has a pool and a putt-putt golf course inside of it, so I'm kinda excited about that part." Johnny smiled as he stared at the bedroom door.

"Well, I know Pops is wanting to leave at the ass-crack of dawn, so I better go ask. I'll probably have a better shot if you ask with me, dude." Johnny knew Jared was right, and he imagined Jackson and Graye would be open to Jared coming along for moral support.

"Well, man, let's get down there and ask," Johnny

said as he picked up his barely touched plate of food and motioned to the door.

Jared was slow to rise as he used Johnny's bed to assist him to his feet.

"Man, I'd be down to play some miniature golf with my homechicken," Jared said, smiling, with a bizarre face and his eyes crossed.

"Homechicken? Who the hell says that?" Johnny asked as the boys made their way out the door and down the hall. Jared was a good distraction for Johnny, and Johnny realized that. The boy felt at ease around his friend because Jared had seen him at his worst, and had never once criticized or withdrew from him. Johnny genuinely wanted Jared to go with them, and was willing to beg. As the boys loudly walked down the stairs, Jackson appeared from the kitchen, holding at least three freshly pressed shirts on hangers.

"How you feeling today, bud?" the man asked as looked up at the boys. Johnny looked at Jared and knew by the look on his face and the way he had his head down, that he wasn't going to ask.

"I'm okay," the boy said quietly, "We actually had a question if you have a minute."

"Yes," Jackson said simply as he flashed a small smile. Jared instantly looked a bit taken aback as he looked at his father.

"Yes what, Pops?" Jared asked as he looked down to his dad.

"Yes, you may go with us to Shreveport. Be sure to pack at least two dress shirts and your swimming trunks." Jackson didn't stick around to see the boys' reactions; he merely retreated to his bedroom.

"That was easy," Jared said.

Johnny felt a sense of relief come over him. "Dude, please tell me you gotta extra pair of trunks," Johnny said as the two boys began walking back to their rooms.

"Oh hell yea, dude. I got you, homechicken."

CHAPTER FORTY-THREE

Taste Of Closure

Graye

Graye watched the boys playing in the large indoor pool. She sat poolside with her husband on extremely comfortable chairs as they enjoyed cocktails. Although they both had their swimsuits on, neither of them wanted to get wet. She found the hotel was gorgeous, and the pool had an almost tropical theme to it. She and Jackson had decided it would be best if everyone stayed in the same room, so they reserved a large room with two queen-sized beds. The day had been long, Johnny had said he had had trouble sleeping the night before. The boy slept most of the drive, as did Jared whom Graye imagined having slept through the night just fine. The group had left at six in the morning, dropping off little Bryce and her beloved Bitty at the sitter's, and then leaving Lake Charles on a nonstop drive to Shreveport.

Graye and Jackson were allowed to be present while Johnny answered questions. She felt that the interviews with the prosecutor and Agent Boudreaux were just about as painless as they possibly could be. Everyone involved seemed to handle Johnny with extreme sensitivity, and would instantly give him space if they noticed any tension at all. The assistant district attorney, Allison Cline, walked Johnny through the process of his testimony, but was most positive he wouldn't be needed, as Doug Davenport was more than likely going to be pleading guilty to every single malicious charge he was accused of. The man had been on suicide watch for several days.

Regardless of whether he was needed or not, Agent Boudreaux highly suggested Johnny attend the trial as a means of closure. Graye felt that decision was one that could be made at a later time.

As the boys splashed around, acting like typical teenage guys in a pool, Johnny's scars were highly visible through his wet white t-shirt. Although Johnny had to have noticed the transparency of his shirt, he didn't seem to care, and if he did it wasn't noticeable as the guys dunked each other's heads under water and wrestled around. Occasionally the two would exit the pool to soak in the hot tub. There was no one else in the swimming area, which was within an attached pool house, so the guys were allowed to be as ridiculously loud as they wanted to be.

Graye knew when they returned home it would be the beginning of a long and painful process for Johnny and the rest of the family. There were several appointments already set up with Brian's colleagues to evaluate the extent of psychosis that was at play. Brian had done a fine job detailing the processes and therapies associated with treating severe post-traumatic stress disorder, but was quick to assure the

Everetts that no case was identical, and this was going to be taxing at best. Graye was certain both she and her husband were ready to devote whatever needed to be done to help Johnny.

"This makes it worth it. Knowing he just wants to be happy, he just needs a shot to be happy and have a normal life. Look at him, he's smiling from ear to ear, laughing, and acting like a normal eighteen-year-old kid. He just needed out of that situation," Jackson said as he sipped on his fourth martini.

Graye watched the boys as they relaxed at the side of the pool engaging in small talk.

"I couldn't agree more, hon. When I look at him I only see a world of potential and one of the sweetest boys I've ever met. I couldn't be happier with our family. I'm not sure what to expect tomorrow. The thought of actually seeing the house, I just don't know what to expect or how I'm going to react," Graye said as she continued to watch the guys relaxing. She grabbed her husband's free hand and raised it to her mouth, kissing it.

"He needs this, he doesn't have a single picture, and I felt like I got punched in the gut when he told me he felt like a bad son because he was forgetting his mother's face. He needs to see that place one more time knowing that he can walk away from it," Jackson said as he polished off his last drink.

"My husband. Always saying the right things regardless of how much he's had to drink." Graye sat up and kissed Jackson on the cheek.

"What time are we supposed to be at the funeral home? I'm not sure how long that's going to take, but I'd like to be back home by sundown tomorrow if you think that's possible," Jackson said.

"They didn't say, I'm assuming whenever we get there because he never once mentioned the need for an appointment. You have a hot date tomorrow night or what?"

"Well, that depends on her I guess, but in other news Johnny is supposed to meet with Brian at nine on Wednesday morning, and I want him to be well rested." Jackson smiled at his wife as a soaking-wet Jared came running happily to his parents, throwing water from his cupped hands on his father and laughing hysterically.

"You little shit," Jackson said smiling as he sat his glass down and sprang from his seat in pursuit of his son.

Graye watched with an amused smile from her chair as Jackson tackled Jared into the water.

The guys both surfaced and everyone began laughing as Jackson made his way to the side of the pool.

Graye sat, watching the three guys conversing and playfully splashing each other in the water. She thought of how perfect the night was. She felt if Bryce were there with them, the family could happily stay at that point in time forever, with everyone happy, and smiling and joking around as if the night wasn't stuck between two points of disparity and hardship. She understood that things would get worse before they got better, but she loved seeing Johnny smile, and it pained her to watch him suffer the mental downfalls that would undoubtedly come with having an abusive excuse for a human being for a father.

At that moment, at least for the next few minutes, everyone was safe and happy. She felt a deep gratitude for Johnny as she watched him with her husband and son. In just a short period of time the boy had come into her life and completely reorganized her priorities and thought processes. She had a deeper appreciation for the gifts she'd been given in life, and genuinely felt she would never take them for granted again. She hadn't known this boy long, but she felt she had known him all his life, like he was supposed to be there with them. She felt this way now, just as she did then when she was washing his tattered and torn clothing. There was a natural fit that had occurred, and each day brought a stronger bond regardless of the trials that had come with taking Johnny in. Graye was genuinely overwhelmed with love for this bus stop refugee that her softhearted husband had brought home on an average July night.

She understood that almost every woman has a naturally ingrained sense within her that drives her to protect her offspring at all cost. This sense is either naturally acquired during childbirth, or is gained through a bond that even nature can't orchestrate. Graye knew that she would die before Johnny was ever hurt again. Perhaps some would argue there hadn't been enough time to develop such devotion, but those people were not her family, so she was less than concerned with what they may or may not have to say regarding the fledgling the family had informally adopted. This young adult, who was wise beyond his years in some aspects, and awkwardly delayed in others, had finally found the mother's love that every child needs to flourish; it had only taken him eighteen years.

CHAPTER FORTY-FOUR

Ashes To Shit

Johnny

His heart was racing and his armpits were wet, even with the truck's air conditioner going full blast. He felt the beads of sweat formulating across his forehead as the familiar surroundings were coming into view one by one. As the truck approached the tiny store on the corner of the road, Johnny softly instructed Jackson to turn left, and then left again. His heart was beating so hard he felt it in his eardrums. Returning to this area with this family seemed beyond surreal, and the morning's events had already proven to be difficult for Johnny as well as the rest of the family.

"Stop. Please just stop. I can't…I don't think I can do this. Please just stop," Johnny blurted out as the Jackson began braking on the parish dirt road, with a freshly cut cornfield on the left side of the truck. Johnny hadn't gone that long, yet everything seemed so different.

"Johnny, sweetheart, you don't have to do this. The

officer is waiting at the house and I'm sure he can get you as many pictures as you like," Graye said in a comforting tone as she placed her hand on Johnny's head.

Johnny knew the officer wouldn't be able to find pictures, he knew Graye more than likely assumed there were family pictures on the walls or displayed elsewhere in the house. That wasn't the case, Johnny knew he would have to look in a special place to find the picture of him with his mother and Jacob. The only pictures Thomas Tregalis had ever seemed to show concern for were the ones Agent Boudreaux had taken as evidence.

"No, I'm sorry. I'm…I'm okay. It's just up here on the right," Johnny said, trembling as he pointed toward the shambled house on the right side of the road. Although the house itself wasn't completely visible, the garbage and numerous car parts had caught the Johnny's eye first as he watched Jared's reaction to viewing his former home. "The driveway is right there," Johnny said as the house came into view, with the patrol car sitting in front of it.

As Jackson drove down the driveway to the house, all were speechless as the drive was lined with mufflers, door panels, and endless garbage that had escaped the burn barrel. As Jackson came to a stop, Johnny watched as the family seemed to stare in horror as they looked at the disgusting, rundown shack. The majority of the paneling had fallen off the side of the house, most of the front windows were boarded up with plywood, and the front door had a large hole kicked through it.

"Sweetheart, the officer is heading this way, would you like us to go in with you?" Graye asked sweetly as Johnny continued staring at the house.

"No, no, I…I wanna go in by myself, if that's all right." Johnny didn't want anyone in the vehicle to see the inside of his nightmares, the place where all his deepest fears originated from.

Jackson rolled down the driver's window as the policeman showed up. "Hello, officer," Jackson said politely as the older officer looked past Jackson and into the backseat of the truck.

"How you folks doin' today? Is Johnny Tregalis in there?" Johnny grabbed the door handle and quickly opened the back door without speaking a word. As the boy exited the truck, he quickly walked past the officer without acknowledging his presence.

"Son," the officer called out, "boy, you're gonna need some of this," the policeman said as he held up a small blue jar.

Johnny turned to the officer and walked slowly back to the man as his emotions were beginning to finally take over. He felt tears pouring down his face as he stood in front of the sympathetic-looking officer.

"I'm gonna dab some of this under your nose, it helps with the smell, okay?" the officer said kindly as he opened the jar and stuck his index finger in, removing a small amount of the thick, semitransparent, substance. "It smells like menthol and it's a little powerful at first. And uh, we talked to Bill Clementine about your request. He ain't home, but he said to come by just the same," the officer continued as he dabbed the substance under the crying boy's nose.

Johnny turned from the officer, drew in a deep breath, and began walking toward the front door of the house. He ducked under the yellow tape surrounding the premises. Staring at the destructed door, Johnny took the time to read the condemned sign posted on it, it pleased him to read the set demolition date of October 2. Pushing the door open, Johnny was hit by an overwhelming stench that seemed to enter his nose thicker than water from the swimming hole.

This wasn't the smell of rotting garbage or months of molded, maggot covered dishes; this was the smell of death and decay. Johnny instantly knew the lingering smell was from his father's bloated corpse, rotting in the shack in the Louisiana summer heat, even though the body had been removed long before this final visit.

The horrendous smell gave Johnny a strange sense of reassurance. He inhaled deeply through his nose, knowing he was breathing in his father's death. The stench made it real, and Johnny could tolerate what several investigators could not because of this.

As he entered the house, he wasted no time in the kitchen as he had no desire to relive anything that ever took place in the filthy area. He walked briskly to the hall and went straight for his father's bedroom, holding both hands up to either side of his head, blocking his peripheral vision like blinders. The only thing that was keeping his anxiety from overtaking him was that sweet stench, reminding him that there would be no drunken, raging man stomping down the hall to bloody him.

As he opened his father's bedroom door, thoughts of Jacob came flooding into his mind. The situation proved too much for the young man as he hit his knees. He remembered how the two would spend hours in this room, playing with beer caps and army men made of old Kleenex. He remembered how Jacob would kiss the scars on his back and tell him he loved him, how he would have to hold his hand in order for the toddler to drift off to sleep, and how Jacob would kiss Johnny all over his face in the mornings to wake him up. Even the morning after a beating, Johnny would always welcome his brother's wakeup kisses as the little boy smiled largely with a mouth full of milk-rotted teeth.

Johnny then realized he was crying rather loudly as he looked up at his father's destroyed bedroom, which had obviously been ravaged by investigators. Although this place never felt like home to Johnny, this visit made him feel as if he were trespassing in someone else's life and house, and this was a good feeling for Johnny. He was beginning to disassociate from the horrors of this hellhole, and soon the house would be nonexistent.

Wiping his eyes, he stood and walked to the corner of the bedroom on the right side of the room. Squatting down, he pulled back the corner of the burnt orange carpet, which came up easily. There it was. The picture Irene took of her and her two boys with the Polaroid camera that Doug Davenport was so fond of. It had been there, hidden since the day she had taken it, which was about a week before she was murdered.

Johnny looked at the picture and realized he hadn't forgotten their faces at all as he smiled through his tears. He wiped his nose with one hand and shoved the picture in his back pocket with the other. As Johnny rose and turned to leave, it caught his attention out of the corner of his eye.

The belt-buckle was large, and was the closest

thing to a family heirloom that Thomas Tregalis had ever owned. An instant anger came over Johnny as he reached for the large, tarnished brass buckle on the floor, squeezing it tightly as he stood, staring at the tarnished buckle within his grasp. He hated this object and wanted nothing more than to destroy it, he knew he couldn't so he did the next thing that came to mind; he threw it right through his father's bedroom window.

As he turned from the shattered glass, he began walking quickly out of the room for the last time, and toward the front door, toward the people that loved him regardless of the labels his father branded on him. Walking out of the front door, Johnny felt a rejuvenating sense of release come over him.

Jackson

From the truck, Jackson saw Johnny exit the dilapidated home. The man was somewhat puzzled by how quickly Johnny was returning.

As Johnny opened the door and climbed in the backseat, no one said a word. Jackson simply put the truck in drive and began turning around in the front yard, hoping he wouldn't run over a nail or some other random piece of metal.

Jackson tried to look at Johnny in the rearview mirror, but Johnny avoided eye contact as he stared out the backseat window and continued to sob. As the truck approached the end of the driveway, Johnny reached up and placed his hand on Jackson's shoulder. "Can…can you please go right? Can you turn right, please?" Johnny muttered in between gasps and sobs.

Jackson said nothing. He only smiled at the boy in the mirror and turned in the direction he requested. He watched Johnny set back as the boy resumed looking out the window, seemingly attempting to compose himself.

Jackson looked toward the large box on the floorboard. Inside the box were two small, beautiful, silver urns and a small coffee can. He and his wife spared no expense for the handling of Irene and Jacob's remains; however, at Johnny's request, Thomas's ashes were placed in an empty tin coffee can.

"Can you stop just up here?" Johnny asked as he pointed to a small farm on the right side of the road. Jackson had no clue what to expect, but he did as the boy asked and pulled into the sloppily kept farmstead that boasted a small, white stucco house, and several livestock pens attached to makeshift wooden and sheet tin shelters. The place appeared run down and dirty.

"Will you guys come with me?" Johnny asked with a red, wet puffy face as he reached over the seat for the coffee can.

Jackson glanced at Johnny in the mirror as he put the truck in park. He looked at Graye briefly and then reached for the door handle, as did the two boys in the backseat.

As Johnny exited the truck, he took the lead in front of Jackson, Graye, and Jared while toting the coffee can, walking from the driveway through the dead crabgrass of the farmyard.

The smell of pig excrement was disgustingly thick as Jackson watched Johnny walk toward the large swine enclosure. The pen housed two plump pigs that were well at home in a disgusting muck of their own waste and fly covered mud puddles. As Johnny reached the wooden railing of the pigpen, he seemed to wait for the remainder of the party to join him.

As Jackson stood next to him, Johnny wiped the tears from his eyes and opened the tin can. Without saying a word, Jackson watched Johnny turn the can over, dumping its contents out directly into the pig pen, watching the pale gray ashes quickly darken in color as they absorbed the mud water and swine urine. Johnny was breathing heavily and rapidly as he threw the coffee can on the ground and was embraced by both Graye and Jackson. The family stood still a few moments more, silently acknowledging the symbolic gesture behind Johnny's actions.

"So, what now?" Johnny asked as Jackson stared out into the pigpen. The three remained in their embrace, Jared at their side, for a few seconds until Graye kissed the boy on his cheek.

"Now we have family game nights, and go school shopping. Now we look at colleges and plan our Halloween party. Now we look forward to years of Christmases and birthdays, and hundreds of home-cooked meals," Jackson heard his wife say softly as she hugged them both tighter.

Jackson sighed as he pondered the events that had led him to this point, to this incredibly odd and uncharacteristic wake in front of the foul-smelling pigpen in rural Louisiana. He found himself once again thankful for his beautiful family—all of them. He looked down at the bravest young man he had ever had the privilege of knowing and smiled.

"Now we go home."

ACKNOWLEDGEMENTS

It was mere seconds after reading a poem to my wife that she looked at me lovingly and said, "You should write a novel." A few days later, she presented me with a brand-new laptop and a mounting support that continues to this day. Thank you, Bethany. Thank you for going to bed alone on countless nights while I completed *just one more chapter'* of edits. Thank you for reading and re-reading my material when I needed a second opinion. Thank you for acting as an underappreciated editor during the days of self-publishing. But mostly, thank you for being proud of me even when I found it difficult to be proud of myself. The literary world is difficult to navigate at times. I'm incredibly blessed to have you by my side on this, and everything else in our incredible journey.

To my mother, Connie and my sister, Tana: Thank you for acting as my original marketing and press release team. You have no idea how powerful your small words of motivation have been. It was as if you could sense the lack of self-confidence in my voice, and were quick to reassure me with every phone call.

My cheeks were literally about to cramp from smiling on the day I received the email from Beacon Publishing Group welcoming me to the family. Team Beacon is without a doubt the best team to be on—I'm confident in that. Thank you, Beacon, for supporting my writing, and for adding my book-baby to the Beacon lineup. I couldn't be happier. The support and camaraderie has been amazing. This has seriously been one of the most awesome experiences of my life.

To Brennon and Blaike, I am so thankful to have such amazing children. There aren't words to appropriately express the depth of my gratitude. You have both been the most loyal of friends, my greatest accomplishments, and major sources of support and motivation. I am the luckiest person alive to have the family I do. I love you all so much.

I have always agreed with the saying, "Without demand, there can be no supply." Without readers, my stories would live in my mind alone. If you are reading this now, thank you. Thank you for acknowledging my hard work, and for placing enough faith in it to allow it to occupy several hours of your life. I would like to give a special thank you to readers.

Lastly, I would like to thank my roots. To the beautiful people of Elkhart, Eva, Yarbrough, and Guymon: I am humbled by your continuous support. So many wonderful things come from our area of the world that often we tend to forget the wonderful things that remain there. The community I grew up in, my community, has been a foundation of solid support. This invaluable platform has allowed me to live the dream and do so with people I know and love.

ABOUT THE AUTHOR

Bradon Nave was born and raised in rural Oklahoma. He attended a small country school during junior high and high school, and graduated with only three people in his class. After graduate school, he decided to devote his spare time to his passion of writing. Bradon currently lives Oklahoma, with his wife and two high-school children.

When he's not writing, he loves running, being with friends and family, and being outdoors.